aftermath

Clara Kensie

MeritPress |

Published by
Merit Press
an imprint of F+W Media, Inc.
10151 Carver Road, Suite 200
Blue Ash, OH 45242. U.S.A.
www.meritpressbooks.com

ISBN 10: 1-4405-9870-3
ISBN 13: 978-1-4405-9870-8
eISBN 10: 1-4405-9871-1
eISBN 13: 978-1-4405-9871-5

Printed in the United States of America.

10   9   8   7   6   5   4   3   2   1

Cover design by Alexandra Artiano.
Cover images © nikoniano/123RF; iStockphoto.com/NK08gerd.

This book is available at quantity discounts for bulk purchases.
For information, please call 1-800-289-0963.

To those who have never been found, and to their families.
I will never lose hope.

acknowledgments

I have wanted to write this book since I was twelve years old. That's pretty young, you're probably thinking, for someone to want to write about such a dark subject. But here it is, almost exactly as I plotted it in my head three decades ago. Now that you're holding *Aftermath* in your hands, Charlotte and Alexa's story is finally complete. Charlotte and Alexa were mine for so long, and now they're yours. I'm having a hard time letting them go.

Writing a book is hard, but writing a good book would be impossible without my insightful, talented, and lightning-quick critique partners, Sonali Dev, Lynne Hartzer, and Bethany Robison. It would be inconceivable to write a book without the support of my incredible author friends, Erica O'Rourke, Heather Marshall, Melonie Johnson, and the Aphrodite Writers.

I am also fortunate enough to have friends who are such experts in their fields that I asked them to be my consultants for this story. Thank you for being so generous with your time and patient with my questions: Greta Lopez for your medical expertise, Patricia Gallarneau and Chad Tompoles for your legal and procedural expertise, and Kathy Mitchem for your educational expertise. Thank you to the Sunday Night Viewing Crew, Mike and Mary Kay and Lisa and Rosie Rosario, for cheering me on every week.

To my husband Glen and our beautiful kids: thank you for supporting this crazy career of mine and for not complaining (too much) when I forget to make dinner because I'm so wrapped up in writing that I lose track of time. I love you with my whole heart.

Thank you to the esteemed Jacquelyn Mitchard and her amazing team at Merit Press for believing in this story. Thank you to Alexandra Artiano for designing such a beautiful, haunting, perfect cover.

As always, thanks to my agent and fearless slayer of dragons and doubts, Laura Bradford.

To those of you who read my books, blog about them, leave reviews, send fan letters, tell your friends to read my books, and basically let my books touch your lives: thank you. You are the best part of being an author.

chapter one

My Keeper left and he hasn't come back.

Through the thin slit between the heavy curtains covering the attic window, I've watched the sky turn from blue to black three times since he left. The sky is a pinkish orange now, which means it's about to be blue again.

He leaves me every day when he goes to work, but he's never left me overnight before.

I drank all my water the first day. Now the last drops that remained along the sides of my water bottle have evaporated, and my tongue is heavy and dry.

I hope he didn't leave to replace me with my sister.

My sister's in high school now. My Keeper has taken the Christmas decorations from the attic's neatly stacked plastic storage bins four times since I've been here, so that means Alexa and I are sixteen. That makes her a sophomore, I think.

Alexa loves school. She gets straight A's, she has lots of friends, and she's a cheerleader. Now that we're sixteen, she can drive. She drives home in her new red convertible to have dinner with Mom and Dad, and then she chats with her boyfriend for hours before falling asleep on her bed in our pink and white bedroom.

I know this because when Alexa and I turned seven, we used some of our birthday money to buy a diary from the bookstore on Chapman Street. It has a bright pink cover, and a little lock and two keys, one for each of us. We used glitter paint pens to write *Charlotte and Alexa's Dream Book* on the cover, and drew flowers and swirls on it. We wrote each dream on its own page and vowed to do them all: Go to Disney World. Lead the Dragonettes to a state cheer championship. Go to Woodland Creek Middle School, then Woodland Creek High School, and make the honor roll every semester. Get matching cars for our sixteenth birthday. Date the cutest, nicest guys. Be co-captains of the high school's cheer squad, the Sparklers. Go to the University of Illinois, where our parents met when they were cast as Romeo and Juliet. Pledge our mom's sorority. Marry handsome, funny, smart men. Live in houses right next to each other.

When we were nine, Alexa and I were supposed to be matching Twix bars for Halloween, but she caught pneumonia and couldn't go trick-or-treating. I didn't want to go without her, but she told me to go to twice as many houses and get twice as much candy. So that's what I did. I did it double, because she couldn't do it at all.

Now Alexa is following the plans in our Dream Book alone. She's doing it double, because I can't do it at all.

My Keeper punched me in the stomach once, and that's how it feels now. Cramping. Rumbling. Sunken and hot. My head is fuzzy and light.

I wonder if Alexa's awake yet. Maybe she's eating breakfast right now, before she goes to school. Our favorite food is oranges. When we were little, we would peel our oranges, pull the sections apart, and arrange them to look like a flower on our plates.

My Keeper gave me an orange one time. I peeled it and made it into a flower. He said it was pretty, just like me.

My Keeper loves me. That's why he took me. That's why I belong to him, and why he'll never share me with anyone.

I wonder if my family ever thinks about me.

I hope so.

I hope not.

My tongue is dry. My throat is dry. Even my eyes are dry. My skin is crackling and my muscles hurt when I move. But in my mind, I'm holding a big, sparkly glass of my mom's homemade lemonade. I bring it to my mouth, and the ice cubes tickle my lips as I take a sip.

I swallow, and it hurts, burning my throat, and I realize there is no lemonade. There's no Mom, no Dad, no Alexa. Just the blue storage bins in the front of the attic, the big bed in the back, the wire crate, and me.

By now, Alexa's probably at school, and my parents are at work. Mom's a fitness instructor at the Woodland Creek community center. Zumba is her specialty. Dad sells insurance to make money, but really, he's an actor. One time he played a chef in a commercial for gourmet spaghetti sauce, and sometimes he's in a big theater production down in Chicago. He always gets a big role in the plays at the community center. Sometimes Mom, Alexa, and I do a play with him.

Well, now just Mom and Alexa do the plays with him.

On our last day together, we left rehearsal early—Dad was the Wizard, Mom was Glinda, Alexa and I were Munchkins—so Alexa and I could cheer in the Dragons Pee Wee football game. Our friends Bailey, Megan, and Amber were on the Dragonettes squad with us. We wore our new blue and white uniforms with pleated skirts, and Alexa and I tied our pigtails with two ribbons: a blue one to match our eyes, and a white one to contrast with our long black hair.

We both had bangs back then, but my Keeper has never cut my hair, so my bangs have grown out. I wonder if Alexa still has bangs.

My cheer uniform fell apart after a few months in the attic, so he gave me three faded nightgowns to wear instead. He let me keep my uniform, though, which was very nice of him. I fold it up and use it as a pillow in the wire crate he puts me in while he's away. Sometimes I press my nose into my uniform and inhale as deeply as I can. Underneath the stench of sweat and dirt, I can smell the springtime detergent my mom uses, or sometimes it's the freshly cut grass of the football field, or the popcorn from the concession stand. Then I hold my breath for as long as I can, because I know the next time I inhale it will be stale attic air, or sometimes my Keeper's coffee-smoky breath, or the sharp bleach he made me use to clean the blood I got all over the wooden floor that one time. There are two big bleach stains on the floor. One is mine. The other is from The One Before.

Outside, across the street, the car with the loud engine rumbles to life and drives away, as it does every morning. I hate the person who drives that car. I hate that person for not knowing that I'm here, that I've been here this whole time, just across the street. I hate that person for never hearing the creaks: the creak of the wooden stairs as my Keeper climbs up to the attic, the creak of the door as he swings it open and quickly locks it shut again, the creak of the bed where he sleeps with me every night.

My head throbs and my joints ache, but I shuffle up to my hands and knees, arching my back to the top of the wire crate and stretching my neck down, chin to chest. My arms are like shaky feathers, and my elbows collapse. There's not enough room to stretch my legs all the way, but if I press against the corner and lean on my hip, I can extend them into the opposite corner, one at a time.

When I stretch my right leg, I knock over the pail I use as a bathroom while I'm in the crate. It clangs against the metal bottom, the sound screeching around the attic. I flinch instinctively, even though he's not here to hear it. *No noise.* He puts his hands around my throat when I make noise. I can feel him now, squeezing, squeezing, squeezing.

One day, he'll squeeze too hard.

My waste from the pail has spilled all over the crate, and I swipe my uniform away just in time. I soak up the mess with my blanket, but now the blanket is wet and smelly. When he comes back, he'll be furious.

He likes his things to be neat and clean, including me. The attic is tidy and dust-free. Every morning he has me make the big bed, tucking in the sheets, plumping up the pillows, smoothing out the quilt. Every night he has me take a bath. The tub has brass feet that look like lion paws, with pipes that go down to the lower part of the house that I have never seen. He installed a tub, sink, and toilet just for me, because The One Before kept trying to run away when he took her down the attic stairs to use the regular bathroom. There are claw marks on the attic door where she tried to scrape her way out. That's why he locks me in the wire crate when he's gone. He says he'll do whatever he can to help me behave, so he doesn't have to punish me like he had to punish her. I try to behave anyway. I replaced The One Before, and I behave so Alexa doesn't have to replace me.

My stomach burns hot and hollow. How many days has it been? Three? Four? A hundred? I don't know anymore. Everything is hazy. The buzzing in my ears won't stop. The halo around the light bulb that hangs from the rafters gets bigger and smaller, bigger and smaller.

Three/four/a hundred mornings ago, just like always, my Keeper gave me his leftover toast and my pill, and I made the bed. He kissed me goodbye before herding me into the crate with my pail and bottle of water, told me he loves me, and locked me in. Then just like always, he locked the attic door behind him. And just like always, I counted his footsteps as he walked down the creaky wooden stairs. Fourteen, thirteen, twelve, eleven. All the way to one.

Except that day three/four/a hundred mornings ago, when I got to nine, I heard him gasp, moan, then tumble down the stairs.

Then I heard nothing.

I'm so tired. I've never been so tired. I'm not even thirsty anymore. I just want to sleep.

I'm pretty sure, if I close my eyes now, that I'll never open them again.

I'm so sorry, Alexa. I'm so sorry you have to do the Dream Book all alone.

chapter two

From far away, a scream. A howl.

I'm so tired. Please. I just want to sleep. I just want to float away.

The screams won't let me. From the other side of the attic door, high-pitched, panicked words trip over themselves, so fast I can't understand them.

Someone's here. A woman.

My eyelids fly open.

A woman is here. In my Keeper's house.

She's shrieking. I try to get my heart to stop drumming so I can hear what she's saying.

"Send an ambulance. I found my brother at the bottom of the stairs. I think he broke his neck. Please come. Oh God, hurry!"

Muscles aching, I haul myself up, hitting my head on the top of the crate. I couldn't have heard that right. This is a dream. A death-dream.

But I can hear a woman. Behind the attic door, on the stairs. Shrieking. Crying.

A whimper escapes from behind my lips, then my throat closes up. *No noise.*

But what if he's lying there at the bottom of the stairs with a broken neck, like that woman said? What if he can't stop me from making noise anymore? What if he's dead?

But what if this is a trick?

He's tricked me before. Telling me he had a son on the Dragons Pee Wee football team was a trick. Asking me to help him go get ice cream for the team was a trick. Bringing me to his house and up to his attic was a trick.

He tricked me again the first time he left me alone in the attic. When I opened the door to escape, he was standing at the top of the stairs. Waiting. He was testing me, and I had failed. He punished me for trying to leave him. Now I can't straighten my left leg all the way and the edge of my vision is blurry in my right eye, and he puts me in the crate every time he leaves.

The woman is still crying.

This is a trick. I know it. He's down there on the other side of the door, raising his voice high to sound like a woman, testing me to see if I'll call for help.

As quietly as I can, I shuffle to the back of the crate and bite my dried lips shut. He'll open the door any moment now and reward me for passing the test. Maybe he'll give me extra food.

The high-pitched crying continues.

A siren wails in the distance, growing louder as it comes closer. It's so loud now that it must be in front of the house.

Seconds later, men's urgent voices join the woman's cries. A walkie-talkie hisses and sputters.

This is a trick. It has to be.

If I call for help, he'll be outraged. He'll punish me again, maybe badly enough that he'll do to me what he did to The One Before, and then he'll have to replace me with Alexa.

But what if it's not a trick? What if there really are people, right outside the attic door? What if they leave without ever knowing I'm here?

I have to make a noise. I have to call for help.

I try to lick my lips, but my tongue is dry and thick and won't move. My jaw aches as I open my mouth wider, and even though I haven't said anything yet, even though he's not here, I feel his hands around my throat.

I force a word through the tiny opening left in my air pipe.

help

Only a pained croak comes out. I try again.

Help

Not loud enough. Even *I* couldn't hear myself. I swipe my hands over my neck, ensuring his hands aren't really there. I take a deeper, stronger breath and push air out of my lungs, trying to get my throat to work, to get my vocal cords to move after so many days of silence.

Help me!

Still not loud enough. His hands won't release my throat.

The men behind the door are leaving.

No! No, please don't go! I rattle the crate. The noise may as well be a whisper. With shaking hands, I take the metal pail and tap it against the bars.

ding

I try again, this time swinging the pail.

clang

I scoot to the back of the crate to make more room, and swing the pail again, using as much force as I can.

Clang!

The noise resonates, shakes me down to my bones. My ears ring.

My arms no longer shaky little feathers, I swing the pail again. And again. Adrenaline seizes me, burns through my veins as I clang the pail over and over again.

There's a thump on the other side of the door, then a bang, making it rattle on its hinges. A louder bang, and the door bursts open.

I freeze.

A man stands in the doorway, huffing, rubbing his shoulder. The bright light of the stairwell behind him shadows his face, but he's short and round.

My Keeper is tall and thin.

The man in the doorway is not my Keeper. He's not my Keeper!

Elated, I swing the pail to clang it again, but wait—what if this man takes me, and Keeps me too?

I shrink to the back of the crate. Hold my breath.

The man looks around the dim attic and shouts over his shoulder. "I don't know, Kev, but it can't be a raccoon. A raccoon wouldn't make noise like that."

Another whimper escapes from behind my lips, and the man's head jerks in the direction of the crate. "Hold on, Kev, I think that guy has a dog back there."

He strides past the rows of shelves to the back of the attic, past the bed, to the crate. I see his black shoes, white socks, black pants as he kneels, then the whites of his eyes as he peers inside. I'm huddled with my knees under my chin, wanting him to see me, not wanting him to see me.

He sees me.

"What the—"

"Please," I croak. Please don't hurt me. Please don't take me. Please don't Keep me. Please bring me home.

"Holy shit." His fingers fumble with the lock on the crate's door. "Kev! Kev! Get up here! It's not a dog. It's a girl!"

This is a trick. It can't be real.

The man tugs at the lock again, then gives up. "Kev! Call for another ambulance and bring me the bolt cutters!" He reaches a finger inside the crate. I'm torn between squirming away from it and grasping on to it like a life preserver.

"Don't be scared, honey," he says. "I'm an EMT. I'll get you out of there, I promise. Are you hurt? What's your name?" He pulls out a penlight and aims it at me, the bright ray piercing through the dim light. "Oh my God," he whispers. "Charlotte Weatherstone?"

I gasp at the sound of my name.

"It's you, isn't it," the man says. "Charlotte Weatherstone."

I dip my head, just the tiniest bit. My Keeper's invisible hands creep around my neck again and squeeze.

The EMT hollers over his shoulder. "Kev! It's Charlotte Weatherstone! She's alive!" He turns back to me. "Have you been here this whole time?"

Another tiny dip.

He lets out a triumphant whoop. "I knew it was you the second I saw your face. Your dad keeps the whole county, the whole *country*, plastered with your picture. No one will believe you've been so close this whole time. Charlotte Weatherstone, holy shit!"

I can't allow myself to believe it's over. I have to believe this is a trick. I can't get my hopes up. I've gotten my hopes up too many times before, only to have them plummet and shatter.

The other EMT runs into the attic, and there's lots of swearing and sharp snapping as they cut the wire bars and lift the top panel off. The first man grabs my blanket, then grimaces when he sees that it's soiled. He tells Kev to get the quilt from the bed, and then he wraps it around me and gently lifts me from the crate. "Another ambulance is coming, Charlotte. Hold on. Shit, Kev, we've got to call the police."

Another ambulance comes, and the EMT places me on a stretcher and straps me in.

The wire crate. The big bed. The lion paws on the tub. The blue storage bins, the bleach stains on the floor, the claw marks on the door. They all disappear behind me as I'm carried out of the attic and down the creaky wooden steps.

Fourteen, thirteen, twelve, eleven . . .

All the way to one.

This isn't a trick. This is real, and I am going home.

chapter three

I don't move as the doctors prod. I don't speak as the police question. It's too much. Too many people, too many hands, too much noise, too much light in this hospital room.

A grandmotherly nurse lifts my arm and takes my pulse. She's wearing light blue scrubs, and over her heart, embroidered in royal blue stitching, are the words "Kendrick County Hospital." I'm in the hospital near my home in Woodland Creek. Alexa and I were born here.

I'd forgotten that my Keeper's house was only a short drive from Woodland Creek. It'd seemed so far away.

Where *is* he? He was gone by the time the ambulance guys carried me out of the attic.

Maybe he's dead.

Maybe he's not.

The needle piercing my arm is connected to an IV that's pumping hydrating fluids into my body. I'm not as thirsty anymore. Not as weak. My tongue is no longer thick and heavy. The ache in my head is lessening and my muscles don't feel as tight. But I can't allow myself to believe this is real until I see my family. Mom, Dad, Alexa.

The nurse makes a note in her chart. Police officers, nurses, doctors rush in and out. Questions, prods, pokes. I don't move, I don't speak.

From the hallway, there's a sound of running footsteps, and someone cries my name. "Charlotte? Charlotte!"

It's my mom, it's my *mom*; I recognize her honey-sweet voice. I struggle to sit up as the nurse fiddles with the needle in my arm.

Mom flies into the room, wavy black hair and big brown eyes, just as I remember. She's beautiful, the most beautiful thing I've ever seen.

She halts, her hands going to her mouth. "Charlotte," she says again, whispering it this time. Her face scrunches up, and with a guttural, primal howl, she throws herself on me, wrapping her arms tight.

"Careful," the nurse warns, but my mom won't let go. She still uses springtime laundry detergent, and she smells like home. She's sobbing so hard that the nurse tries to pull her away, but I cry out and cling to her, and the nurse retreats.

Mom finally draws back and cups my face in her hands. Her hair has lots of gray in it, I notice now. It hangs limply around her face. Her eyelashes are light—this is the first time I've seen her in the daytime without makeup. She has deep shadows under her eyes, and she's heavier now, too. Rounder. But she's still my mom.

She kisses my cheeks, fiercely, then sobs again. "Were you there, in that man's house, this whole time? Only twenty minutes away? Did he hurt you? Of course he hurt you. They found you in an attic, locked in a metal crate. Oh . . . oh God . . ." Her words tumble out of her mouth between sobs and heaving gasps. The more she cries, the more I cry.

More noise from the hallway interrupts us: a stampede of rushing, stomping feet. Sharp, shouting voices. Flashing lights. A tall man rushes into the room—Dad!—and bolts over to me.

He presses both hands over his heart like he's trying to keep it from bursting out of his chest. Broad shoulders, strong jaw, golden-brown hair: he still looks more like a movie star than an insurance salesman. Maybe he *is* a movie star now.

"It's really you," he says. "Charlotte." He reaches for me, then hesitates, unease crossing his face.

Can he tell, just by looking, what kind of things happened to me in the attic? Damaged, dirty, disgusting: is that what he thinks of me?

"We never stopped looking for you, never stopped hoping," he says. "But I was so sure you were—" His face crumples, and he pulls my mom into the tightest of hugs. "We have our baby girl back, Vickie."

A female voice calls from the hallway, "Mr. Weatherstone! Can you confirm the rumors? Is it her?"

Mom goes rigid and pulls away from him. "How did those reporters get in here, Cory?"

"They followed me. They just want to know—"

"Get them out of here," Mom hisses, almost growls. "This is *private*."

Dad's lips go straight, but he nods. "Be right back, sweetheart," he murmurs to me. He wipes tears from his cheeks as he walks out of the room. "It's true, it's true!" he declares, throwing his arms up in victory. "She's alive! Charlotte Grace Weatherstone is alive!"

More cheers and questions come from the hallway, more flashing lights. Mom shoves the wooden door shut. "*I* knew you were alive, Charlotte. I never stopped believing it." I want to hug her again, but my arms feel too weak now.

The din in the hallway fades as the parade of reporters shuffle away. Dad comes back in, and more tears have replaced the ones he wiped away. He sits on one side of my bed, Mom sits on the other, and they stare at me, soak me in. Mom takes my hand. I'm still weak, but I curl my fingers around hers. She's solid and warm.

I close my eyes for a second, and when I open them, my parents are still here. Amazing.

I try to speak, but my voice won't work yet. I mouth it instead. "Where's Alexa?"

Before they can answer, a woman in a white lab coat enters the room and introduces herself. Dr. Chen. She's going to examine me, she says. She's young, and little, and she speaks in a soft, high voice. Not threatening at all. I wonder if that's why they picked her.

Her hair is straight and black. My hair is thicker than hers, a lot longer, a little wavier. But just as black.

My Keeper loves my hair. After my baths, he brushes it until it's dry.

I want to ask Dr. Chen if I can go home now, but I can't get the words out. She scrapes under my fingernails, swabs a Q-tip inside my cheeks, draws vials of blood from my arm. I used to be scared of needles and shots when I was younger, but these tiny pinpricks of pain are nothing now. She takes me for X-rays and scans, and she probes and prods every inch of my body, looking for injuries and evidence. I let her do what she wants. "You're being very cooperative, Charlotte," she says.

Of course I cooperate. Resistance means punishment.

At one point during the exam, Dr. Chen asks my father to leave. Dad nods, seeming relieved, and his phone is up to his ear before he reaches the door. Then the doctor examines me between my legs, and even though she's very gentle and my mom's sitting right next to me holding my hand, I separate my mind from my body the way I do when my Keeper touches me there, and take myself far away. The doctor asks me questions but I pretend I don't hear them.

My mother weeps.

Dr. Chen leaves, and my father comes back. He and Mom take their previous positions on either side of my bed. Mom fusses with the blanket, tucking me in, and smooths my hair. Dad simply stares at me again.

My eyelids are heavy now. I'm not used to so much activity in a single day—I sleep most of the day while my Keeper's at work—but I won't let myself fall asleep until I see my sister. I lick my lips, and my question comes out in a breathy exhale. "Where's Alexa?"

Mom's gaze flies up to meet my dad's. They don't reply.

"Where's Alexa?" I say again, louder this time. My voice is still raspy from disuse. "Is she at school?"

Pain weaves its way across Mom's face, and when I look at Dad, he has the same expression. "Sweetheart, she's . . . she's not . . ."

Alarm zips through me and I shoot up straight. "He took her?" I behaved so he *wouldn't* take Alexa. But I *didn't* behave—I called for help, I escaped, I left him. And now he's replaced me with Alexa, just like he said he would, the same way he replaced The One Before with me. Or maybe he's had her all along, in a different house, in a different attic.

Mom and Dad say something, but all I can hear is the blood rushing in my ears. No, no, no, I shouldn't have called for help. I shouldn't have left him. He escaped from the ambulance, or maybe he was testing me all along and this is just a trick, and now he has Alexa. "He took her," I shriek. Every nerve is ablaze with panic. I thrash and scream, the howls hurt my throat, but I'm unable to stop. His hands are around my neck, he's squeezing, and I can only breathe in high-pitched wheezes.

Mom and Dad cry out, and the nurse rushes back in. They hold me down as I struggle against them. "He replaced me with her, the way I replaced The One Before. I left him, and now he took her, he took Alexa!"

"Charlotte, no!" Dad cries. "Alexa is safe. He didn't take her." He repeats it over and over again. "No one took her. Your sister is safe."

Exhausted, drained, unable to breathe, I have to stop struggling. My Keeper's hands slowly release my throat. "Then where is she?" I ask. "Why isn't she here?"

"She's coming." Mom shoots a narrowed glance at Dad. "Your father will do whatever it takes to get her here."

Dad's lips go back in that straight line, and he nods.

"He didn't take her?" My heart pounds in my ears. "You're sure?"

"I'm one hundred percent positive," Dad says. "Alexa is safe. She'll be here soon. Tomorrow. Next day at the latest."

I nod and sniffle, and my heart rate slowly returns to normal. The nurse fiddles with the IV before leaving again.

"Where's Alexa?" I ask, but my voice doesn't work anymore. Every muscle in my body is heavy, and I'm sinking and floating at the same time. That nurse must have given me a sedative. I fight it, but my eyelids close without my permission.

Just as I'm about to slip away, my mother's trembling voice breaks the silence. "Charlotte? Who's The One Before?"

chapter four

Light penetrates my closed eyelids when I wake up the next morning. Light so bright that it can only be sun rays shining through a big window, not the dim light that comes from a bare bulb hanging from the rafters.

Instead of silence, there's hushed chatter. A far-away ding, like an elevator. The muffled rolling of a cart on wheels.

My Keeper, with his coffee-smoky breath and his rough roaming hands, is not lying next to me.

I'm not in the attic anymore. I'm in the hospital. I'm free.

I open my eyes. Mom is curled up in a chair next to me, asleep, wearing the same blue sweater and jeans she wore yesterday. I reach out to touch her, just to make sure she's real, and she is.

Dad's awake, pacing, murmuring into a cell phone. He's also in the same suit he wore yesterday, but he's taken off the jacket and rolled up the sleeves of his button-down shirt. His pink tie is loose and thrown over his shoulder.

My hospital room exploded with gifts while I slept. They cover every surface. Bouquets of flowers, bundles of balloons. At least a dozen teddy bears, small, medium, large, every single one of them pink.

I have a pink teddy bear at home. Wiggles. I slept with it every night since I was little, even when I was too old to admit that I slept with a teddy bear. Alexa has a matching bear in purple named Giggles.

I haven't thought about Wiggles and Giggles in a long time.

When Dad sees I'm awake he clicks off his phone call and comes to the side of my bed. He pushes his hands into his pockets. "Good morning, sweetheart. I still can't believe you're here. It feels like a dream."

I try to give him a smile as bright as the one he gives me, and gesture to all the gifts.

"They're from your supporters," he says. "People from all over the country. There are more bears at home. They keep coming."

Wow. For years, the only person who knew where I was, was my Keeper. Now the entire country knows where I am, and they're sending me presents.

It takes me a few tries, but I finally get the words out, though they're soft and raspy. "Were you just talking to Alexa? Is she on her way?" My voice sounds odd, and alien, and much too loud, and now he'll punish me—

"Your sister can't come just yet." Dad's gaze flickers away for a split second before coming back. "Are you okay? Do you hurt anywhere? Do you want anything?"

"I just want to go home."

"I know. But you're not strong enough yet, and the police need to talk to you. Lots of people want to talk to you."

Mom lifts her head. "She'll talk to the police. No reporters. No cameras." She cups my cheek in her hand, kisses my forehead. "Good morning, my darling, sweet, precious girl."

"Those reporters care about Charlotte, Vickie," Dad says. "The whole country cares about her." He nods his head at the teddy bears and flowers. "They deserve to know how she's doing."

"Then issue a press release."

The door opens, and Dr. Chen enters. "Good morning," she chirps. Her hair is tied back in a low ponytail today. She draws my parents to the other side of the room for a murmured conversation, but I can hear her tell them that my test results are back: I'm dehydrated and malnourished, so I'll need to spend a couple more days hooked up to the IV. Plus she's worried about my left knee and my right eye and something called rickets, which, she explains, is caused by a lack of vitamin D—all those years in the attic without sunlight.

With every word the doctor says, my dad's face gets redder and my mom's face gets whiter.

"But you'll be happy to know the tests came back negative for STDs," Dr. Chen says. "The pregnancy test was negative too. And there's evidence of birth control pills in her blood. He must have ordered them online from a foreign distributor."

Exhaling a shaky breath, Mom sinks to the chair. "Thank God," she whispers, wiping her eyes with trembling hands. "No diseases. No babies. Thank God, thank God."

I could have told them about the birth control pills. He made me take one every morning. I belong to my Keeper, and he is never going to share me with anyone, not even a baby.

Alan Shaw.

That's my Keeper's name. He never told me his name, not once the entire time.

Alan Shaw. Eight letters. I have more letters in my first name than he has in both of his.

Slumped in an avocado-colored chair in my hospital room, a scruffy FBI investigator named Agent Lindo is telling Mom, Dad, and me what he's learned about Alan Shaw.

Agent Lindo is a big man, but he doesn't look like an agent. Instead of a dark jacket with "FBI" in yellow letters, he's wearing a wrinkled plaid shirt. Instead of flashing a gold badge and a gun, he's holding a little spiral notebook and a stubby pencil in his massive hands. When he looks at me, there's pity behind his eyes, which are the color of warm maple syrup.

He calls my parents Cory and Vickie. They call him Rick. When he came in earlier, he and my dad gave each other wide grins and congratulatory pats on the shoulder. He gave my mom a hug. He gave me a big pink teddy bear. "I've wanted to give this to you for a long time, Charlotte," he'd said, all choked up. "Welcome back."

He acts like he knows me, as if he cares about me as much as my parents do. It's strange, having someone I've never met before care about me so much.

Agent Lindo says I need to give a statement, but I don't want to talk about what happened in the attic. I don't want anyone to know. But compliance is the only way to avoid punishment, so I separate my mind from my body and take myself far away, and answer his questions. I do what he says.

He records me on camera and takes notes as I tell him how my Keeper lured me away after the football game that last day by asking me to help him get ice cream for the team. How I trusted him because he was wearing a Dragons cap, so he must have a son on the team. How I got in his car. How he drove off, and when we stopped, it wasn't at the ice cream shop.

Lindo asks me more questions, and from a distance, I hear myself answering him. I hear myself tell him about the attic. The locked door. The beatings. The bed.

I'm far away from myself, but I hear Mom crying the entire time, feel her crushing my hand. I see that Dad is ghostly white. I watch once as he dashes to the bathroom, hear him retch and vomit.

When I return to myself, Dad is back, sitting at my side. Mom's wiping her eyes. Agent Lindo is writing in his little notebook.

"I'll, um . . ." He clears his throat, blinking rapidly. "I'll tell you what I found out about Alan Shaw." He flips his notebook back to the first page. "He grew up in Pleasantview, in the same house where Charlotte was found. He's lived in Pleasantview his whole life."

Pleasantview. Locked in the attic of my Keeper's house, there was nothing pleasant about my view.

"He was married for two years, divorced for thirty," Agent Lindo continues. "No children. Never remarried."

Lindo keeps his gaze fixed on his notebook, reading his notes one by one, speaking like a robot: flat and emotionless.

Alan Shaw has never been in trouble with the law. Not even a traffic ticket. By all accounts, he was a model citizen. Involved in the community. His neighbors say he always contributed to their kids' fundraisers. He owns a small chain of copy stores called Print For Less, along with his sister, Donna Hogan, who lives nearby. He rarely missed work, so when he didn't show up for three days, his sister went to his house to check on him. She found him unconscious at the bottom of the attic stairs.

Dad sits up straight. "Wait. Rick, go back a second. The name of that copy store—did you say Print For Less?"

Agent Lindo takes another glance at his notebook. "Print For Less. Yeah."

"Oh God." Dad puts his head in his hands. "He's tall, thin, short gray hair?"

My breath catches. Tall. Thin. Short gray hair. Long nose. Muddy, close-set eyes. Pointy chin with a white scar. One front tooth that slightly overlays the other. Thin pale lips. Dry, rough skin. Calloused hands with ink-stained cuticles and knobby-knuckled fingers that clamp around my neck and squeeze, squeeze, squeeze.

Agent Lindo asks my father, "You know Alan Shaw?"

Dad nods miserably. "I went to his shop once, back in the beginning, to print up some of Charlotte's missing posters. He didn't charge me. He donated the entire order. He even made an extra one to put up in the storefront window. And I thanked him. I *thanked* him." He cups his hands over his mouth like he's trying not to vomit again. "That son of a bitch."

"He—he printed posters about me?" I ask. My voice is high and squeaky.

"Three hundred posters," Dad chokes.

"But that means . . ."

"What, honey?" Mom asks.

"That means he knew my name. The whole time. He knew my name."

"He didn't call you Charlotte?" she asks. "What did he call you?"

Girl, come over here for a second. Want to help me get ice cream for the football team?

Take off your skirt, girl.

Don't be afraid, girl. I won't leave you alone at night. I'll sleep with you, right here in this bed. See, isn't this nice?

Girl! Look what you made me do! Now your blood is all over the floor. Clean it up!

"He called me girl," I said. "Just . . . girl."

Agent Lindo flips his notebook closed.

I blink at him. He's not done yet. There's still so much I need to know, one thing in particular. But he's not saying anything, so I have to ask. "Is he dead?"

Again, my parents shoot each other looks. "No, but he's badly injured," Dad says. "He had a stroke, which is probably why he fell down the stairs. He's paralyzed now. He can't move the right side of his body. He can't hurt you, sweetheart. He's all the way on the other side of the building."

My stomach lurches. "*This* building? He's *here*? In this hospital?"

"I'm not happy about that either," Dad says, "but the doctors say he's too injured to keep him in the jail. He's handcuffed to the bedrails, and there's a guard outside his room." His hands curl into fists as he growls, "That guard is keeping him in, and keeping me out."

"Is he awake?" I ask. "Can he talk?"

"He's in and out of consciousness," Agent Lindo says.

"You have to wake him up. You have to make him talk."

"Why?"

Those hands are around my throat again, but before they can squeeze, I blurt, "There was another girl."

He goes rigid. "Another girl? Who?"

"The One Before."

"She was in the attic with you?"

I shake my head. "Not with me. Before me."

"Did she run away? Escape?"

Again, I shake my head. "She . . . she tried."

"Charlotte." He leans forward, unblinking and serious. "Did Alan Shaw kill her?"

I nod as hands seize my throat.

All three—Mom, Dad, Agent Lindo—sip in air. "You witnessed this?" the agent barks.

"No," I squeak. "It happened before me."

The questions fire from his mouth like bullets, demanding and urgent. What's her name? Where is she from? How long did he keep her? How did he kill her? When did it happen? Where is her body?

But the only answer I have for every single question is a choked, strangled, "I don't know."

And suddenly I'm crying. Crying for The One Before, who never escaped, who will never see her parents again, who will never finish the plans she made with her sister in their Dream Book. In death, The One Before saved my life. Our Keeper taught me not to be loud like her, not to try to leave him, not to do the things that made him angry enough to kill her.

"Please." I reach out to the detective. "You have to wake him up. You have to make him talk. You have to make him tell you who she is."

chapter five

He's still alive. He's in this building. He's paralyzed. Can't move. Can't speak. Barely conscious. He's all the way on the other side of the hospital, handcuffed and guarded.

But he's still alive, just a few hundred feet away.

To help me feel safer, Agent Lindo arranges for an off-duty police officer to stand outside my room. But still, when Dr. Chen comes to check on me, I beg her to please let me go home.

"Soon," she says. I'm not strong enough yet. I still have to see lots of specialists and a crisis counselor.

Mom sits next to me, holding my hand. She never leaves my side. Dad paces the room as he talks on his phone, or to the doctors, or to Agent Lindo. Sometimes he leaves to talk to the reporters who are milling in the lobby.

Alexa still hasn't come.

I just want to go home.

The mustached off-duty police officer stationed outside my door pops his head in. "Orderly's here. Lunch."

My father allows the orderly to enter, and a slender woman in bright blue scrubs brings me a tray. Chicken noodle soup, a turkey sandwich, green beans, apple slices, cherry Jell-O, a little box of milk with a straw. A colossal amount of food.

My parents watch as I take the spoon, watch as I slurp as quietly as I can, watch as I chew each bite. I try to eat slowly, to not scarf the food down before my Keeper snatches it away.

"Oh!" Mom says. "There's tomato and lettuce on the sandwich. I'm sorry. I should have checked."

I'd forgotten that I don't like tomatoes and lettuce. I eat what he gives me, or I don't eat at all.

But I can eat what I want now. I remove the limp lettuce from the sandwich. "Can I—can I have an orange?" I ask. "And maybe some lemonade?"

"Of course," Mom says, brightening. She's quick to ring for the orderly. But when the door opens, it's the guard, who says someone's here to see me. Les E-something. A doctor, maybe? Another FBI agent?

Mom and Dad shoot each other that look again: dread. Dad says, "Let me talk to her first—"

But it's too late. With a strangled wail, a flash of black and white flies into the room and pounces on me. I stiffen, then my body automatically goes limp, waiting for the first blow. Resisting only makes him hit harder.

But the person on me isn't beating me. She's hugging me. Sobbing. Blubbering.

She lifts her head. Pure white spiky hair. A ring through her bottom lip, one through her nose. A safety pin through her eyebrow. Behind layers of thick, black, tear-streaked makeup are big blue eyes.

Oh my God. Alexa.

Elation shoots through me, and I squeal and grab her, and we're sobbing and hugging and blubbering, and then we're sobbing and hugging and laughing. It's Alexa, my sister, my twin, my best friend, half of me.

We finally pull away, wiping our tears with the back of our hands at the exact same time, and laugh again. We still have it.

I can't stop smiling. It's Alexa.

Alexa is safe. He didn't take her. Until now, until this moment, I didn't fully believe it. But I believe it now.

I draw away, just far enough to look at her. Her round cheeks have slimmed since I saw her last, and the sparkling, brilliant blue eyes I remember are now clouded and troubled.

We're twins, so I know what I look like now, too.

It hurts to see what I look like now.

Alexa crawls all the way into the hospital bed and curls up into me, ignoring Mom's warning to be careful. She *is* careful. She takes my hand and we fit perfectly, just like we used to. I can see her black roots from this angle, and I take a lock of her white hair and weave my fingers through it. The safety pin in her eyebrow catches the sunlight.

She tilts her head up to look at me, a million questions behind her eyes.

"Lex," Dad says. "We need to talk."

Alexa's expression goes hard. She hauls her combat-booted feet off the bed and sits up. "Nice to see you too, Dad. Rehab was horrible. Thanks for asking."

"How about thanking me for pulling strings to get you released early so you can see your sister?" he replies.

"How about *not* thanking you for putting me there, even though I don't do drugs anymore?"

"You were drinking at a party. I had to do something."

"Yes, God forbid the country finds out that one of Cory Weatherstone's daughters isn't a perfect little angel," Alexa sneers. "I said hi to all the reporters in the waiting room, by the way. Introduced them to the counselor who drove me here because neither of my parents cared enough to pick me up."

"We weren't going to leave Charlotte to drive two hours each way to get you," Dad says. "Keep this up, young lady, and I'll send you right back to Bright Futures."

"Mom's the one who should be at Bright Futures, not me."

"Lex!" Dad roars, and slaps the wall with an open palm.

I flinch. Alexa doesn't. I've never seen my father angry before, but she's clearly used to it.

"Cory. Lex," Mom says, her chin quivering. "Charlotte's back. Can't we please put all this stuff aside for now? Please?"

Alexa snorts.

Rehab?

"What happened to you guys?" I ask.

Alexa shrugs. "Mom's a drunk. Dad's a fame whore." She flops back onto the bed and crosses her ankles. "And I'm a juvenile delinquent. Welcome home, sis."

"Damn it, Lex." Trembling, Mom rises, then rushes from the room.

"Oh, is your flask empty, Mom?" Alexa calls after her. "That's okay. There's a liquor store down the street."

"Mom!" I call out, but I'm tethered to the bed by the stupid IV. I may as well be locked back in the attic.

"Let her go, Charlotte," Dad says. "I'll go talk to her in a minute." He glares at Alexa. "Your mother is not a drunk."

Alexa glares back at him. "You don't know—"

"And I," Dad continues, "am not a fame whore. I was keeping Charlotte's story alive."

"And in doing so," Alexa says, "you became famous. Just like you always wanted."

Aggravated, Dad pulls a chair over to me. "Sweetheart, after you disappeared, I felt so helpless. The few leads we had were dead ends. I couldn't just sit around and hope that you'd come home one day, so I started a foundation. We raise money to search for missing children and to provide emotional and financial support to their families. We've raised over ten million dollars so far, and we've financed the searches for over a thousand missing children. We've helped recover many of them. We're in newspapers and magazines and on TV. HBO did a documentary on us. The president invited me to the White House."

For the first time since my return, my dad's blue eyes sparkle. He's truly excited about this foundation of his. "What about your insurance agency?" I ask. "What about acting?"

"I still have my insurance agency," he says. "I have to. I don't earn a penny from the foundation. And acting . . ." He dismisses it with a wave. "There's no time for that. I spend every last minute of my time on the foundation."

"Tell her the name of your foundation, Dad," Alexa says. Her eyes aren't sparkling, they're radiating with contempt.

Our father beams at me. "I named it after you, sweetheart. The Charlotte Weatherstone Foundation. Everyone in the country knows who you were. Who you *are*."

I am flabbergasted. Proud of my dad. Horrified for myself.

Dad jumps to his feet. "There're so many people who want to meet you, Charlotte. The entire country. All those reporters out there? Some of them have been covering this story since the day you disappeared. At first it was reporters from local papers like the *Kendrick County Reader*, but now we have journalists from *USA Today* and the *New York Times*. *People* magazine, *Time* magazine. The *Chicago Tribune* and the *Sun-Times* always get first dibs, of course. *Dateline, 60 Minutes,* and *The Shannon Symond Show* called me earlier today. Shannon Symond, can you believe it? I'm having my PR person figure out which one would be best to do first."

He looks at me expectantly.

What am I supposed to say? "I—Dad, that's . . . great about the foundation, but I just want to go home."

"You don't have to give the interviews if you don't want to," he says. "Maybe in a few weeks, after you've acclimated to everything."

"Jesus, Dad!" Alexa stands and tugs at her black skirt. She's wearing thick black tights with holes in them and a black T-shirt. "Leave Charlotte the fuck alone! She doesn't want to talk about what kind of disgusting things that guy did to her, and no one wants to hear it. Everyone can already guess. Let her go home and get on with her life."

"Alexa—" I say, but she whirls around.

"Lex," she snaps. "It's Lex now." And then she says that strange word the off-duty police officer had said just before she burst into the room. E-something.

"What does that mean?" I ask.

"It's my last name." She takes a napkin from my tray and writes five block letters on it. "E-N-O-L-A. Enola."

Dad throws his hands up with an exasperated sigh. "A jumble of random letters. It means nothing."

"It means *everything*," she snarls.

"You know you can't legally change your name until you're eighteen," he says.

"But Alexa—" At her sharp glance, I try again. "Lex. Why did you change your name?"

My sister crumples the napkin into a tiny ball, then blinking hard, she bends down to tie the shoelaces on her boots, even though they're already tied. "Because the day Charlotte Weatherstone disappeared," she mumbles from the floor, "was the day Alexa Weatherstone died."

chapter six

After three days, a bunch of specialists, and dozens of examinations, Dr. Chen declares I can go home to finish my recovery. Everyone is relieved, especially me. I'm desperate to put some distance between myself and my Keeper, who is still here, and still alive.

Mom hasn't looked me in the eye since Alexa called her a drunk. I guess that means it's true. But I haven't seen that flask Alexa taunted her about. I haven't seen her drink anything other than water and juice.

I have no clothes, and I assume I'll have to go home in a hospital gown, but Mom hands me a shopping bag. "I picked up a few things for you. Your old clothes are too small," she says, "and Lex's will be too big." She looks at Alexa with disapproval, like she wouldn't want me to wear her clothes anyway.

She's right, though. Alexa's clothes would be too big on me. My sister is at least three inches taller than I am. She's heavier, too. It's not that she's overweight; I'm underweight. Four years without nutrition, exercise, and sunshine have stunted my growth.

Even without her piercings and bleached hair, Alexa and I no longer look like twins.

Dad leaves so I can change, but I don't want to change in front of my mom or sister either. Trying not to limp on my bad leg, I take the shopping bag and go to the bathroom, shutting the door behind me. A mirror hangs over the sink. I avoid looking in it as I reach into the bag.

A package of underwear. Cotton. Eight pairs in assorted colors.

I had no underwear for four years, and now I have eight pairs in assorted colors. Which one should I choose? I finally decide on the light pink ones and pull them on. They feel good. Like . . . protection. Like a shield.

I let out air with a huff when I pull a bra from the bag.

My first bra.

When he took me, I didn't need a bra yet. I have breasts now, but barely. I fumble with the straps and hooks of the little white bra. I hear Mom hovering outside the door, but I refuse to ask for help. A sixteen-year-old girl should not need help putting on a bra.

I finally figure it out. The bra is small, but it's still too big. I wear it anyway.

He would hate this. He'd be furious if he knew I was wearing these things. The only clothes he ever lets me wear are those three faded and frayed little-girl nightgowns. One yellow, one white, and the blue one I was wearing when the ambulance guys found me. I wonder where it is now? Maybe Agent Lindo took it for evidence.

Next in the bag is a three-pack of socks. Thick, cotton, white socks. I pull on a pair and wiggle my toes. I never realized how luxurious socks are, how warm and cozy.

Folded at the bottom of the bag are three sets of hoodies and sweatpants: bright pink, light pink, and royal blue. I snap off the tags from the bright pink set and put them on. I pull the cuffs over my fingertips and bring them to my nose, and inhale. They smell new. Fresh. Soft, warm, and safe.

Alexa, Mom, and Dad, each lugging armfuls of pink teddy bears, flowers, and balloons, walk beside me as an orderly, her hair back in a long blond braid, pushes me in a wheelchair down the hall. I'm so excited I can't sit still. I can barely stop myself from darting out of the chair and running home. I'm strong enough to walk, even hide my limp, but it's a rule that they have to wheel me out.

The closer we get to the lobby, the louder it gets. Reporters.

Mom falters. "Did you tell them she was going home today, Cory?"

"Wait here." With a big smile, Dad rushes over to speak to them.

Alexa grabs my wheelchair from the orderly. "I'll take her from here," she says. She tells Mom to get the car and come pick us up in the back of the building. Mom gives her a conspiratorial nod and dashes off.

"If those bloodsucking reporters see you, they'll be all over you," Alexa says as she quickly piles teddy bears onto my lap.

As she whisks me down the hall, my throat closes up. *He's* here somewhere, in one of these rooms. Which one? This one? This one? What will he do if he sees me rushing past his room, leaving him forever?

I hug the teddy bears to my chest.

A left, a right, and another right, through some doors, and suddenly we're in the back lot of the hospital. Outside. Free. Sunny blue sky. Fresh chilly air. Red and yellow leaves scattered on the asphalt.

It's autumn, and I didn't even know it. It's beautiful.

Alexa parks my wheelchair next to the ramp to wait for Mom. I tilt my head up to the sun and soak it in.

"Alexa—Lex?" I ask.

"Yeah?"

"What's today's date?"

She doesn't answer, and when I look at her, she's staring at a dumpster like it's the most interesting thing she's ever seen. The rings in her nose and lip sparkle in the sun, and the breeze brushes through her white spiky hair. Finally she says, "October twenty-fifth. It's a Sunday."

"Oh."

"We're sixteen."

"I thought so."

"I'm a sophomore."

"I thought so."

"School sucks."

"Oh."

After another long pause, she says, "You were gone for over four years."

"How long, exactly?"

"Four years, two months, and seven days."

We're silent for a minute, then I ask, "How's everyone on the squad?"

She blinks. "Hmm?"

"The Dragonettes. Bailey, Megan, Amber."

She finally looks at me. "I don't know."

"They don't cheer anymore? They're not on the high school squad?"

"I think some of them might be."

"You're not on the squad?"

"The Sparklers?" She huffs. "God, no."

"What about theater? Are you in any plays?"

"Charlotte, no. No cheerleading. No plays. Everything is different now."

My throat closes up. "I know."

"You don't know everything. Not yet."

"What else is different?"

"Mom and Dad won't let me tell you," she says. "They want you to get stronger first. They said if I tell you anything before you're ready, they'll send me back to Bright Futures."

"Can they do that?"

"Dad and Lindo are like best friends now," she says with a shrug. "Lindo got me out early. One word from Dad, and Lindo will send me back." She stares at the dumpster again.

Alexa has never *not* told me something before. We used to share every secret, every thought. While I was in the attic, I was only twenty minutes away from Alexa, but it felt like forever far away. Now I'm with her again, outside here in the back lot of the hospital. We're so close that her leg is touching my arm, but there's still a distance between us.

"Rehab wasn't that bad, actually," she says. "Better than being home. But you're back now, and I would never leave you." Suddenly she throws her arms around me, sealing us together, her white hair mixing with my black hair. "I still can't believe you're here, Charlotte. I'm so happy you're home. I missed you. Every single day. Every single minute."

chapter seven

Mom still has the same navy minivan she had before. It's the same car she drove to the football game that last day. I left my house in this minivan, and now I'm coming home in it, four years, two months, and seven days later.

I can't stop staring out the windows as we drive through Woodland Creek. Everything—the streets, the stores, the parks— is exactly the same as it was four years ago, with only a few new things. Dudley's Donuts is gone, replaced by a Starbucks. The community center has a new addition. Woodland Creek High School, where I'll attend as soon as my doctors give me the go-ahead, has a new marquee out front. The stop sign at the intersection of Chapman Street and Crane Avenue is now a stoplight.

My heart drums double-time when we turn into our neighborhood, and triple-time when we turn onto our street, Robin's Nest Lane. All the houses look the same as before, exactly as I remember. Everything is so crisp and sharp and clear, like when Dad bought our high-def TV. I want to reach out and touch the bark on the trees, run through the piles of autumn leaves on the ground, jump in puddles.

I remember everything about our house. Sunny and clean. Tiny, but perfect for the four of us. Our house has yellow siding with black shutters and bright white trim, and a white porch with baskets of geraniums hanging from hooks. A sign on the porch says *Welcome!* in bright mosaic tiles. Mulberry bushes grow under the front windows. Mom's flower garden blooms along the sides—tulips and daffodils in the spring, asters and black-eyed Susans in the fall. The front and back yards are shaded by towering oak trees. Inside, all of the rooms are painted yellow, except for the bedroom I share with Alexa, which is pink.

Our yellow house is a single-story home. There are no narrow, wooden stairways that lead up to an attic.

We turn onto our driveway and I see the paint is chipped on the porch and trim, and the flower garden is weedy and brown. The mosaic *Welcome!* sign has been replaced with three others in bold black letters, staked in the ground by the front walk: *No Trespassing. Private Property. Violators Will Be Prosecuted.* But I'm so excited I can't stop shaking.

Dad pulls in behind us in a white car. Before, he had a silver one.

Alexa takes my arm to help me out of the minivan, but I shake her off to show her I'm not a frail little bird. I burst inside, followed closely by my family, and as I enter the kitchen, the memories inside my head collide with what my eyes are seeing. It's exactly the same.

I fly through the kitchen and family room—there's the comfy couch with the yellow throw pillows and the fleece blanket Mom bought at a craft fair—to the back of the house where the bedrooms are. I pass Mom and Dad's bedroom—same pale yellow comforter on the bed. Past the bathroom—oh! I can take a shower, not a bath, by myself, without anyone watching—and go straight to the bedroom I share with Alexa. Our pink and white bedroom. I wonder if our Dream Book is still on the shelf with our Dragonettes trophies. I wonder if Alexa still keeps her key hidden in the back of our sock drawer. I wonder if my key is still taped to the back of the mirror.

The door to our bedroom is closed. When I try to open it, I can't. The knob won't turn.

"Lex keeps it locked," Mom says from behind me.

"Why? I want to go in."

"It's too messy," she says. "I'll tell her to clean it. Let's go."

"But I—" Hands creep up around my neck, cutting off my protest. I nod in meek obedience instead, and the hands go away. I follow Mom back to the family room.

There, Dad and Alexa are sitting on opposite ends of the couch. He's perched on the edge with his elbows on his knees. She's twisting a lock of her white hair around her finger and staring hard at the TV, which is off. The pink teddy bears are dumped between them and spill to the floor.

Mom sits in the armchair, and I make room among the bears to sit between Dad and Alexa.

The family room, where the four of us had spent so many hours together, seems the same as it does in my memory. The big comfy couch, the coffee table, the bookshelves, the beige carpet. But something is off. The air is so fragile in here that I'm certain if anyone speaks, it will shatter like glass.

This is not the homecoming I was expecting.

Alexa slides a glance at me, and her features soften. "I know! Let's look at pictures. Mom, where are your scrapbooks?"

Dad looks relieved, and appreciative of Alexa for the first time since she came back from rehab. Mom claps her hands and dashes off, returning with a big stack of scrapbooks. We spend the next few hours going over every page, every photo, starting with the pictures of Alexa and me on the day we were born, all tiny, pink, and squirmy in the same bassinet.

When the sun sets, Mom orders a pizza. We eat it on paper plates at the couch, and still, we aren't done looking at the photos. Our first birthday. Getting on the bus on the first day of kindergarten. Mom in her workout clothes and a perky ponytail, heading to the gym to lead a Zumba class. The four of us in the community theater production of *Seussical the Musical.* Dad was the Cat in the Hat, Mom was Mayzie, and Alexa and I were Thing 1 and Thing 2.

We pass the scrapbooks back and forth, and laugh, and reminisce, and laugh some more. I've eaten so much pizza that my stomach hurts, or maybe it's from laughing so hard. I never thought it was possible for anyone to be so happy.

And then my gaze lands on the bookshelf next to the TV, and I realize what's different: my parents' wedding photo isn't there.

Their unity candle isn't there either.

The little bottle of sand from their Cancun honeymoon is gone.

Those items have been on display on that second-to-the-top shelf of the bookcase since before Alexa and I were born. The wedding portrait, the unity candle, the bottle of sand. And now that shelf is empty.

My legs are unsteady as I rise and make my way to my parents' bedroom. "Charlotte?" Mom calls, but I can't respond. The nightstand on my dad's side of the bed is devoid of his alarm clock, his bowl of change, his stack of books.

I go to their closet and open it. My dad's clothes are gone. All of them. No suits, no ties, no button-downs, no golf shirts. Only Mom's sweaters and dresses hang from the rods. Only her sneakers and sandals are hanging on the shoe rack. The edge of my vision is blurry in my right eye, so I close my lids and open them again. But Dad's clothes are still gone.

"Charlotte." Dad's voice, behind me, heavy and sad.

Head swimming, not wanting to believe it, unable to believe it, I turn around. "Dad?" I am drowning.

His mouth opens and closes, but I'm under water and his words are warped and wavy and far away. "We wanted you to get adjusted before we told you . . . not your fault, it's ours . . . we handled your disappearance in different ways . . . a wedge we couldn't overcome . . ."

Through the tidal wave I see Mom and Alexa have come in. The storm has returned to Alexa's expression, and she glares at Mom, then Dad, then Mom again, like she can't decide which of them she hates more. Mom is crying and looking at her shoes, then glances at her nightstand where an empty wine glass sits, then back to her shoes. Dad looks at me, and only at me, and his eyes are full of agony.

When Alexa and I were little, we called our parents Mommydaddy, one word like that, because they were always together. Inseparable, like Alexa and me. Two, but one. Charlottealexa, Mommydaddy.

Dad's still talking, but I only hear one word:

"Divorced."

Dad continues talking, but I can't hear, can't breathe, can't think about anything except that my dad doesn't live here anymore, that they're *divorced*, there's now a space between Mommydaddy, and my disappearance was the cause of it all.

I'm back on the family room couch, Mom and Dad on either side of me, and I don't remember how I got here. Alexa stands in front of us and continues to glare at them behind her white hair, her arms crossed, breathing hard through her pierced nose.

The only thing that gave me comfort in the attic was thinking about my family. It hurt too much to think of them being sad, so I imagined them happy. But they weren't happy. They were a mess.

I'm home, but it's not the home I imagined. Not the family I imagined. Not the family I convinced myself they were. I'd convinced myself that they'd continued on with their happy, carefree lives without me, that they were doing it double, because I couldn't do it at all.

I was wrong.

Finally Mom squeezes her eyes shut and rubs her fingertips in little circles over her eyebrows. "The plan was for your dad to stay here for a few days until you get adjusted. But there's no longer a reason to keep up the charade. Cory, you should go."

"Dad, no," I say, even though protesting makes those hands creep up around my throat.

Dad gives a heavy sigh and drags himself up. "Stay here tonight, Charlotte. Reunite with your mom and sister. I'll come pick up you and Lex in the morning. Explain things further. Show you where I live." He turns to Mom. "Vickie? That okay with you?"

She gives him a tiny, reluctant nod.

Dad gives Alexa a stern look, and she rolls her eyes, then gives him her own tiny, reluctant nod. A silent conversation I don't understand. Another thing that distances me from my family.

Dad reaches for me, then stops. He reaches for Alexa, but she jerks away.

With slumped shoulders and a dejected sigh . . . he leaves.

Watching him walk out the front door is such an unbelievable sight that it can only be a dream. A nightmare. But it's real. He really, really left.

Mom and Alexa didn't even watch him go.

Mom rubs her palms on her jeans. Closes the scrapbooks and stacks them up. Takes the pizza box and paper plates to the kitchen. Returns to the armchair and rubs her palms on her jeans again.

Alexa plops on the couch, shoves all the pink teddy bears to the floor, then twists a lock of her white hair around her finger.

I want them to say something. To explain. I open my mouth to ask, but Mom says, "Are you still hungry, Charlotte? I have ice cream in the freezer. Do you want ice cream?"

I haven't had ice cream in over four years—why does Mom have ice cream, anyway? She only bought low-fat frozen yogurt before—but I don't think I could get anything past the lump in my throat. "No, thanks."

"Do you, um . . ." She rubs her palms on her jeans again, back and forth, again and again. "Do you want to talk about what that man . . . did to you?"

Alexa cringes. "We already know what he did to her. He locked her up and beat her and raped her. That's all we need to know." She yanks at the lock of hair twisted around her finger. "No one wants to hear the details."

Mom gives her the same tiny nod she gave to Dad a few minutes ago. She clearly doesn't want to talk about the divorce. Alexa clearly doesn't want to hear about the attic.

"Please, Mom, can we just go to bed?" Alexa says. "It's Charlotte's first night home, I'm sure she's exhausted, and it's my first night home from Bright Futures. I'm exhausted too."

Mom finally stops rubbing her jeans. "Okay. Good idea. Go to bed, get some rest, and we'll have a nice big breakfast in the morning. Something healthy. Lots of protein. Charlotte needs to get her strength back up."

She gives me a good-night kiss. "I'm so happy you're home, Charlotte," she says. "I'm sorry it's not . . ." Her voice trails off, and she escapes to her bedroom.

chapter eight

I follow Alexa to our bedroom, my mind filled with questions I don't know if I want the answers to. I pause at the locked door, but she walks past it without a glance. She stops at the room at the end of the hall: the extra bedroom Dad uses as his home office for his insurance business.

But he doesn't live here now, so it's not his office anymore. The walls are still painted a light yellow, the curtains are still white, and his L-shaped desk is still there in the corner, but a laptop is on it instead of his big computer. The family photos he had hanging on the wall have been replaced by several large maps with pins stuck in them. There's an old dresser in here now, and a bed. One bed. Unmade, with a rumpled navy comforter, one beige sheet, and one light blue sheet. It smells kind of musty in here, like dirty laundry and discarded food wrappers.

"You can take the bed," Alexa says. "I'll sleep on the floor."

"What about our room?"

"I need to clean it first."

"I don't care if it's messy," I say. "I just want to sleep in our room again."

She still won't look at me. "Maybe tomorrow, okay?"

She's lying. There's something in there she doesn't want me to see. Drugs?

No one in my family is willing to talk about anything.

She digs through the closet, which is stuffed with messy piles of black clothes, pulls out a ratty sleeping bag, and lays it on the floor.

"You can have your bed," I say. "It's your first night home too."

"Seriously, Charlotte, it's fine. Take the bed. I'm sure my bed in rehab was better than however you had to sleep for the past four years."

"There was a bed in the attic. I slept there. With him."

Alexa balks, so I change the subject. "What happened with Mom and Dad?"

She sighs and crawls into the sleeping bag. "It happened pretty soon after you disappeared," she says, folding her hands behind her head. "Less than a year. Dad was organizing search parties, doing press conferences, hanging 'missing' posters all over the place. Mom just . . . she just waited for you to come home. She was a robot. She walked around and did what she was supposed to do, but it was like she was empty inside. She'd look at me but not see me. I'd wake up in the morning and Mom would still be sitting in the same place she was the night before."

"Didn't Dad try to get her help?"

"He tried everything. Took her a therapist. They went to group counseling. But nothing worked. It's like Mom was stuck. She couldn't move on."

"And that's why Dad left?"

"No, he didn't want to leave. Mom kicked him out."

"Why, because of the foundation?"

"She kicked him out because he had a memorial service for you."

I gasp. "Like a funeral?"

"It was easier for him to think of you as dead than suffering somewhere. And after so many months, it seemed like you probably *were* dead. He said it would be healthier for all of us if we just accepted it." Alexa shrugs. "But Mom couldn't forgive him for that. It was the one time she wasn't a robot. She screamed at him, threw things, tossed his stuff out on the front lawn. She was vicious, Charlotte. Like a wild animal. That's when the drinking started, after that. I think it's to help her sleep. Dad doesn't know how bad it is."

Oh, God. Poor Mom. Poor Dad. Poor Alexa.

I wonder if The One Before's parents are divorced now, too, if her mother threw her father out in a fit of wild rage. I wonder if her mom is now an alcoholic. I wonder if they had a memorial service for her. Or maybe her parents believe she's still alive somewhere, and they're determined to stay together so when she finally comes home, it won't be to a broken family.

"Did you go?" I ask my sister. "To my memorial?"

"Yeah," she says. "We did it at the church on Chapman Street. We lit candles, said a few prayers, things like that. But it became this huge controversy. The local papers picked it up, then TV, then the Internet. Some said Dad was right to want closure so he could move on, and some thought he was horrible. But after that, his foundation really picked up steam. People began donating like crazy. He started going all over the country, holding fundraisers, giving speeches, organizing search parties for missing kids."

"Why do you hate Dad? The foundation—it sounds like a good thing."

"I don't hate Dad because of the foundation," she says. "I don't hate Dad for assuming you were dead, either, if that's what you think. I hate Dad because, well, for lots of reasons, but it started because he used *you* to get famous. Every time the media attention dies down, he does something to get it back. He says it's to keep the public aware of his cause." Her lip curls into a snarl. "I say that's bullshit. I say everything he does is to keep the public aware of *him*."

Her breath is huffy, and I wish I could've been here with her so she didn't have to go through it all alone. But of course, none of this would have happened if I hadn't disappeared. "What were you doing while all of that was happening?" I ask.

"Having sex, doing drugs, being your basic menace to society." She says it so candidly, almost as if she's bragging. She thrusts out her chin, daring me to ask about it.

I don't want to ask about the sex, so I ask, "Do you really do drugs?"

"I did. Mostly pot. But I've done ecstasy, coke, whatever. Shot heroin once or twice. That's what got me shipped off to Bright Futures the first time. I was never an addict, though. Dad just wanted to scare me. I went back this time because I came home drunk from a party. If it was Mom's weekend she wouldn't have noticed, but it was Dad's weekend. He went ballistic and had his buddy Lindo throw me in there again."

My sister is a stranger. On the outside, on the inside. Lex Enola: she's a stranger to herself, too.

"Hey," she says, clearing her throat. "Want to see something?" She hops up and brings the laptop to me on the bed. On the lid, drawn with a Sharpie, is a doodle of an old-fashioned airplane with a large circled R on its tail. "Look how many websites there are about you."

She powers on the computer and starts clicking. My smiling eleven-year-old Dragonettes portrait with my hair up in long black pigtails flashes at me over and over again. "I bookmark all the sites about you. Dad's foundation is the biggest one, but you're on Wikipedia and all the usual ones. There are articles and blog posts about you everywhere. I'm sure hundreds more have popped up in the last few days, since you were found. I even set up a Facebook page about you. It got thousands of likes. But I haven't looked at it in a couple of years."

She clicks over to a Facebook page titled "Charlotte Weatherstone, My Twin Sister - I Will Never Forget You." She quickly scans the page and snorts. "God, how childish. You can totally tell a kid did this."

Mom and Dad never allowed us to use all those social media sites before. We didn't have our own computer, and the family computer had parental controls to keep us off of them. And now Alexa is clicking through all of them with expertise. Her cell phone dings—it must have been a thirteenth birthday gift; Mom and Dad said we had to be thirteen to have a cell phone—and she texts something so fast her fingers are a blur, then goes back to the laptop.

On the Facebook page, she hovers the pointer over the status update box and types in, *My sister is home! Charlotte is home! :-)* "And wait 'til you see how many hits you got on YouTube," she says, clicking over. "All of the newscasts about you are here, the press conferences, things like that. The cast of a Disney Channel show did a bunch of stranger danger and self-defense videos for Dad's foundation. Dad's gone on a bunch of talk shows, and those are on YouTube too." She clicks on the top link. "But this video, this is the main one. Almost a million hits." She hits Play.

A video of a football game appears. Half of the players are in blue and white uniforms. "This is the Bantam Dragons team," Alexa says. "The team that played after ours that day."

That day. The last day. I recognize Greenfield Park, where the Dragons play.

"The cops asked all the parents who recorded the games that day to turn in their videos," Alexa continues. "They found this on one of them. It was the only clue to your disappearance."

The football game plays in the foreground, but the video darkens except for a circle in the upper right corner, highlighting the blurry patch of trees in the background.

Standing in the patch of trees, barely visible, are two people.

A man in jeans, a Dragons baseball cap, and sunglasses.

A girl in a blue and white cheerleader uniform, her black hair in pigtails tied with blue and white ribbons.

She's looking up at him and nodding, then together they walk away, until they're no longer on camera.

"That's how we knew you didn't run away or wander off and get lost," Alexa says. "We knew you walked off with that guy."

I can't breathe. I can't breathe. His hands are around my neck, and they squeeze, squeeze, squeeze.

Alexa stares hard at me through her black makeup. "They interviewed every single dad who had a football player or cheerleader on the Dragons league because of that baseball cap he wore. Uncles, grandfathers, too. But eventually, they had to rule everyone out. They figured that guy probably wasn't a real Dragon dad, that he just got the hat from somewhere. Apparently they were right."

I can't even nod.

Alexa clicks on a few more videos. The self-defense and stranger danger clips. Interviews with Dad, clutching Wiggles, my old pink teddy bear, and pleading for whoever had taken me to let me go. Reporters standing with microphones outside our house and on the football field. Dad on news programs and talk shows.

"What about you and Mom?" I ask. "Didn't you go on the shows too?"

"Mom did in the beginning. They interviewed me in the beginning too, but then I dyed my hair and got my piercings and changed my name to Lex Enola, and Dad wouldn't let me anywhere near the cameras."

She clicks back to the Facebook page, and there are already over a hundred comments on her status update. Lots of exclamation points. Everyone is welcoming me home. Some of them said they prayed for me. "Wow." Alexa turns off the computer and returns it to the desk.

"So . . . with all this going on," I say carefully, because I think I already know the answer, "that's why you're not doing cheerleading or anything else in the Dream Book?"

"The what?"

I blink at her. "That pink diary we had with the little lock and the two keys? We wrote everything we wanted to do in it. The *Dream* Book."

She twists her hair around her finger. "Oh. Yeah. I forgot about that."

A punch to the gut: that's what those words are. I hide the tears in my eyes by crossing the room to study the maps on her wall. She marked the maps with lots of blue pins, some green, and a few red. "What's all this for?" I ask.

"These are maps of Woodland Creek and the towns surrounding us." She comes over and points to the map in the center, smiling for the first time in hours. "See? This is our house." Our neighborhood is neatly outlined, each street labeled, each house represented by a little square with its address printed in tiny numbers. Our house, 1453 Robin's Nest Lane, is circled in black and has a single black pin stuck in the middle.

"The blue pins are where the sex offenders live," Alexa says.

She watches me carefully as I look at all the blue pins. Too many to count.

"In Kendrick County alone, there are two hundred and twenty-six registered sex offenders," she says. She goes to her laptop and opens it again. "I wasn't able to check the registry in rehab. There's probably more now." She clicks on a website, then scrolls down a long list that appears on her monitor. "Yep. Two more. That brings it to two hundred and twenty-eight."

She digs two blue pins from a box on the desk, finds the addresses on the map, and sticks them in. "Most of the sex offenders live in the bad neighborhoods, like these two new guys. But every town has at least a few. You'd be surprised."

Not really. Not anymore. "What about the other colors?" I say.

"The greens are for the ones who got sent back to prison. The reds . . . those are the child sex offenders." There are a lot fewer red pins than blue, but enough to make me shudder. "Those are the ones I watch the most," Alexa says.

"What do you mean, watch?"

"I go watch their houses. Make sure they're not, you know, holding some kid captive."

I suck in air. "You were looking for me."

Her gaze flits away.

"How did you know I was so close to home?" I ask.

"I didn't know you were close," she says. "I thought you were dead. Anyway, everyone assumed that if you were still alive, that guy would have taken you far away or sold you off to some other pervert. But it's not like I had a car and could go driving around the country to look for you. I did what I could do."

"Oh." Then: "That was sweet of you. To look for me."

"I was arrested twice," she says, snickering. "For harassing them. Like *I'm* the menace to society."

"You were *arrested?*"

She waves me off. "I followed them around and told everyone they talked to that they were sex offenders. Also I egged someone's house and keyed *Sex Offender* into someone's car. Misdemeanors. I had to pay for the damages and do community service. Totally worth it. I'd do it again, and worse, if Dad and Lindo weren't always on my case."

She runs her finger over the maps, up and down, traveling the paths of the streets. She stops, then sticks a black pin in one of the houses. "This is where you were," she murmurs. "2339 Mill Road, Pleasantview, Illinois." She puts the finger of one hand on the black pin that marks our house in Woodland Creek, and puts the finger of her other hand on the black pin of Alan Shaw's house. The two pins are less than three feet from each other.

Alexa takes a black marker and draws a circle around his house, then scribbles it in. She doesn't stop, making the circle bigger and bigger, digging harder and harder, until the map gets a hole in it.

Without stopping her circles, she gestures to the dresser with her head. "I have some T-shirts and sweats in the top drawer if you want to use them as pajamas." Her voice is strained and I can tell she's trying to get rid of me so I won't see her cry.

I stop watching her and go open the drawer. Everything is black and ripped and held together with safety pins.

Our Dream Book said we were going to wear the trendiest fashions. I doubt I'd see anything like these clothes in *Teen Vogue*.

When I come back from the bathroom wearing her black T-shirt and sweats, Alexa is still drawing the circle.

A shuffling wakes me up with a start.

shuffle shuffle

I go rigid. Something's different.

That's right: I'm home. Sleeping in a soft bed, with thick warm covers. Alone. My twin sister is sleeping on the floor next to me. My mother is sleeping down the hall.

My father is sleeping somewhere else.

shuffle shuffle

I go rigid again.

The shuffling is coming from the other side of the wall, from my pink and white bedroom, that I haven't seen yet.

"Alexa?" I whisper it.

She doesn't answer.

"Lex?"

No answer. I squint through the darkness and see the sleeping bag on the floor, but she's not in it.

Oh god oh god oh god, it's *him*, he's in my bedroom, I *know* it. He woke up, escaped the handcuffs, escaped the guard, escaped the hospital, and came here. I was bad, I didn't behave, I called for help, I left him, and now he's replacing me with her, just like he promised he would.

His hands are around my throat, cutting off my air, but I jump out of bed and run from the room, limbs burning with fear. Maybe it's not too late. Maybe I can catch them before he takes her away. I'll promise to go back to him, promise to be good, I'll stay with him forever, if only he'll let her go . . .

The door to my room is opened a crack and I burst inside. "Wait!"

Alexa. She's still here, thank God. White spiky hair, dressed in black, eyes wide and startled.

But I don't see him.

He's not here. He is *not* here. He's in the hospital, handcuffed to the bed rails and guarded by an armed police officer.

The fear drains from me in a rush, turning my muscles to jelly, and I slide down the wall to the floor. I sob with relief, then look up.

Clothes I wore when I was eleven are strewn all over the room, some ripped to pieces.

Closet doors flung open and hanging by a hinge.

Mirrors shattered.

Drawers pulled open, some pulled out completely. One lies broken on the floor.

Dragonettes cheer trophies on the floor on the other side of the room, as if they'd been hurled against the wall.

Every single photo that had been hanging on my bulletin board lies in crumpled pieces on the floor.

Wiggles, my pink teddy bear, lies discarded in the corner, limbs askew.

The pink covers from my bed have been torn off. The mattress lopsided, angled, pulled off its frame, one corner on the floor.

Alexa's bed, next to it, is made up neatly, its pink covers perfectly straight. Pillows plumped. Her purple bear, Giggles, sits between them.

Alexa is looking at me, frozen, eyes wide with guilt.

I look at those three last things, over and over again.

My bed: destroyed. Alexa's bed: neat. Alexa's eyes: wide with guilt.

She did this. Alexa. Alexa destroyed my things.

"I—I did this a long time ago," she says. "That's why I kept the room locked. I was trying to fix it before you woke up."

In her hands is our Dream Book. It's torn in half, straight down the spine.

My Keeper's hands squeeze my throat and all I can squeak out is, "Why?"

Silence. Then her jaw clenches and her guilty eyes narrow into rage. She hurls the Dream Book and it hits the wall right over my head, and its pages flutter over me like dozens of brittle, dead butterfly wings.

"Why did you go off with that man, Charlotte?" she screams. "You just walked away with him! How could you do something so stupid? You ruined everything. *You ruined everything!*"

Invisible hands are at my throat, and Alexa and the ransacked room and the pages of the Dream Book rush down a long dark tunnel, and I can't breathe, I can't breathe, I can't breathe.

chapter nine

I spend the rest of the night in a stupor of disbelief. Alexa spends the rest of the night crying. She clings to me on her bed in Dad's old office, choking on her sobs, begging me to forgive her.

By the time the sun rises, I realize that I do forgive her. Alexa is my sister. My Keeper may not have taken her, but he broke her as badly as he broke me.

If Mom overheard what happened between Alexa and me, she doesn't mention it at breakfast. She's sluggish as she gives me a dose of pills from the arsenal of antibiotics and vitamins the doctors prescribed. She moves like an arthritic old woman as she scrambles egg whites on the stove and heats turkey sausage patties in the microwave. She makes three plates, but doesn't touch her food. "You eat mine, honey," she says, sliding her plate over to me. "I'm not hungry anyway, and you need to build up your strength." She downs four aspirin instead.

I remember my parents drinking the occasional glass of wine or champagne to celebrate something, but they never got drunk. And the only things my Keeper ever drinks are soda and coffee. I've never seen anyone with a hangover before, but there's no mistaking that my mother is indeed hung over.

Dad comes to pick us up while we're still eating, and Alexa and I go to get dressed. It's Monday, a school day, but she's coming with me to his house. Mom and Dad decided that they don't want to separate us so soon after we got each other back. They're letting her stay with me until after Thanksgiving.

I'm relieved, because even though she destroyed my things and threw the Dream Book at me and said I ruined everything, I don't want to go to Dad's new house without her.

She spikes her white hair, smears black makeup under her eyes, and pushes the safety pin through her eyebrow before changing into another all-black uniform. "You can wear my stuff if you want," she offers with a casual wave at her dresser, but all of her clothes are short and tight, designed to draw attention to her body. I don't want to draw attention to my body, so I wear the light pink hoodie and sweatpants that Mom brought for me at the hospital.

"Girls!" Dad jingles his keys in the foyer, anxious to leave. But I linger in the front doorway, a ball of anxiety and dread settling in my stomach. I don't want to leave my house. I don't want to leave my mom.

"Call if you need me, Charlotte," she says, placing her palms on my cheeks. "My phone number is the same as it was before. I never changed it, in case you were able to call. Do you remember it?"

I reach into my memory, then recite the number to her. It rolls easily off my tongue.

"Good," she says. "If you call, I'll drop everything and come get you." She kisses my forehead, then gives me a hug so tight I begin to think she'll never let go. I don't really want her to. "You just got home, and now you have to leave again." She looks accusingly at Dad.

But that's okay. I'm back now, and soon Mom will stop drinking, Alexa will stop causing trouble, and Dad will come home.

For now, though, Dad lives on the far side of Woodland Creek, on Greenleaf Avenue. He drives Alexa and me there in his white sedan. As much as I don't want to like it, Dad's house is pretty. It's small, like Mom's—how weird to think of it as just Mom's house—but it has two stories. It's white with forest-green shutters, and mums bloom under the windows. A harvest wreath hangs on the front door.

Dad pulls into the garage. "I have something to show you." He seems a little nervous as he quickly guides me through a shiny blue kitchen and into a large open room at the back of the house. An office: computers, printers, phones, tables covered with papers. Alexa stays close at my side, the grumpy, defensive anger back in her eyes.

"This," Dad says, gesturing to the room, "is the headquarters of the Charlotte Weatherstone Foundation. We knocked down the wall between the living room and dining room. Cheaper than renting a place."

One wall is papered with hundreds of children's faces, all under the words NEVER LOSE HOPE, stenciled in big blue letters. The opposite wall is papered with more faces of children under the word FOUND! Smack-dab in the middle is that photo of me from the Internet, eleven years old in my cheer uniform, innocent and untarnished.

But mostly I see teddy bears. At least a hundred of them. All pink. Stuffed onto shelves from floor to ceiling.

"I told you there were more teddy bears waiting for you at home," Dad says. He pulls an extra-furry pink bear with a magenta bow tie from the shelf and hands it to me. "When you disappeared with that man, I went on TV to beg for your release. I was holding the pink teddy bear from your bed. People started leaving pink teddy bears at the football field where you disappeared, along with notes and prayers, and other people sent them from around the country. Now it's the official symbol of the Charlotte Weatherstone Foundation. We get so many that we give one to every family we help."

A chubby young woman with a tangled mess of blond curls and a freckled nose smiles at me from behind a computer. She walks over, wringing her hands. "Charlotte, it's so wonderful to meet you. Welcome home."

I nod at her, disconcerted that she knows who I am even though I don't know who she is. I hate that she knows what happened to me.

She gives Alexa a smile that seems over-eager. "Lex, hi!" Her tone is over-eager too. False.

Alexa replies with an unimpressed grunt.

"Charlotte, this is Marissa," Dad says. "She's the foundation's biggest volunteer. She's in charge of PR and publicity. Newsletters, media coverage, things like that."

I don't know what to say. I finally decide on, "Thank you. It must be a lot of work."

"Cory," Marissa says, "you've gotten about twenty more e-mails in the last half hour, and six voicemails. You'll have to do another press conference soon. They want to interview Charlotte, but I'm telling everyone she needs her privacy."

She's not bad, this Marissa. I kind of like her.

She's got hazel eyes, and she flashes them at my dad before quickly lowering them. Her cheeks flush and she hides them behind her curls.

I think . . . yeah, I'm pretty sure she has a crush on my dad.

It's understandable, really. My dad has always been very charming, and he's very handsome. But Marissa has to know that now that I'm back, Dad's coming home to Mom and Alexa and me. Maybe not right away, but eventually. Soon. I need him at home. I need my family together. Marissa has to understand that.

"There's more, Charlotte," Dad says. He leads me through the foundation's office, followed by Alexa and Marissa, and sits me on a couch in the family room. Marissa hesitates in the doorway. Alexa sits right next to me, stiff like a bodyguard, a snake ready to strike at the slightest provocation.

I only have time to notice more pink teddy bears all over the room before Dad clears his throat. "You're so strong, Charlotte," he says. "Strong for surviving that ordeal, strong for calling for help. It was a mistake to assume that you weren't strong enough to hear about the divorce, so I'm not going to hide this next piece of news from you. It's better if you find out from me than someone else."

"Don't you dare, Dad," Alexa says. "She's not ready. You said you were going to wait."

The air turns heavy and thick. I take the biggest teddy bear and put it on my lap, like a shield.

Dad waves Marissa over, and she comes.

No.

He takes her hand.

No. No, no, no.

"Charlotte," he begins.

I sit there dumbly, clutching the teddy bear in both hands while my Keeper clutches my neck in both of his. I know what Dad's going to say: *Marissa is my girlfriend.*

"Marissa," Dad says, "is my wife."

I blink. Wife? As in *married*?

Dad searches my face. But I must be frozen, because his anxiety melts into relief. He puts his arm around Marissa, his wife. "Our second anniversary is in February."

Alexa puts her arm around me, and I'm glad she's holding me, because I'm spiraling. I can't feel the couch beneath me.

Dad tells me how they met. He was organizing the search for a missing child a few towns away, and she was a volunteer. She used to do PR and publicity for the county's crisis center. She's twenty-six. Ten years older than Alexa and me. Thirteen years younger than Mom.

He rubs his hand up and down Marissa's arm. My blurry eye is tricking me: I'm seeing everything opposite. Mom has wavy black hair, not curly blond. Mom's eyes are brown, not hazel. Mom is tall and lean, not short and plump. Mom's nose is long and regal, not stubby and freckled.

But Dad is rubbing this blond-haired, hazel-eyed, short and chubby woman's arm, all proud and protective, the way he used to do with Mom. He loves this woman.

How can I put my family back together when my father is married to someone else?

Dad frowns at me. "This is a lot for you to take in in such a short time . . . it's too much. We should have waited."

"You *think*?" snaps Alexa. "Let's leave," she says to me. "Right now. We can leave and never come back."

"No," I squeak, because Dad thinks I'm strong. "I'm fine. Just . . . surprised. I'm fine, really." I force a smile and keep it there until Dad smiles back.

Dad's new wife, the traitor named Marissa, gives me a trembly smile. Dad whispers into her ear, and she nods uncertainly, then goes upstairs.

Alexa tightens her arm around me. "I hate you, Dad," she mutters. "I hate you so much."

Dad ignores her.

Marissa comes down the stairs, and she's carrying something on her hip.

Something tiny.

Something pink.

Something with rosy cheeks and blond curls and a toothless smile.

Something that reaches out to my father with pudgy little hands. "*Da*da!"

I've never seen Dad's smile so wide before. "Charlotte," he says, "this is your baby sister." He takes the baby, my baby *sister*, and sits next to me. He jostles her in his lap and she squeals with delight.

"Her name," he says, "is CiGi Hope. CiGi, for Charlotte Grace. We named her after you, sweetheart. In your memory."

Alexa's fingers dig into my shoulder.

I start to sweat. My throat closes up and I can't swallow. My heart pounds in my ears.

Dad thought I was dead, so he made someone to replace me. I behaved for my Keeper, I behaved so he wouldn't replace me, and I was replaced after all.

CiGi gurgles.

My Keeper's invisible hands punch me, strangle me, throttle me. He kicks me in the gut.

My stomach clenches, and I throw up.

chapter ten

Vomit is all over me, all over the couch, all over the teddy bear, all over Alexa. She gags. Dad swoops CiGi away as Marissa rushes from the room.

"Jesus, Dad!" Alexa yells. "You and Mom made me promise not to say anything, but then you shoved your new family in her face. What did you think would happen? It makes *me* want to puke too. If I'd known you were going to do it like this, I would have told her last night."

"I'm sorry, Charlotte," Dad says. "You're all over the news, TV, online . . . the reporters . . . I had to tell you before you found out from someone else." He's pale and shaking, and he looks like he's about to crumble. He reaches for me with the arm that's not holding the baby, but stops short.

"I'm fine," I lie. "It's all the food I've been eating. All that pizza last night. Two servings of breakfast this morning." Those hands are around my throat. I can feel them. My stomach churns, then clenches, and I dry heave. Dad hollers for Marissa to hurry.

Marissa rushes back with a can of ginger ale and an armful of towels. I should apologize for puking all over her couch, but I can't get the words out. While I was locked away in that attic and forced to do awful, horrible, disgusting things, Marissa married my dad, and then she had a baby with him.

The baby is wailing, and Dad is bouncing her, looking worriedly at me. "I'm taking you to the doctor," he says.

"I'm fine," I say, then dry-heave again. "I just need . . ." To get out of here. ". . . to clean up."

Marissa reaches to help me up, but I let Alexa help me instead. The can of ginger ale hisses when Marissa opens it. "Take this," she says, handing it to me. "It'll settle your stomach. I'll clean up in here. Lex, show Charlotte where your room is so you can both change. Just toss your clothes in the hamper and I'll be right up to wash them."

As Alexa takes me upstairs, I notice the pictures lining the staircase walls. Most of them are of CiGi. Some of them are of Dad, Marissa, and CiGi. One of them is of Dad, Marissa, CiGi, and Alexa. Alexa and her dyed-white hair fit right in with the golden-haired family, but she's the only one who's not smiling.

There are lots of photos of me, too: candids, posed, school portraits. They stop at fifth grade.

Alexa brings me to the first bedroom. "This is ours," she says with a sigh. "Your bed must be new." Against opposite walls are two beds, made up neatly with pretty paisley comforters with matching pillowcases. Other than that, there are no signs that this is a teenage girls' room. The walls are white and plain, and there's nothing on the dresser or desk.

Alexa peels off her pukey clothes right in front of me. "I'm sorry I didn't tell you." Under her breath she adds, "I hate him so much."

"Is there anything else I need to know, Alexa?" I say. "I can't handle any more surprises. If Dad tries to send you back to rehab for telling me, I'll say that I made you do it."

"Nothing else. I swear."

I don't know if I believe her.

"Do you like Marissa?" I ask.

"No. She sucks."

I believe her on that one. Alexa doesn't like anybody. I can't even be sure she likes me. Her words from last night—*you ruined everything!*—still echo in my head.

The closet in our little bedroom is filled with clothes. Jeans in a variety of sizes. Sweaters and tops in all colors. "Are these yours?" I ask Alexa.

She snorts. "No way. Marissa must have bought them for you while you were in the hospital. She must have cleaned out the juniors department."

She opens a drawer of ripped black clothes. "You can wear my stuff, if you want."

I shake my head. From the closet, I choose a pair of jeans that I think will fit and a bulky blue sweater, then find the bathroom so I can change in private. The tub is a regular, modern tub—no old-fashioned lion paws—and it's cluttered with bottles of baby shampoo and baby soap and baby bath toys. A rubber ducky smiles at me. I draw the curtain closed over it.

On the sink are a brand-new toothbrush, a tube of toothpaste, and a hairbrush. I assume they're for me. Marissa has done more to prepare for my homecoming than my own mother has.

I resent her for that. My mom was in the hospital with me, and Marissa was out shopping.

I pull off my pukey pink sweatshirt.

Good girl. See, that wasn't hard. Now take off your skirt.

No. He's not here. He is *not* here. I shake his voice from my head, then turn off the light so I can change my clothes and brush my teeth without seeing myself in the mirror.

I wonder if The One Before has a new baby sister too. A replacement baby.

If she does have a new baby sister, she'll never get to meet her.

chapter eleven

Dad made appointments for me that fill up the rest of the day: a dentist for my teeth, an orthopedist for my knee, an optometrist for my eye. Alexa comes with, and watches over everything with crossed arms and a scowl. I have six cavities, a left knee that requires intense physical therapy, and a right eye that will always be blurry on the edges.

The entire time, Dad rambles proudly about how strong and brave I am. It's almost dinner time by the time we get back to his house. I'm exhausted. I want to go home to Mom, or maybe I just want to avoid Marissa and the replacement baby, but Dad's not taking us back until tomorrow.

When we walk in, Agent Lindo is there, drinking coffee with Marissa in the family room, which has no sign of my earlier puking incident. Lindo's massive form fills the entire armchair, and the coffee mug looks tiny in his hand. He and Marissa are shuffling through a stack of papers on the coffee table and murmuring to each other. I don't see CiGi. Good. Even thinking about her makes me queasy again.

As soon as Dad and I sit on the couch across from Lindo, my air is cut off. The top paper in the stack is a photograph.

A man lying in a hospital bed. Connected to tubes. Gray. Frowning.

His eyes are open, hard, cold. Staring directly at me.

I can't move. I can't take my eyes off the photo. Off of *him*. He knows I ran away, he knows I left him, and he's furious.

His hands creep up around my throat.

The photo is swept away by a hand with chipped black polish. Alexa's. "Get this picture out of here, Lindo. It's traumatizing her, can't you see that?"

"Lex," Dad warns. "Watch your tone."

But without my Keeper staring at me, I can blink. I can breathe.

Dad thinks I'm strong. Strong and brave. Too strong and brave to be traumatized by a stupid photograph.

"Sorry, Charlotte," Lindo says. "I stopped by because I have news. As you saw in the photo, Shaw woke up today."

Dad lets out a slow breath while I gasp.

"Don't worry," Lindo says. "He's still under guard. You're safe."

"There's going to be a trial now, right?" I say. "I have to testify, and he'll be there?"

"You don't need to worry about that," Dad says. "You can do your testimony on video. You'll never see that man again, Charlotte, I promise. Not even in court."

The last time I saw him, he locked me in the wire crate, told me he loved me, and left. And now I'll never see him again, not even in court.

"It'll be a while before a trial," Lindo says. "He's still too weak to transfer out of the hospital, and we're still building our case. He's saying he's innocent."

Dad slaps his hand on the table. "You mean he denies he kidnapped my daughter? Jesus, they found her locked in a crate in his attic! Is he saying she put herself in there?"

I flinch. I don't want my dad to think of me in the attic. I don't want anyone to think of me in the attic.

"He can proclaim his innocence all he wants when it comes to Charlotte," Lindo says. "We have enough proof to send him away for the rest of his life and beyond. But he's not answering our questions about the girl before Charlotte. He's denying he kidnapped another girl."

"But he did," I say. "He told me so."

"What exactly did he tell you?" the detective asks. "Did he ever tell you her name? Did he mention where she was from, what she looked like? How old she was? Anything?"

"He called her 'The One Before,'" I say. "He never said what she looked like or anything. He only said that she never behaved and she kept trying to leave him. He said that if I didn't behave, he'll have to do to me what he did to her, and then he'll have to get my sister to replace me." It's the same information I gave at the hospital, but it's all I have.

"Unfortunately, that's not enough information," Lindo says. "We can't charge him with a second victim without proof that one existed."

"What about DNA?" Dad asks.

"The only viable DNA we've found belongs to either Charlotte or Shaw."

"Fingerprints?"

Agent Lindo shakes his head. "We've found a few partial prints in the attic, but that house is seventy years old. Two families lived in it before the Shaws moved in. Who knows how many people have been in that house over the years? It would be impossible to find a match for every one of those partial prints."

"I didn't make her up," I say. "I'm not lying."

"No one's accusing you of lying," Lindo says. "But it's likely he fabricated her to scare you into behaving."

It takes a few moments to sink in: The One Before was fabricated. He made her up. She never existed. He was tricking me the whole time.

She isn't real! He never snatched anyone else away from her family and locked her up and beat her and made her do things she should never have to do.

He only did those things to me. I'm his only victim.
There is no One Before. She's not real. She never existed.
I'm so happy for her.

chapter twelve

I can't sleep.

Alexa is sleeping in the bed next to mine. Dad and Marissa are sleeping in the room next to ours. CiGi is sleeping in the room across the hall. Everything is quiet, everything is peaceful, except inside my mind.

Each second of my four years, two months, and seven days in the attic dragged on forever, and nothing ever changed. But outside the attic, everything changed, and so violently fast. Destruction and devastation for all of us, whether we were in the attic or out.

I want to curl into a tight little ball and forget about my Keeper. I want to forget about my broken family. I want to forget about The One Before, who never existed, and the replacement baby, who does. I want to forget everything.

Something is churning inside of me, a storm fierce and howling and dark. But I can't let it take over. I can't let myself cry. If I start crying, my tears will turn into a tsunami, and it will sweep me away.

chapter thirteen

Dad drops Alexa and me off at home the next morning. After telling me to call him every day, as many times as I want, and promising to pick us up again this weekend, he reluctantly lets us out of the car, then watches until we're inside the house before he drives away.

The first thing I notice upon entering is the kitchen is clean. Uncluttered. Bright. Even Mom's eyes sparkle. The recycle bin is filled with empty liquor bottles; she must have poured it all down the sink. "Come on, girls," she says, her voice clear and smooth. "Let's go sit outside. It's such a nice day."

Her enthusiasm is contagious enough to quiet the storm in my mind, and I eagerly agree. But Alexa makes a face. "It's too cold."

"We'll bundle up and drink hot tea," Mom says. "Charlotte needs fresh air and sunshine."

Alexa mumbles something about bleaching her roots and goes to her room, slamming the door behind her. I start to go after her, but Mom says to leave her be. "I want some alone time with you anyway."

While Mom makes tea, I notice that a new pink teddy bear has been added to the pile in the family room. What makes this one stand out are the blue and white pompoms attached to its paws. Next to it is an envelope covered with hearts and smiley faces and *Welcome Home Charlotte!!!!!* in big fat bubble letters, and I know immediately who it's from: Bailey Brandis, my friend from

Dragonettes. I tear open the envelope and pull out the card. The note contains more exclamation points than words.

Charlotte!!!!!
I'm so happy you're home!!!!
I missed you soooo much!!!! Call me!!!
xoxo,
Bailey

"She dropped that off for you yesterday," Mom says. "I told her you'll call her when you're ready."

I'm ready now, but Mom hands me her yellow wool coat and a steaming mug of tea, and we go outside to sit on the glider in our backyard. Our oak trees tower over us, their trunks surrounded by leaves of crimson and gold. The tree house Dad built for us is still there, and our tire swing, too.

Mom and I warm our hands by cupping them around the mugs. The air is crisp and cool and fresh, and I love every molecule of it. I can't believe I'm sitting outside. Free.

The One Before was always free, because she never existed. She was just a lie. A threat. A trick.

Mom takes a sip of her tea. "Your dad told me you know about Marissa and the baby. You okay?"

I shrug. "Are *you* okay?"

"You're home," she says. "I've never been happier in my life."

"But before," I insist.

She looks down at her mug, and it takes her a long time to answer. "The last four years were . . . hard. But that's over now."

"You had no one to help you," I say.

"My friends helped. Uncle Tim and Aunt Dina helped. They even asked Lex and me to come live with them."

Uncle Tim is Mom's brother. He and Aunt Dina and my cousins Nick and Jason live in Georgia. "How come you didn't go?"

"Because," she says, "I kept imagining you escaping, and coming home, looking for us, but the house was empty. I couldn't leave. So I got a new job, and . . . waited for you to come home."

"You're not a fitness instructor anymore?"

"I haven't done that since you disappeared," she says. "Besides, I needed a full-time job with benefits. My friend Aubrey hired me as an accounting clerk at her law firm in town. It pays well. The people are nice. On the tough days, when I can't get myself to leave the house, she lets me work from home."

I put my head on Mom's shoulder as we rock gently back and forth in the glider. I don't know if other sixteen-year-olds sit like this with their moms, but they should.

"I'm sorry about your bedroom," she says. "Lex did that one night three years ago. I was so upset. I wanted to keep your room exactly as it was the day you disappeared. But when I saw what she did, I just locked the door. I could never bring myself to open it again. It was too painful. I'm so sorry I didn't clean your room before you came home. I'm sorry for lots of things."

"So it's true, then," I say. "About the drinking."

I take her hand, and we rock back and forth, back and forth, before she answers.

"The worst part was knowing you were suffering," she says. "Someone had taken you away, and all I could think about was what could be happening to you. You had to be scared. You had to be suffering. Day after day, year after year. I felt so helpless. I joined a support group for parents of missing children, and whenever one of their children was found dead—" She inhales a sharp, squeaky breath. "I shouldn't be telling you this. It's too much."

"No, Mom. Tell me. I want to know."

She sniffles. "I envied them," she whispers. "Their child was dead, but at least they knew where they were now. At least they knew their child was no longer suffering. At least they could visit their child's grave."

There is a lump in my throat so large that I can barely speak around it. "Did you wish I was dead?"

"Charlotte, no, of course not!" she says. "I wished that you would come home. I wished that I could turn back time so I could stop that man from taking you. I wished that he had taken me in your place. I wished, hoped, prayed for so many things, but I never, ever wished that you were dead."

"Dad thought I was dead," I say.

"I'll never forgive him for that. We had no proof you were dead. I told him, I told everybody, that until we had proof, we needed to believe that you were still alive. And look, here you are. Alive, and home. My wish came true." She kisses the top of my head. "I love you so much."

"I love you too."

Somewhere overhead, perhaps from a branch of the tire-swing tree, a bird chirps. High and sweet.

Mom and I rock for a long time, our fingers entwined.

chapter fourteen

Our feet crunch on the gravel parking lot as Dad leads Alexa and me to a big white building shaped like a barn. Alexa grabs my arm and whispers into my ear. "When you're talking to the therapist, just sit there and don't say anything."

"Why?"

"Because therapists are full of shit," she says. "All she's going to do is give you a naked Barbie and say, 'Show me on the dolly where the bad man touched you.' Do you really want to talk about that?"

Actually, no, I don't want to talk about that. Not at all. And besides, those hands are back around my throat, so I couldn't talk about it, even if I wanted to.

But the hands disappear the moment we step inside. This place is shaped like a barn on the outside, but inside it's a bright, open space with shiny wooden floors, lavender walls that stretch two stories high, and wide windows with sheer lavender curtains. Even the air smells like lavender, not the usual barn smell of horse and hay.

The close end of the room is set up for little kids, with a wooden chest of toys and a dollhouse in the corner. In the middle of the space is an easel and a long table covered with art supplies—paints, brushes, crayons, clay. The far end is dominated by a velvet lavender sofa surrounded by large floor pillows and soft shaggy rugs in light purples. A stack of glossy magazines on the floor. A stereo and a pile of CDs. A bookshelf stacked with books.

A woman in a flowing lavender dress steps forward. "Hello, Charlotte. Welcome. I'm Talia Goldbloom."

Her voice is soft and warm and feminine, with a slight clipped accent. It's November, and chilly, but she's barefoot. Lavender toenails peek out from under her skirt, along with an ankle charm bracelet that whisper-jingles with each step. Her hair is long and silver and wavy, like she braided it when it was wet and let it dry that way.

She and Dad give each other a professional hug. "Your girl is home," she says. "Congratulations, Cory."

Dad nods, and I can tell he's trying not to cry.

Alexa, in her oversized black coat, black eye makeup, and white spiky hair, hangs back by the barn door with crossed arms and a scowl.

"Lex, it's lovely to see you again," Dr. Goldbloom says to her. "I hope you've been well."

"I've been great," Alexa says dully.

"You're welcome to come back any time, whether you talk or not."

Alexa grunts.

Dad glowers at her, then turns to Dr. Goldbloom and me. "Lex and I will be in the sitting room across the way. We'll be back in an hour."

They leave, and I follow Dr. Goldbloom to the lavender couch at the back of the barn. Am I supposed to lie on it while she sits behind me, taking notes? I don't know a lot about therapists, but I know enough to realize she's probably analyzing my every word, my every movement.

I don't want her to analyze me. I want her to tell my dad that I'm fine, that what happened to me didn't affect me at all. I want her to tell my dad that I'm ready to go back to school, that I'm ready to join the cheerleading squad and go out with my friends.

The doctor sits on the couch first, curling her legs under her. She gestures to the space next to her.

The couch *does* look comfortable. Tentatively, stiffly, I perch on the opposite end, but the cushion is so plush that I sink all the way back. My feet dangle awkwardly off the edge. I slide off my sneakers and tuck my feet under me. My knee hurts, sitting like this, but I don't let it show. There are several plump throw pillows on the couch, and I take one and hold it in my lap.

Dr. Goldbloom says nothing, just gazes at me, an approving smile on her face.

I smile back, brightly, to show her how well adjusted and un-damaged I am.

"Would you like to pick out some music?" she asks. "Look through some magazines? Paint? We can go for a walk if you'd prefer. The leaves are so pretty this time of year."

"I thought I was supposed to talk about what happened to me."

"We can do that too."

"We don't need to talk about that, though," I say.

"We can talk about whatever you'd like."

I like Dr. Goldbloom.

But I like her too instantly to trust her. I liked Marissa instantly, and she turned out to be my dad's wife. I liked my Keeper instantly, that day on the football field, when he smiled and asked me to help him get ice cream for the team.

"What would you like to talk about?" Dr. Goldbloom asks. Her voice is soft and sweet, like a lullaby.

I struggle for a moment in the silence, wondering what to say that won't make her analyze me. "Where are you from?"

"Israel. Tel Aviv. I've lived in the United States for twenty years."

"Why is your office in a barn?"

"I used to have a traditional office in Chicago, right in the heart of downtown. But it felt too frantic and constricting. When this place went up for sale a few years ago, I bought it and converted it." She looks around and sighs happily.

"Why is everything lavender?" I ask.

"It's my favorite color. I find it soothing. Do you like it?"

"Yes." That's the truth. It is soothing in here. Peaceful. Dr. Goldbloom is very soothing and peaceful, too. It's all I can do not to throw myself into her arms and start bawling. I hold my breath until the urge passes.

"Why don't you want to talk about what happened to you?" she asks.

"Because it's in the past," I say with a shrug that I hope is casual. "It happened, it's over, and I'm ready to move on."

"I can see that," she says. "So, there is no need to talk about your past. Why don't we talk about your present, then. You're back home. How are you adjusting?"

It takes me a while to think of an answer. "I'm very happy to be home," I say. "Very grateful."

Her face remains open, her eyes remain friendly and warm. "There have been a lot of changes at home. Changes you weren't expecting. Changes you probably never imagined."

I take the throw pillow from my lap and hug it to my chest.

"Your parents got divorced," she says. "I'm sure you didn't expect that."

My lip trembles, so I bite it. "No."

"How do you feel about it?"

"My disappearance drove a wedge between them that they couldn't overcome." I parrot the words my dad said the night I returned home and found his stuff gone.

"That is correct. But how do you feel about it?"

"My dad's already remarried, and they have a baby," is my reply.

Dr. Goldbloom's eyes are blue and deep. Warm and kind. There is no judgment in them, or pity. "You must be feeling quite powerless right now," she says. "Which is probably the way you felt when you were with Alan Shaw. Is that right, Charlotte?"

Dr. Goldbloom analyzed me, as easy as that.

I push the pillow away and pick up a magazine. *Seventeen*, the current issue. I flip through the pages one by one, recognizing none of the actors and pop stars. My eyes keep going blurry, so I just skim the headlines and look at the photos. One double-page layout is a tutorial of how to braid your hair into a crown. An article lists nine fun fall date ideas. The couples in the photos are having such a good time, picking apples and getting lost in corn mazes together.

"But I'm happy to be home," I tell Dr. Goldbloom when I get to the last page, just before it's time to leave. It's very important she knows that. "It's not like I wish I was back there in the attic with him. I'm sure any other missing kid would be happy to be back home, even if her disappearance caused her parents' divorce. Even if her dad got married to a woman who's only ten years older than she is, and they had a new baby to replace her." I hear the words falling out of my mouth, but I'm helpless to stop them. "Even if her mother became an alcoholic and wants to move to Georgia. Even if her twin sister turned into this angry stranger who hates everybody and who blames her for making their family fall apart. Even if she finds out The One Before never existed, but she can't stop thinking about her."

Slowly, Dr. Goldbloom nods. "Well then, Charlotte. It looks like we have plenty of things to discuss."

chapter fifteen

Powerless. Powerless.

Dr. Goldbloom's words echo in my ears the rest of the day, even after Dad takes Alexa and me back to Mom's.

After dinner, Mom opens her computer in the living room to finish up a financial report for work, so I go see what Alexa's doing. She's in her room, Dad's old office, with the door closed. Next to it, the door to our pink bedroom is closed, too. It's still locked.

At my Keeper's house, I was locked in. At my own house, I'm locked out.

Powerless.

I run my fingers down the doorframe. Our doors at home are white. The door of the attic was white too. In some places, around the doorknob and near the hinges on the doorframe, the white paint was scratched away.

Scratched away by fingernails.

Oh my God.

Hands creep up around my throat and I stumble back.

"Mom?" I call. "Mom!"

Alexa's door flies open and Mom comes running. "What is it?" they both ask. "Are you hurt? Is it your knee? What's wrong?"

"Agent Lindo," I gasp. "Do you know his number? Can you call him? Now? Please?"

"Of course," Mom says. She pulls her phone from her pocket and presses one button. "Hello, Rick? I'm fine. But Charlotte wants to t—."

I grab the phone from her and try to speak. I have to bring my own hand to my neck to convince myself my Keeper's hands aren't really there. I choke out, "She's real."

"Charlotte?" Lindo sounds muffled, and something clinks in the background, like utensils.

"There are claw marks on the attic door," I say. "I didn't make them. The One Before did. There were bleach stains on the floor, too. One from me, and one from her." Mom and Alexa whiten, their faces sick with horror.

"I saw the claw marks and the bleach stains," Lindo says. "But they don't give us the proof we need."

"It proves she's real," I say. "It proves he didn't make her up just to threaten me. It proves you need to look harder for evidence."

"We *are* looking for evidence, Charlotte, but we haven't found anything conclusive."

"She was a real person," I say, "and she's been missing for so long, longer than I was. Her family doesn't know if she's alive or dead. They can't stop imagining what kind of horrible things are happening to her. They're suffering as much as she did."

Alexa's gaze falls to her boots. Mom brings her hands to her mouth.

My father needed to assume I was dead and give me a memorial so he could move on. My sister masked her grief with drugs and rebellion. My mother was in so much pain that she envied the parents of children who were found dead.

My fingers clutch the phone so tightly that my knuckles hurt. "You need to find out who she is, Agent Lindo, and you need to tell her family she's dead. They'll be sad, they'll be devastated, but it's better than not knowing. At least they'll know she's no longer suffering. At least they'll know where she is now. At least they can visit her grave."

Alexa looks up, shocked. Mom begins to cry.

"Make him tell you," I say to Lindo. "I don't care what it takes, but you need to make him tell you who she is. The One Before wouldn't want her family to fall apart because of her."

I grip the phone but I can no longer speak; the air around me has jagged edges, and I drag it painfully into my lungs.

Trembling, Mom takes the phone from my hand, mumbles a goodbye to Agent Lindo, and hangs up. Her cheeks are wet with tears. Alexa swipes hers away, smearing her black makeup.

There's a threatening pressure behind my eyes, a thunderstorm swirling in my mind. But if I start crying, I'll never stop. I turn my back, press my forehead against the locked door, dig my nails into my palms. I will *not* cry.

Alan Shaw took everything from me: my home, my family, my voice. He made me powerless.

But I'm home now. It may be split in two, but I'm home. My family may be broken, but I have it back. I have my voice back. I am not powerless anymore.

I turn around and face my mom and sister. "No more locked doors."

Alexa, cheeks hot with blood, dashes to her room. She returns with a key, and fingers shaking, presses it into my palm. I unlock the door and push it open, revealing the destruction she wreaked three years ago in a fit of rage and recrimination, blaming me for ruining everything because I walked off with a man in a Dragons cap.

"Come on, Alexa," I say. "I'll help you clean this place up. I'm sleeping in my own bed tonight."

chapter sixteen

Without a word, Alexa follows me into our bedroom. The air is musty and stale. I turn on all the lights, even the one in the closet. Alexa kneels, then carefully plucks pieces of broken glass from the carpet and drops them into our old pink wastebasket.

The pages of our Dream Book are still scattered on the floor near where she'd hurled it at me. I take all the pages, smooth them out, and stack them in chronological order.

Lead the Dragonettes to a state championship
Go to Disney World
Go on shopping sprees at the mall
Have lots of friends
Have all-night movie marathons
Make the Woodland Creek High Sparklers cheer squad
Go on lots of dates
Go to a Made for Yesterday concert
Hang out at Stubby's
Go to homecoming and prom
Get matching red convertibles

My bad eye goes blurry as I compile the pages. A dozen more, two dozen more. The pink cover with *Charlotte and Alexa's Dream Book* written in glitter paint is still whole, although the strap with the lock is torn. The little padlock dangles from the clasp. I tear the rest of the strap off, then toss the lock in the wastebasket. It makes a quiet clink as it hits the broken glass.

I place our pages of dreams between the covers. In the corner of the room is a pile of hair ribbons Alexa and I used to wear. White, blue, red, yellow. Every color, every pattern. I take a silky blue one and use it to tie the Dream Book closed.

From the periphery of my vision, I can see Alexa watching me. "Do you remember what we wrote on these pages?" I ask her.

She turns away and resumes cleaning. "No."

"Yes you do."

"I can't believe you even remember that book," she says.

"I never forgot about this book. I thought about it every day."

Her eyebrows lift, but she still won't look at me.

I don't quit. "I thought you were doing the things we wrote in here. I was sure of it."

"Why?"

"Because these are our plans. Our dreams. Even though I couldn't follow them, I was sure you were."

She snorts. "Why would I do that stuff without you?"

"Because you *could.*"

"Well," she says, thrusting out her chin, "you were wrong."

"Why did you stop following them?"

"Because I wasn't going to do them without you, okay? How could I go out there and cheer and have fun, when you were being tortured by some pedophile? Or dead?"

"Did you really think I was dead?"

A muscle twitches in Alexa's jaw. "Yeah. I thought you were dead." The words sound like she's ripping them from her throat. "It was easier to think of you as, like, an angel in heaven than it was to think of you being raped every day by that old guy you walked off with, or being rented out as a child prostitute or whatever. I didn't think you would ever come home, and I didn't want you to suffer for years and years and years for the rest of your life. So yeah. I hoped you were dead. I hoped he killed you the day he took you."

Something contracts in my chest.

The air shifts, stills, grows heavy and dense as mud. Alexa twists her white hair around her finger and whispers, "Didn't you even *try* to escape, Charlotte?"

"Once," I tell her. "In the beginning."

"What happened?"

"He said he was going to work and would be back later. It was the first time he left the house. I waited a few minutes, then tried to open the attic door. But it was a test. A trick."

Alexa is staring at me, not moving, breathing deeply. The air is still thick.

"He was standing at the top of the attic stairs," I continue. "As soon as I tried to turn the knob, he burst back in."

I thought you were a good girl!

I can still see the betrayed fury in his eyes, hear his belt snap as he chases me to the back of the attic, feel his fists as they pummel me to the floor.

"That's how my knee got twisted," I say. "Why my vision is blurry."

Alexa cringes and tugs hard at her hair.

The One Before kept trying to leave me too. But she was bad. I'll help you be good.

". . . and then he dragged out the crate."

You have a sister. A twin sister. I know where she lives.

"He said if I didn't get in," I tell Alexa, "that he would have to do to me what he did to The One Before, and then—" I have to suck in air, because it's getting hard to breathe again. "He would replace me with you."

Alexa's face whitens, her eyes darken. The coil of hair loosens itself from her finger. "You did it for me. You never fought back. Because you thought you were keeping me safe."

I pull up my gaze to meet hers. "Yeah."

"I—" It's a strangled, high-pitched word, laced with shock and grief. Then she bites her lips shut. Her chin trembles, just once, before she turns and starts cleaning the room again.

⟋⟍

It's after midnight before everything is put back in place. All of the broken things are in the garbage, our cheerleading trophies are back on the shelves, my bed is made back up as neatly as Alexa's. Wiggles sits on my bed, and Giggles sits on hers. I take all of the pink teddy bears I'd gotten at the hospital and arrange them on my bed, and pin Bailey's card to the bulletin board.

Alexa takes the Dream Book from where I'd placed it on the shelf with the trophies. Now it's my turn to watch her as she sits on her bed, unties the ribbon, and goes through each page. She breaks her silence with a chuckle. "Go on lots of dates," she says, reading one of our dreams. "Well, I *have* done that one."

That's exactly what I'd hoped for her. "You have a boyfriend?"

"No," she says with a shrug. "I just go out with lots of guys."

"Have you gone to homecoming or anything?"

"High school isn't like it is in the movies, you know," she says. "Homecoming and prom and all that? Totally lame. When I go out with guys, we hang out, drive around, party, things like that."

That's disappointing, and I don't know if I believe the dances are lame. But I don't want to seem naive, so I say nothing.

She turns back to the Dream Book, and laughs aloud at the next page. "Go to a Made for Yesterday concert? Charlotte, that band broke up years ago. One of them has a stupid reality show now, I think. It's embarrassing to even admit we once liked them."

"Well, these are the things I need to know," I say.

"Hang out at Stubby's," she continues reading with a snort. "Only the Peps hang out at that place."

"Who are the Peps?"

"Oh, you know. Bailey, Megan, Amber and the rest of them."

"You mean our friends."

"I *told* you," she says, "I'm not friends with them anymore. You know what they did two weeks after you disappeared? They went to a cheer competition in Joliet. You were missing, probably dead, and they went to a fucking cheer competition." Viciously, she turns the page, almost ripping it. "And you can forget about getting matching red convertibles. Dad won't even let me get my license, not after all the drinking and drugs and stuff. Maybe you could get your license. But a red convertible? No way."

She slams the Dream Book shut, grips it between both hands. "Charlotte, all these things in here—we wrote this stuff when we were little kids. Everything's different now. Dad's never going to divorce Marissa and forget about CiGi and give up his foundation and come back to Mom. Things will never go back to the way they were, just because you're back."

"I know," I say, although I don't mean it. "But we can still do the things in this book."

That's why we *have* to do the things in our Dream Book. Alexa needs to do them as much as I do. And I will do them double, because The One Before can't do them at all.

chapter seventeen

Alexa and I sleep in our pink bedroom that night.

With my sister in her bed next to mine and the Dream Book tucked under my pillow, I sleep as if I'd been drugged: deeply, fully, soundly.

I am not powerless anymore.

The next morning, Mom hands me a pink smoothie when Alexa and I enter the kitchen. "Protein shake," she says, and gives me a bowl of oatmeal with blueberries and sliced bananas on top. Alexa makes herself a bowl of Cheerios.

As Mom dispenses my antibiotics and vitamins, I sneak a peek at the recycle bin: no empty liquor bottles. No wine glasses in the sink. I eat my oatmeal and wash my pills down with the protein shake. It tastes like chalk.

"I have to hop on the computer to finish up some work." Mom leans against the counter and twists her shiny black hair into a bun. "But after that, how about a movie marathon? We'll pop some popcorn, camp out on the couch, watch a bunch of DVDs."

"How about going to the mall?" I say.

Both Alexa and Mom raise their brows. "The mall?" Mom asks. "Why?"

I pinch my pink hoodie between my fingers. "I need clothes that aren't sweats. Alexa said I could wear her things, but I want my own." Plus, a shopping spree is something Alexa and I can easily do from our Dream Book.

"We can order more clothes for you online," Mom says. "Whatever clothes you want. Next day delivery."

I don't want to buy my clothes online. As much as I'd wished to come home, I don't want to stay here forever. I can't follow the Dream Book if all I do is rotate between Mom's house, Dad's house, and doctor visits.

Alexa slurps her cereal and looks at me, at Mom, and back to me. "You know what, Mom? Charlotte wants to pick out her own clothes, and she needs to try them on. We should go to the mall."

Mom shakes her head. "I don't think you can handle the mall, Charlotte."

"Why not?" I ask.

"It's so big. You'll get tired."

"But—" my protest sticks in my throat, and I nod meekly.

Good girl.

No. I'm not in the attic; I'm home. I'm not powerless anymore. "If I get tired," I say, "we can take a break."

"It's a lot of walking. Your knee will hurt."

I straighten my leg, ignoring the pain. "I can handle it. I should exercise it anyway."

"It'll be crowded."

I slide a glance at Alexa, silently imploring her to help. She does not disappoint. She pokes her finger through a rip in her black jeans and says, "I could use some new things too. Then we can have lunch in the food court. The three of us." She jacks up the corners of her mouth into a smile. "It'll be fun."

Two hours later, Alexa, Mom, and I step into Gracemeadow Mall.

Alexa leads Mom and me across the mall. Dizziness washes over me as my brain tries to take everything in. Music blares from somewhere, perfume mixes with the scent of hot pretzels, lights flash in store windows. Everyone looks at us as we walk past them. Of course they do—Alexa's spiky white hair and facial piercings would draw anyone's attention. Not only is her hair different than it used to be, her walk is different too. She used to skip and toss her hair, her entire being filled with playfulness and joy. Now she pushes through the crowd with her head down, her eyes darting back and forth, anger radiating from the inside out.

Mom holds tight to my arm, as if she's afraid I'll believe someone else's lies about needing help getting ice cream and walk off with them again. If anyone gets too close to us, she stiffens and draws me even closer.

Alexa takes us to the juniors department at Macy's, and we survey the racks of clothes. "Pick out whatever you like," Mom says.

But I don't know what I like. Jeans or skirts? Sweaters or tops? Vests? Boots or sneakers? I can't decide; there are too many choices. What was fashionable four years ago is not stylish now, and eleven-year-olds dress differently from sixteen-year-olds. Childish and cutesy has been replaced by sophisticated and sexy. I don't want to look childish *or* sexy. But I don't want to keep wearing bulky sweats, either. Finally I choose everything the mannequins are wearing, as long as it's not tight or revealing.

I won't let Mom or Alexa in the dressing room with me, and I have to trust their opinions on what looks good on me because I can't bring myself to look in the mirror. But it *is* fun, modeling for them. I twirl to make the skirts flare out, posing and preening in the colorful, stylish outfits. Alexa goes back and forth to get me different sizes if I need them. Mom relaxes a bit eventually, and she even laughs a few times.

We leave the store weighed down with nine huge bags of clothes, accessories, shoes and sneakers and boots, and a soft wool coat the color of pink cotton candy. All of it's for me, except for one thing Alexa chose: a thin black T-shirt with a melting skull on it. I didn't expect us to still dress alike now that we're sixteen, but I wish she would dress in clothes that weren't so angry.

Taking the lead again, Alexa heads out of Macy's. We walk past the men's department and—

I see him. Ducking behind the tie rack. He's here.

My blood goes icy. My insides knot. My throat closes up.

"Charlotte?" Mom says. "Honey? What's wrong?"

He turns, steps toward me . . .

It's just a man with gray hair. His face is round with sagging jowls, not long with a pointed chin.

My Keeper is in the hospital, handcuffed to the bed rail, guarded by a police officer. He's not here. He is *not* here.

"Charlotte?" Mom says again. "Are you okay?"

"I, um . . ." My insides untangle themselves, but I can't speak until the jowled man strolls away. "I'm just hungry."

"Let's go eat," Alexa says. "Food court's this way."

It's not quite noon yet, but the food court is already crowded, mostly with moms and preschoolers. There's one table of older teenagers, dressed in the kind of clothes Alexa wears. They give each other bored nods as we walk by.

I wonder how she knows them. Friends from school? From rehab? She has a whole life that doesn't include me, a life I know nothing about.

But that's going to change now that I'm back. Soon we'll be hanging out at the mall with Bailey, Megan, and the rest of the Dragonettes—well, now they're Woodland Creek Sparklers. I should call them when I get home, tell them I'm coming back to school soon.

I wonder what grade The One Before would have been in this year.

Mom, Alexa, and I find a table in the corner of the food court. I think I've been doing a pretty good job of not letting Mom see how exhausted I am, but I can no longer hide my limp. My knee is throbbing, and I'm relieved to sit down.

With a glance at my knee, Alexa says, "You two stay here. I'll get the food. Subs and chips okay?" Mom gives Alexa some cash and reminds her that I don't like lettuce and tomato. Alexa takes off, pausing to say hi to her friends.

A pudgy woman is sitting at the next table next to Mom and me, wiping ketchup from the face of a squirmy little girl with blond hair. Then she leans toward us. "Excuse me, I hate to bother you, but are you Charlotte Weatherstone?"

Mom grabs my arm. I freeze for a millisecond, then nod.

"You poor, poor thing." The woman sighs. "I helped look for you. In the woods. I went to one of the candlelight vigils, too. I donate to your foundation whenever I can."

I'm half horrified that this woman knows who I am and what happened to me, and half touched by her generosity. "Th-thank you," I say. Mom murmurs a thank you too.

"To think it happened right here in our town," she continues. "That man took you in the middle of all those people, and no one noticed. It made me realize how unsafe this world really is." She smooths her daughter's wispy hair before turning back to me. "Anyway. Welcome home, Charlotte."

As she leaves, she takes her daughter's hand so tightly the little girl cries out and tries to pull away. "No, no, Sophie," the woman scolds as they walk away. "You must always, always hold Mommy's hand. I don't want you walking off with a stranger."

The color leaches from Mom's cheeks. "She blames me."

"She blames you?" I ask. "For what?"

"After the game. When you disappeared." A tremble starts in her chin and travels to her lip. "I was talking to the other moms.

I should have been watching you. I should have seen you talking with that man. I would have stopped you from going off with him. I could have stopped—"

"Mom, what happened, it wasn't your fault," I say.

"I'm your mother. I'm supposed to protect you. I'm supposed to keep you safe."

"Mom." If I let her keep going down this path, she'll start drinking herself to sleep again. "That woman doesn't blame you. I don't blame you. No one blames you."

She swallows hard. Gives me a tentative smile. Rifles through the bags. "Let's see, what else do you need?" she squeaks, blinking rapidly. "Did we get you enough pajamas? Oh! And purses— you've never had a purse. We'll have to get you makeup, too. Do you want makeup? We can stop at the cosmetics counter and ask the lady to show you how—"

"Charlotte Weatherstone?" A microphone suddenly materializes in front of my face. Holding the mic is a hand with long red nails. I look up to see a thin woman wearing a red blouse and bright red lipstick. "Lisa Lloyd, reporter for *Chicago Today*," she says. "Will you answer a few questions for our viewers." She's asking a question, but it sounds like a demand.

Behind her is a frumpy man holding a video camera, aimed at me. How did they know I was here? Did a shopper recognize me and call them? Did they follow us from our house?

Mom immediately shields me behind her arm. "If you want an interview," she says, "you must first call my lawyer to make an appointment." Her words are strained and obviously rehearsed.

And ineffective. The reporter shoves the microphone closer to me. "Charlotte, tell us about your years of imprisonment by a pedophile."

My muscles are stone. My lungs are rocks.

"No comment," Mom says.

The people at the tables surrounding us grow quiet. From my narrowing peripheral vision, I can see them watching.

"Describe the attic for us," the reporter says. Her nails, her voice, her eyes: they are all sharp.

"No comment," Mom says.

The reporter is a shark. "Did he ever let you out, or were you in the attic the entire time?"

"No *comment*," Mom says.

"Will you confirm that the EMTs found you naked and locked in a dog cage?"

The crowd gives a collective gasp. A couple of people step forward, tell the woman to stop, but she ignores them, stepping even closer to me. The assault of questions whirl around, battering, crushing, bruising, and invisible hands creep up around my neck. Mom cries, "No comment, no comment!" over and over again as she takes my arm and pulls me up, but the reporter blocks her path.

"Hey!" A shriek, and a flash of white and black: Alexa, her hair bristling as she shoves through the crowd. "Leave her alone!" She snarls at the reporter, and her lip ring sparkles. "Get the fuck out of here, you insensitive bitch."

I cannot breathe. I cannot breathe.

The reporter aims the microphone at Alexa and bares her teeth through a sickeningly sweet smile. "You're the twin, aren't you. Lex, right? This is all on camera, Lex."

"Good. Go ahead and air it," Alexa says. The air around her crackles with fury. "Here, I'll even give you an exclusive." She grabs the mic and speaks directly into the camera. "Lisa Lloyd is a talentless, diseased whore who is so desperate to get viewers for her pathetic tabloid news show that she harassed Charlotte Weatherstone. You heard it here first, folks. Lisa Lloyd of *Chicago Today*: picking on the victim for your entertainment."

Alexa shoves the microphone back at the reporter. Everything is blurry. I cannot breathe. I cannot move. The world rushes at me, then retreats. Rushes, retreats.

Someone takes my arm—Mom, Alexa, both, I don't know—and pulls me away. They tow me from the food court, past the stores, down the escalator, past the perfume ladies and the pretzel stand. Everyone watches, everyone stares, everyone whispers.

They all know who I am.

No. They all know *what* I am: The girl in the attic. The naked, beaten girl they found locked in a cage like a dog. A cautionary tale, a thing to be pitied, a victim.

"That was exactly what I was afraid would happen if you went out in public," Mom cries as she drives us home. When we get there, she makes a hysterical call to Dad, shouting, crying, blaming him for turning me into a circus freak for the media.

She hands me the phone, and Dad vows he'll make some calls to stop that video from airing; he'll put out a statement to remind reporters that they need to contact him first if they want to do a story on me; we really should have a press conference to stop things like this from happening. But I can't reply—those hands are still around my neck.

At five o'clock, Alexa snaps on the TV and turns it to *Chicago Today*. I'm the second story, after news of a truck accident on the tollway. An anchorman in a gray suit and black tie cheerfully welcomes me home. In the square over his left shoulder is that photo of eleven-year-old me smiling in pigtails and my Dragonettes uniform, followed by a clip of my mom and me sitting in the food court that afternoon, my mom refusing comment. Alexa's venomous monologue is not shown. The food court clip is followed by the blurry YouTube video of me walking off with Alan Shaw at the football game. After that is a video of his house: brown shingles, dark red shutters, cordoned off with yellow-and-black police tape. The camera zooms in on the single window in the attic.

His hands are still around my neck, and as each image appears on the TV screen, his grip gets tighter.

chapter eighteen

That night, Alexa tosses and turns in her bed a few feet away from mine. Today's shopping spree was supposed to be fun, a page from our Dream Book. But it was a nightmare. Unable to sleep at all, I slip out of bed and leave the room.

How amazing, that I can just get up and walk around the house like this. So much freedom.

Mom's door is wide open; her room is dark except for the flickering TV. She's in bed, asleep, but she must sense me in her doorway because she jolts awake. "Charlotte? What's wrong?"

"Nothing." I do a quick scan of her nightstand, but I don't see a wine glass. "Can't sleep."

She pats the bed next to her. "Do you want to sleep in here with me?"

I kind of do, but sixteen-year-olds shouldn't need to sleep with their mothers. I'm sure Mom would never consider asking Alexa if she wanted to sleep with her. "No thanks," I say. "I'll just get a glass of water and go back to bed."

"We don't have to stay here, you know," she says. "I talked to Uncle Tim a couple hours ago. He said his offer still stands. We can move in anytime we want."

"You mean, move to Georgia?"

"Your father has made a media spectacle out of you here in Woodland Creek. It'll be so much easier in Georgia."

My family is already split between two houses. I don't want them to be split between two states, too. If we move to Georgia, it'll be harder than ever for Alexa and me to follow the plans we made in our Dream Book. *This* is the house I dreamed about while I was in the attic. *This* is the house I thought I'd never see again.

I'm not leaving Woodland Creek. I am home, and it may be broken, but I am not leaving it.

"I want to stay here," I say.

She bites her lip. "You sure? After everything that happened today?"

"I'm sure. I want to stay here. Please don't make me leave."

She stares at me for a long time. I know she's disappointed, but eventually, she gives a small nod.

"Thank you, Mom."

She glances at her nightstand, and I wonder if she wishes she hadn't dumped all her alcohol down the sink. With a sigh, she lies back down. "Call for me if you need anything. I'll come check on you soon."

Relieved that we're staying in Woodland Creek, I get some water from the kitchen. But instead of going back to bed, I turn into Alexa's old room, Dad's old office. I sit at the desk and run my index finger along the little airplane she doodled on her laptop, then open the lid. It's been a long time since I've used a computer, but I haven't forgotten how.

My fingers are much slower on the keyboard than Alexa's were the other night. I type one letter at a time, hunt-and-peck style, slower than I was when I was eleven. I key *Charlotte Weatherstone* into the Google search bar and hit Enter.

The top search result is The Charlotte Weatherstone Foundation. I click on it, and it takes me to the homepage, which features that same cheerleading portrait of me, and a graphic of Wiggles, my pink teddy bear. An announcement is underneath.

My reading skills are rusty, but after a few blinks to clear my vision, it comes easily to me again:

We are thrilled beyond words to announce that after more than four long years, our dear Charlotte Grace Weatherstone has been found alive. She is now recovering at home with her family at her side. Thank you all for your support and prayers over the years.

Charlotte's rescue has motivated and inspired us to redouble our mission's efforts. The Charlotte Weatherstone Foundation will never stop in its quest to help families in crisis. Let's bring all of our missing children home. Never, never lose hope.

The website has pages for the kids the foundation has helped recover; children who are still missing; self-defense and safety skills. Links to various child and family advocacy programs. A page on how communities can organize a search party. How to recognize signs of abuse. How to help families in crisis. A page to make donations. On every page is a graphic of Wiggles.

I go back to Google and click on a YouTube link with my name in the title. It brings me to a local news broadcast from Channel 7. I hit Play, and Mom, Dad, and Alexa are on camera, being interviewed by a reporter. Mom is crying. Alexa, young, her hair long and black and her face piercing-free, is crying too. Dad is holding Wiggles. Agent Lindo is standing next to them. "As of this point, three weeks after she disappeared, no one has contacted her parents for ransom."

The next video, a news clip from yesterday, shows a portrait of Alan Shaw. The voice-over says, "His Pleasantview neighbors had no idea that the friendly owner of the local Print For Less copy shop was hiding a terrible secret in his attic . . ."

Immediately I click away from that video and land on a new one that posted two days ago. It's from CNN, and the anchor is interviewing the two ambulance guys who found me in the attic. They're wearing the same white shirts and black pants. The short, round one who found me first—Joel Bracco is his name, according to the banner at the bottom of the screen—rubs the back of his neck. "Yeah, we were carrying the guy out on a stretcher when we heard this clanging noise coming from the attic. Kev here said it was probably just a raccoon, but I said raccoons don't make that kind of noise . . ."

I watch the whole thing. Joel reveals that my mom sent him and Kev bouquets of thank-you flowers on my behalf, and my dad gave them a plaque from the foundation.

The next video features a trauma specialist, a woman with thin, colorless lips and hair slicked back in a tight bun. "Charlotte is back home, but she still has a long road ahead of her," she says to an off-screen interviewer. "Victims of pedophiles often suffer from nightmares, panic attacks, flashbacks, sometimes for the rest of their lives . . ."

I click through video after video. I read blog after blog, article after article, until my eyes burn and the screen is blurry, even out of my good eye. Finally I've had enough. I shut off Alexa's computer and sneak back to bed. She's deep asleep now, no longer restless.

I'm still wide awake.

I read some ugly words tonight, going through those videos and articles. Ugly, terrible words.

Abducted. Pedophile. Captivity. Subjugation. Rape.

And more. Words for things he did to me. Words for things he made me do to him. Words for things I couldn't have imagined existed before he took me. When he did those things to me, I didn't know there were actual words for them.

Giving those things names makes them more real. Makes them permanent. I'm labeled with them now, branded. They radiate off me like a flashing neon sign: Victim. Victim. Victim.

I take one of the teddy bears from the pile at the edge of my bed, a bright pink one the size of a football. The stitching along a seam on one of its legs is loose, and I pick at it. Pull at it.

Victim. Victim. Victim.

Pick-pull. Pick-pull. Pick-pull.

The seam finally opens up enough to form a little hole. With my thumb and index finger, I reach inside and pluck out a tiny bit of stuffing. I tear the hole a little bit bigger, reach inside for the stuffing, and pull out a little bit more.

chapter nineteen

CiGi's squealing laughter turns my blood to ice, my stomach to rocks.

The replacement baby is sitting in her high chair, directly across from me at Dad's kitchen table. She's chucked her baby spoon and instead takes handfuls of her mushed carrots and smooshes it between her fingers. Dad and Marissa laugh like it's the cutest thing they've ever seen. Even Alexa gives a chuckle, and it feels like a betrayal. Their laughter eggs CiGi on, and she does it over and over again. The orange glop gets all over her face, all over her bib, and even in her hair. It's disgusting. Nauseating. I try, I really try, but I can't possibly eat.

Next to me, Alexa stabs her fork into her dinner, pushes it around her plate, buries the broccoli under the meatloaf. She doesn't eat anything either.

The doorbell rings.

"Probably another reporter," Marissa says, pushing herself up from the table. With a dismissive wave at a glaring Alexa, she adds, "Don't worry, I'll send them away."

She hurries from the kitchen, and I hear her open the front door. A raspy, feminine voice says, "I'm sorry to bother you . . . I was hoping . . . I need to speak with Charlotte, please? Is she here?"

"We're not giving exclusives at this time," I hear Marissa reply. "We'll put an announcement on the website with the date of our next press conference."

"Please," the woman says. "I'm not a reporter. My name is Donna Hogan. Alan Shaw is my brother."

The blood drains from my face, and invisible hands creep up around my throat. But my legs lift me up and walk me to the foyer. Dad and Alexa follow, and I shake Alexa's hand from my arm when she tries to hold me back.

Alan Shaw's sister stands in the doorway in a bulky navy coat. Her hair, a drab brown, is in a loose bun at the back of her neck. She looks like him, kind of. Brown eyes. Long nose. Pointy chin. But he has a scar on his.

"Please," she says to Marissa. "If I could just . . . I need to apologize to her. I never knew . . ."

Her watery gaze lifts and lands on me. "Oh!" Her face scrunches up and she stifles a sob behind her hand. "Ch—Charlotte? Please? May I come in?"

Unable to speak, I nod. Marissa looks to my dad.

"Fine," he says. His voice and his expression are stone. I can't tell if he's angry or curious or sympathetic. Alexa puts her arm tightly around me, and as the woman steps in, she moves me back.

From the kitchen, CiGi howls, curdling my blood. Marissa rushes to get her.

Dad gestures to the family room. "We can sit in there," he says. We push some pink teddy bears out of the way and settle on the couch, except for Alexa, who stands guard at my side. Donna Hogan perches on the edge of the armchair across from us, knees together. Shaking, crumpled, broken.

With one hand, she clutches her purse on her lap. With the other, she clutches her coat closed at her chest. She has the same spindly fingers, the same knobby knuckles, as her brother. There's a single gray hair on her head, thick and wiry. It darts up from her scalp, then bends like a zigzag, as if it's trying to escape.

"Charlotte," she quivers, "I know apologies won't make up for the years that you lost . . . but please, please know that I was as shocked as everyone else . . . doubly so . . . that my brother was the one who did this to you."

She sniffles. "I thought I knew him. Alan. We grew up together, of course. And then we owned a business together. He came over for holidays. I saw him almost every day. And all this time . . . He didn't invite me over very often, but I went in his house a few times to drop off papers or checks. Did you ever hear me?"

"No. He never mentioned you," I say. "He never talked about the outside."

She stifles another sob. "Our mother died when we were young. Our father didn't know how to raise children. He was very hard on Alan. He would beat him with a belt for the slightest infraction. Alan was terrified of him. He would . . . he would hide up in our attic. When he was fifteen, he moved his bed up there and that's where he slept."

I take a teddy bear and hold it to my chest as Dad bristles. "Lex, take your sister to the other room. She shouldn't hear this."

Alexa takes my arm to pull me up, but I shake her off again. I try, but I cannot picture my Keeper as a boy, weak, terrified, overpowered, beaten. All I can picture is the white scar on his chin, his one front tooth that slightly overlays the other, his thin pale lips. His muddy eyes turning from emotionless to angry. I can smell his coffee-smoky breath, feel his weight on top of me, hear the snap of his belt.

I wonder if the belt he used on me was the same belt his father used on him.

"I'm sorry you had a difficult childhood, Mrs. Hogan," Dad says. "But we're not going to feel any sympathy for your brother."

"I don't expect you to," she says. "I'm just trying to come to terms with this. I'm trying to understand why Alan . . . turned out the way he did."

She releases her grip on her coat, and her hands tremble. "I have a daughter," she says in a small voice. "Julia. She's grown now. Such a beautiful child. Happy, cheery." From her purse, she pulls out a faded school portrait of a smiling little girl. "But then she changed. Angry, sullen, withdrawn. When she was seventeen she ran away to live with her father in California. But he couldn't control her either. She dropped out of high school, she's been in and out of jail for drugs, can't keep a job, never married, won't let anyone near her. Not even me."

"Mrs. Hogan," Dad says, shifting in his seat. "Did you ever consider that your brother may have been—"

"It never occurred to me." She sniffles and wipes her eyes. "But after all this," she gestures to me, "I made the connection. I contacted her and asked if her uncle Alan had ever . . ."

I look at Julia's photograph, and the room narrows until I can't see anything else.

"He did," I say. I know exactly what he did to Julia.

"She denied it at first," Mrs. Hogan says from far away. "But then she told me everything. He'd been . . ." She takes a deep breath, tries to say those awful words, and fails. "Since she was twelve," she whispers.

"In his house? In the attic?" I ask. Despite the ache my heart feels for Julia, hope blooms there too. Could Julia be The One Before? Is The One Before still alive?

But my hope withers when Mrs. Hogan shakes her head. "She says she was never in the attic. The . . . abuse . . . happened downstairs, and at my house."

The sobs she'd been stifling win the war. "She never told me. She never told anyone. She's been carrying this horrible secret around with her all these years. If I'd known, if I'd asked more questions, been more observant . . ."

She doesn't say it, but the guilt in her eyes finishes her sentence for her. *None of this would have happened. He never would have taken you.*

Or, I add silently, The One Before.

chapter twenty

Pick-pull.

Alexa sleeps on her side of our bedroom at Dad's house, facing the wall. I lie on my bed, and pick-pull at a seam in the leg of a pink teddy bear.

I'd tried to sleep, but when I close my eyes all I can see is Julia Hogan's photograph, along with The One Before. I don't know who The One Before was, but now, after seeing Julia's photo, I have an idea of what she looked like.

I slip out of bed and go downstairs to the foundation office. Pink teddy bears are everywhere, even more than before. My cheerleading, pigtailed photograph is still in the center of the wall stenciled with FOUND! But the wall I study is the one labeled NEVER LOSE HOPE. Or rather, I study the photographs displayed on that wall.

There are hundreds of them. Boys and girls. Infants, toddlers, school kids, teens.

Many of the photos are school portraits. Some are candids. All of them state the child's date of birth, and date and place they disappeared. Many of the missing were taken by a noncustodial parent. Some of them, mostly older ones, are suspected runaways. Only a very few of them are believed to have been snatched off the street, kidnapped by a stranger.

I go through each of them, one by one, blinking frequently to clear my vision.

At some point, I'm not sure when, Alexa appears next to me. "What are you doing?"

I tell her what I'm looking for. She nods, then starts going through the photographs too.

CiGi cries from upstairs. Above us, footsteps shuffle from Dad and Marissa's room to hers. A few minutes later, maybe more, maybe less, CiGi stops crying, and the footsteps shuffle back. Alexa and I continue searching through the photographs, pulling down the ones we need.

The sun is just beginning to rise when we finish.

Later that morning, I call Agent Lindo and ask him to come. When he does, I hand him a file containing the photographs Alexa and I pulled from the NEVER LOSE HOPE wall.

Of the hundreds of pictures, Alexa and I found six that match my criteria.

They are all girls. All from the Chicago area. All disappeared between five and ten years ago. All have never been found.

And like Julia Hogan and me, they all have long, black hair.

"The One Before might be one of these girls," I tell Agent Lindo.

He flips through them, nods solemnly, and promises to check.

chapter twenty-one

In the attic, it was hard to have an idea of time. Days blurred together, always the same: quiet, dim, cramped and looming, until nighttime, when he would climb the fourteen creaky wooden steps and unlock the attic door.

The nighttimes . . . well. Those were always the same, too.

But sometimes, little things happened to remind me that the world outside was plodding along without me, that time was passing, that days had become weeks, months, years. I knew it was the Fourth of July when I heard fireworks. I knew it was nearing Christmas when he brought down his blue bins of lights from the shelves.

I knew it was Thanksgiving when he came up to the attic with plastic containers of real, home-cooked food instead of the usual leftover fast food or frozen meals he gave me. He never told me it was Thanksgiving; I'd made the conclusion based on the food in the containers: turkey, mashed potatoes, stuffing, pumpkin pie. He also had never told me where he spent his Thanksgivings, but I know now that he'd gone to his sister's house.

How could he have gone to his sister's house for Thanksgiving every year, and worked with her every day at their copy shop, knowing what he had done to her daughter, his own niece? Knowing that his abuse is what caused Julia's sudden turn from cheery and happy to depression and despair; that it was his abuse that caused her to turn to drugs and to drop out of high school and to run away? How could he look his sister in the eye? Did he even feel guilty about what he had done to Julia?

No. No, I don't think he felt guilty about it. I think he felt that Julia belonged to him, and only to him, and that she had betrayed him when she ran away. That was why he was so hurt when The One Before tried to run away, too. That was why he threatened to replace me with my sister, so I wouldn't even try. I belong to my Keeper, and only to him, and he will never, ever let me go.

While I ate Thanksgiving dinner with him, on paper plates up in the attic, I would imagine my family having their own Thanksgiving dinner at our little yellow home in Woodland Creek. My dad doesn't usually cook, but he loves to grill the turkey. Mom makes the most delicious mashed sweet potatoes. She puts butter and cream in them, and whips them until they're creamy. It's amazing how they're thick and airy at the same time.

In the attic, if I closed my eyes and concentrated hard enough, I could taste those mashed sweet potatoes. I could see Mom, Dad, and Alexa sitting at our dining room table. Dad caresses Mom's hand with his thumb as they sit next to each other, so casually and naturally that he doesn't even realize he's doing it. Alexa teases them about it, her black hair tumbling down her back, and she occasionally sneaks away to text Bailey and the rest of the cheerleaders and her boyfriend about the pep rally they're going to next week.

"Charlotte?" Dr. Goldbloom asks. "Did you hear me? I asked how your first Thanksgiving back home was."

I blink, coming back to the present: on Dr. Goldbloom's lavender sofa in her sunny white barn, the day after Thanksgiving. "It was really good," I say. "Great."

"You don't sound very convincing."

"It *was* great," I insist. "In fact, I had two Thanksgivings. First with my mom, and then another one with my dad." I don't tell her that I'd hoped my parents would put aside their differences, just for one day, so we could have my first Thanksgiving back home together.

Dr. Goldbloom nods, as if she knew I'd omitted something. "Tell me about the one with your mom."

"She made her mashed sweet potatoes," I say. "I ate almost the entire pot all by myself. It was delicious. Better than I even remembered."

She smiles encouragingly, and waits, which compels me to say more. "My uncle Tim and his family came in from Georgia just to have Thanksgiving with me."

"It must have been nice to see them again."

"It was."

Again she waits, so I add, "They said that they want us to move to Georgia with them."

"What do you think of that?" she asks.

"My mom would do it if I wanted to. But I want to stay in Woodland Creek."

Dr. Goldbloom has decorated the barn with pumpkins covered in sparkly lavender glitter. I pick up a mini pumpkin by the stem and spin it. "My cousins, Nick and Jason?" I say. "They were . . . I don't know. Uncomfortable around me, I guess."

"In what way?" she asks.

"Before I went away, they were always goofy, always joking around, teasing Alexa and me. But yesterday, they were quiet. They kept looking at me, but when I met their eyes, they looked away."

"Ah." She nods. "They treat you differently now."

I twirl the pumpkin and watch the sparkles reflect on the wall. "Aunt Dina and Uncle Tim, they were kind of awkward around me too. With them, it was more like they felt sorry for me. With Nick and Jason, when they looked at me, it was like they didn't see *me*. All they saw were the disgusting things that happened to me."

She waits for me to continue. When I don't, she says, "What about your sister? Did they treat her differently too, or did they joke around with her?"

"No one would dare joke around with Alexa," I say. "Not anymore. She's always so angry all the time. She didn't talk much. No one talked much."

Dr. Goldbloom's hair catches a sun ray, and the gray turns to silver. "How was Thanksgiving with your dad?"

"It was okay. Good. Noisy."

"Noisy? Were a lot of people there?"

"Dad wanted to invite a lot of people," I say. "Marissa's family, Agent Lindo and his family, some board members from the foundation. But Marissa convinced him that it would be better to have a quiet, calm Thanksgiving. It was just Alexa and me, and Dad and Marissa. And the baby."

"But it wasn't quiet or calm after all?"

I shake my head. "CiGi screamed the entire time. I thought there was something wrong with her, like she was sick or hurt or something, but she was just teething. Dad soaked a washcloth in cold chamomile tea and let her chew on it. It's what he did for Alexa and me when we were teething."

Even now, the next day, it brings a sour taste to my mouth. CiGi was cranky and sticky and covered in drool, and refused to go down for a nap. Each one of her screeches was like a punch to the gut. It made the mashed sweet potatoes I'd eaten earlier curdle in my stomach.

In the attic, I'd imagined my family so, so happy on Thanksgiving. And now I know that I was only tricking myself.

chapter twenty-two

I'm not sure what to wear today. I could just wear sweats. Actually, I could just stay in my pajamas. I'm not leaving the house, so who cares if I stay in my pj's?

No. My parents may think I'm not ready to go to Woodland Creek High, but I'm not going to be a slob on my first day of homeschool. The One Before would be grateful to go to school, even if it was just homeschool with a tutor.

I shower, then comb my hair and brush my teeth with the lights off. In my bedroom, I pull on a pair of jeans and a pink sweater. It takes me fifteen steps to walk to my new school: the dining room.

Mom is talking to a skeletal woman wearing a green cardigan over a floral, collared shirt that's buttoned all the way up. They stop talking when they see me. "Charlotte," Mom says, "this is your tutor, Mrs. Ridge."

Mrs. Ridge gives me a smile. It's not a warm smile, but it's not a trembly, oh-look-at-the-poor-victim smile that everyone else gives me. Maybe she doesn't know who I am.

"Wonderful to meet you, Charlotte," she says. She shakes my hand, and her skin is loose and soft. She's so thin I'm afraid her bones will break if I squeeze even the tiniest bit.

Alexa's going back to school today too, but she gets to go to Woodland Creek High. Her tattered backpack is slung over her shoulder, and as usual, she's wearing all black. She watches us with narrowed eyes and her almost-permanent scowl and crossed arms.

Mom puts her hands on her hips and looks around. "I had everything set up on the kitchen table, but Mrs. Ridge thought the dining room would be better. I think she's right. It's nice and bright in here, and this table is so much bigger." She gestures to the yellow walls, which used to have wedding and family photos hanging on them, and now have nothing. "I'll order some whiteboards to hang on the walls, and you can use the china cabinet to store all your textbooks and school supplies."

The two women continue discussing how to convert the dining room into a classroom, and I realize how naive I've been: I knew I'd need a tutor for a few weeks to get me caught up enough to go to Woodland Creek High, but Mom and Mrs. Ridge are talking like they expect this homeschool thing to last for a long, long time. Don't my parents *ever* want me to go to regular school?

"We're all set," Mrs. Ridge says primly to my mother. "Why don't you get going so Charlotte and I can start."

Mom chews her lip. "Maybe I should stay," she says. "It's her first day."

If I want to go to Woodland Creek High anytime soon, I need to show my mother that I'm strong. I lift myself up as tall as I can, ignoring the pain in my knee as I straighten my left leg. "We're good here, Mom. You can go."

"Okay, well, I made you lunch. It's in the fridge," Mom quivers. Behind her, Alexa rolls her eyes. "You'll tell Mrs. Ridge if you get too tired, right? If it's too much for you, or if you don't understand something—"

"It won't be too much for me," I promise. "I'm good at school, remember? Straight A's."

Mom nods, then slowly slides on her coat. She gets as far as the garage door before turning back. "No. I just don't think you're ready to be away from a parent," she says. "I can work from home a few weeks longer. My boss will understand."

If my mom stays home, she'll hover over me the entire time, anxious and fussing. I look to Alexa for support, to jump in the way she did when I asked to go to the mall, but she only gives me a shrug. She agrees with Mom.

A few seconds later, a car horn beeps from the driveway. "That's Jen," Alexa says. "Gotta go." She sticks out her tongue and screws up her face like going to school is the last thing she wants to do, but that look turns to relief as she turns away.

Mom settles in the kitchen with her computer and paperwork, in sight of me, while Mrs. Ridge hauls a wheeled bag to the dining room table. She unpacks a stack of textbooks: Math. English. Science. Social Studies.

I recognize those textbooks. They're the same ones the sixth graders use at Woodland Creek Elementary School.

I sit in a chair at the middle of the table, and I feel very small.

chapter twenty-three

My schedule goes like this:

Monday through Friday, I have homeschool at the dining room table while Alexa goes to Woodland Creek High.

Wednesday nights and every other weekend, Alexa and I go to Dad's house.

Mondays, Tuesdays, and Thursdays after homeschool, Mom takes me to physical therapy and to various doctors as necessary.

Wednesday nights and Saturday afternoons, Dad takes me to see Dr. Goldbloom.

Every night at eight o'clock, I call Agent Lindo to ask for updates. He gives me either no news, or bad news. Alan Shaw is still in the hospital, still under guard. He's been formally charged with my kidnapping and sexual assault and dozens of other crimes, but he vacillates between being too weak to speak and refusing to speak. Lindo was unable to connect him to any of the six missing girls in the file I gave him. None of their fingerprints match the ones in the attic.

Every night, I ask Lindo to look harder. I tell him to get Alan Shaw to speak, to force him to confess, to do whatever he has to do to find The One Before. I remind Lindo how important it is to find her, that she existed, that she's *real*, and that somewhere out there, her family is wondering where she is.

Every night, after Alexa has fallen asleep in her bed across the room and the house is quiet, I pick at the seam of a pink teddy bear, pull out tiny bits of stuffing, and send a silent apology to The One Before that I haven't been able to find her.

Every night, much, much later, when Mom thinks I'm sleeping, she slides my bedroom door open and tiptoes to my bedside. I hear her gentle breath as she stands over me. Sometimes she cups her hand lightly on my cheek before she tiptoes out.

And every night, the Dream Book sits on the dresser, its plans un-followed.

chapter twenty-four

I sit on the bed in Dad and Marissa's room as he hurriedly, expertly, packs his suitcase. We had to rush back to his house after my appointment with Dr. Goldbloom because the foundation got a call about another missing child. Now he's flying to Texas to help organize the search efforts for a little boy who went to the park two days ago and never came back. Another photo for the NEVER LOSE HOPE wall.

The walls in Dad and Marissa's bedroom are painted a soft sage green. There are pink teddy bears in here, too. They've taken over the whole house.

CiGi's on the floor at my feet, trying to pull herself up using my legs. I swing them back and forth to discourage her while trying to quell my nausea. She's got a cold, not a bad one, but her nose is somehow stuffy and runny at the same time. She's got drool on her chin.

"I was thinking, Charlotte," Dad says. "Why don't you come with me?"

"To Texas? To look for that missing boy?"

"The Charlotte Weatherstone Foundation is helping to finance and organize the search. Charlotte Weatherstone should be there."

I try not to cringe as Dad coils a belt around his fingers, and I can only breathe again after he packs it away in a pocket of the suitcase. "You can personally give his parents a pink teddy bear," he adds.

"I don't know how a pink teddy bear would help find him," I say.

Dad reaches to put his hand on my shoulder, then retracts, discomfort flitting across his face.

It's the bed. I'm sitting on his bed. It makes him think of me in the attic bed, and all the dirty, disgusting things that happened there. No wonder he's uncomfortable with me sitting here, on his own bed. I push myself off and move to the armchair across the room. There are two teddy bears on it, and I take one and hold it in my lap.

Dad zips up his suitcase. "I know firsthand how that boy's parents are feeling right now, Charlotte," he says. "They've never been so scared. They've never felt so helpless. They're at the lowest point in their lives. A visit from you would give them hope."

CiGi is back at my feet; she puts her slimy, germ-ridden hand on my knee, the left one, my bad one. I cross my legs so she can't reach me, ignoring the pain when I bend my knee so much.

"I don't think you realize what a huge opportunity you have to help people," Dad continues. "If you're there, leading the search, we'll get dozens more volunteers. We'll get thousands more in donations, which will help us find even more missing children. You have no idea how powerful your image is."

Me? Powerful? I may not be powerless anymore, but I'm not power*ful*.

"In fact," Dad says, "I was thinking you should come with me to all of the foundation's events. You would be our ambassador of hope."

I can hear the capital letters in those words: Ambassador of Hope.

While I was in the attic, I lost hope of ever going home. My mother hoped that I was still alive and would come home. But days and weeks and years of not seeing that hope realized had turned her into a robot who divorced my father and needed alcohol to fall asleep. My father believed I was dead. He hoped he was wrong, but he replaced me with a new baby, whom he named CiGi Hope. And my twin sister hoped that I was dead.

Hope is made of air, and wishes. An empty box wrapped in shiny paper.

And now Dad wants me to be the *ambassador* of hope. How can I be the ambassador of hope, when hope doesn't change anything? When unrealized hopes bring only pain and despair?

Hope won't bring that missing boy home. Hope won't bring The One Before home, either.

I pick at the seams of the teddy bear in my lap. "I can't go," I mumble. "I have a lot of studying to do."

"You can study on the plane and in the hotel. I'll help you."

"I really need to concentrate on school, Dad, so I can get caught up." It's true, but I can't look him in the eye as I say it.

But from my peripheral vision, I can see his resigned nod. "You're right, sweetheart. Of course. School is important." He swoops up CiGi and wipes her nose, then kisses the top of her head. She plops her tiny thumb in her mouth and nestles her head on his shoulder. She fits perfectly in his arms.

I don't want to disappoint my dad, and I don't want to disappoint the parents of that missing boy, or the parents of any missing child. I squeeze the pink teddy bear. Someone sent this bear to the foundation while I was missing, someone who had been hoping for my safe return.

"Maybe . . ." I take a deep breath and let it out. "Maybe when you get back, we can have a press conference."

Dad lights up, his blue eyes sparkling. "That would be wonderful, Charlotte. I'll have Marissa set it up."

chapter twenty-five

Dad says he likes to have the foundation's press conferences outside on the patio, using Marissa's flower garden as a backdrop. But it's the middle of December, and it's snowing, so today we're doing it inside, in the foundation's office. Bouncing the messy blond curls on her head and bouncing CiGi on her hip, Marissa directs a crew to set up lights and microphones. She acts like she's done this a million times before. She probably has: she's in charge of publicity and PR, after all.

Mom, Alexa, and I watch from the corner. Mom shifts uncomfortably, smoothing her skirt over and over again. Alexa leans on a desk, dressed in her usual all-black, tight clothes and texting someone on her phone. Dad, in a gray suit and pink tie, sets up the microphones on the long table where we'll sit as we answer questions from the reporters. Even though he's assured me that he will do most of the talking and I'll only have to give a short statement, Dad wants all of us to be part of the press conference. Mom, Alexa, even Marissa and CiGi. The whole family. Neither Mom nor Alexa want to do it, but I begged them to come. I need them here, at my side.

The table is set in front of the wall stenciled with FOUND! and papered with photos of all the kids who are no longer missing. My photo is still in the center. I'm happy to see the photo of the little boy from Texas underneath mine. "Hey, Dad?" I ask. "Can we move the table to the other side? To the NEVER LOSE HOPE wall?"

Dad adjusts his tie as he shakes his head. "We'd have to move the computers and file cabinets to make room for the table."

"But the photos of the missing kids should be on camera," I say. "Not the ones who've already been found."

Dad gives me that look again, that look of amazement. He's so proud of me. He thinks I'm the Ambassador of Hope. He gives a little whistle to the crew and uses his finger to make a circle in the air. "Okay, guys, let's switch things around."

Marissa nods her approval, then looks me up and down. "Charlotte, come with me. I need to get you ready."

Oh, no. Dad is busy, and Alexa is texting. I have to go with Marissa alone.

I follow her from the office. CiGi is still on her hip. I expect her to take me to the family room to rehearse my statement, but she takes me upstairs to the bedroom I share with Alexa. "Let's find you something to wear." With one hand, she rifles through the closet. The baby reaches for me like she wants me to hold her, but I back away. She smells like talcum powder and it's suffocating. Her sticky hands make me queasy.

"What's wrong with what I have on now?" I'm wearing my mom's black skirt, her white ironed button-down shirt, and her black pumps. It's too loose, but I specifically chose this outfit so I would look grown up at the press conference.

"It's very nice," Marissa says, taking out a peach shirt, then putting it back before rifling again. "But you look like you're wearing your mom's clothes for a job interview. Don't you want to look like a teenager? Like yourself?"

Yes. I do want to look like a teenager. A normal, well-adjusted teenager who has no reason whatsoever to have a press conference.

"Ah." Marissa takes a red sweater dress from the closet. "What do you think?"

"I like it." I really do. A normal, well-adjusted teenager would totally wear that. I'm trying hard not to like Marissa, but she's not making it easy.

She hands me the dress and a cropped denim jacket to go over it. "I have boots that would be so cute with this," she says, grinning. "Hold on." She sets CiGi on the floor and dashes from the room.

Crawling, the baby makes a beeline to a pile of pink teddy bears in the corner. She takes one in her sticky little hands and holds it up to me. "Broo!" she exclaims. I pull the bear away from her. I do *not* want her touching those pink teddy bears.

Marissa returns with knee-high chocolate-brown boots. I don't want to change in front of her, so I take the clothes and change in the bathroom.

A few minutes later, Marissa knocks. "I found a headband that would be perfect with your outfit. Want it?"

"Okay," I call, and open the door.

She holds out a wide red headband, then stops. "Aren't the lights working in here?" She snaps on the switch and I blink against the sudden brightness.

Her brows knit for a moment, and when she speaks, it's softer than before. "Your hair got messy when you changed. Can I help you style it?"

Unable to speak, I nod, then stiffen when she runs a brush through my hair. She's gentle, timid, but as she brushes, my mind separates itself from my body, and I take myself far away.

He sits on the bed, and I kneel on the floor between his legs, my back to him. My skin is still cold and damp from the bath, my wet hair making me even colder. I separate my mind from my body and take myself far away as he brushes my hair, over and over again, taking hours, it seems, running his fingers through it, until it's dry.

Then his lips are on my neck, his coffee-smoky breath is in my nostrils, his rough hands are on my shoulders. He leans back, and I hear his zipper open. "Turn around, girl."

"Charlotte?" Marissa's voice brings me back. "Are you—sweetie, are you crying?"

I wipe my eyes and my fingers come back wet. "No," I say anyway.

"Did I hurt you?"

"No," I say again.

In a whisper: "Do you want me to cancel the press conference? I will. I'll do anything—"

I shake my head again. "No."

"Charlotte, I . . ."

I shake my head. Whatever question she's about to ask, whatever kind words she's about to say, I don't want to hear them. If she says them, I'll break. I swear to God, I will break.

She clamps her lips shut, stuffing those words back down and trapping them inside.

By the time we get back downstairs, the foundation office is crowded with Dad's most trusted reporters. He squeezes his way among them, shaking their hands and calling them by name, his smile alone bright enough to light up the room. Mom shakes their hands too, although with much less enthusiasm.

When Dad sees me, he lights up even more. "Perfect, Charlotte. You look beautiful." He's beaming. "Marissa, did you bring something down for Lex?"

Marissa hands Alexa a purple cardigan and a purple knit cap. Alexa grimaces. "What's this for?"

"I just thought . . ." Marissa says, faltering. "Your dad wants . . . It'll look cute."

"I am not *cute*. I don't want to look *cute*."

With a glance at the reporters, Dad frowns. "I rarely tell you what to wear, Lex," he mutters. "But for this press conference, I am *asking* you to put on the sweater and the hat. And take those piercings out of your face."

Alexa glares at him. "Why, so your *fans* won't see how fucked up I am?"

He meets her gaze steadily. "Yes. That's exactly why."

She draws herself up, about to explode.

"Alexa, please," I say. "I just want to get through this. Just do it. Please."

"Fine," she hisses. She pushes her arms through the sleeves of the cardigan and shoves the hat on her head, covering most of her white spikes. She pulls the hardware from her lip, eyebrow, and nose.

Without her armor, Alexa looks . . . cute.

But also vulnerable. Defeated.

It hurts to see her that way. I want her to take the hat off and put the piercings back in. We're twins. It hurts to look at myself.

Alexa shuffles to the press table, which Dad has dutifully moved to under the NEVER LOSE HOPE wall, and takes a seat at the end.

"Um, no . . ." Marissa says. "Charlotte and Lex, I think you two should sit in the middle. You know, twin sisters, united again. Cory should sit on the other side of Charlotte. Vickie, you sit next to Lex." She hoists CiGi higher on her hip. "And CiGi and I will sit on the other side of Cory."

I expect Alexa to say something snarky, or refuse to move, or at least roll her eyes, but she simply moves to her assigned seat. Unable to twist her white hair around her fingers, she picks at the black paint on her fingernails.

I go to sit next to her and nudge her a little. "Thank you," I whisper.

"I'm doing this for *you*," she says. "Not *them*."

Mom and Dad take their seats, Dad next to me, and Mom next to Alexa. Mom hasn't spoken at all. She's arranged her lips into a smile. She hates this even more than Alexa does.

Marissa adjusts some microphones, then speaks into one of them. "Good afternoon, everyone. We're ready to begin. Please take your seats." She hustles to her chair next to Dad and plops CiGi on her lap.

The reporters' idle chatter hushes. Cameramen lift their cameras. I count: only seven reporters and six cameramen, but squished together in front of me like this, they look like a hungry monster made of eyes and microphones.

Dad gives them his patented smile, more comfortable in front of a camera than anywhere else. "We'd like to thank you all for coming. You supported us in our time of crisis, and now you're celebrating with us in our time of joy."

He goes on, using his stage training to project his voice to the back corners of the room. He talks about how grateful he is to have me home. How very, very proud he is of me, how strong and brave I am. How I've given him hope, how I've given everyone hope. He doesn't mention that he'd believed I was dead.

Mom goes next. Though she's been in several theater productions too, she doesn't project her voice like Dad did. She speaks to her hands, which are folded primly on the table. "I'd like to give my most sincere thanks to everyone who prayed for us while Charlotte was missing. She's home now, and I'd appreciate you giving our family privacy while she recovers. She still has a long road ahead of her."

She stops. That's it. That's all she says.

Dad thinks I'm ready to fly around the country as the Ambassador of Hope, but Mom thinks I'm a frail little bird with broken wings.

Silence has blanketed the room, and everyone is looking at me.

Oh. My turn. I take a deep breath and, remembering my own stage training, force myself to look directly at the reporters and smile. I recite my statement, which I wrote last night with Mom's help. "I'd like to thank everyone for their thoughts and prayers. I'm so happy to be back home with my family. It's . . ."

The rest of my speech disappears from my head. So many cameras are on me. This press conference is going to be on television, broadcast on every news channel, posted on the Internet. Thousands, maybe millions of people will see me. And they will all be thinking: Victim. Victim. Victim.

I swallow, lick my lips, try again. "I'm so happy to be back home with my family . . ."

He could be watching this press conference, too. He's going to see me, too.

His hands creep up around my neck.

"It's, um . . ." I inhale, but air won't get through and it comes out as a panicked squeak.

Alexa is on me then, grabbing me, hugging me, making a sobbing noise. I hide my face in her shoulder.

The reporters go *aww*.

They don't see hands around my neck, cutting off my air. They think I'm so overcome with love for my family that I can't even speak.

Alexa sobs again, then whispers into my ear, "Just say the word and I'll end this. I'll throw a fit and get you out of here. And then I'll come back and smash every one of those cameras." She sobs again, loudly.

That's when I realize: Alexa's sobs are an act. The reporters don't know I'm about to lose it, but she knows. She's trying to help me.

And that's all I need. My throat opens up, and I can breathe again. "I'm okay," I whisper back. I clutch her tightly for one second, then we slowly release each other. At the same time, we sniffle and wipe our fingers under our eyes. My tears are real, and I think Alexa's are too.

The reporters *aww* again. A smattering of applause.

Marissa dabs her eyes and leans toward her microphone. "I think that says everything you need to know about how Charlotte and Lex feel about being reunited. Cory will answer a few questions now."

All of the reporters raise their hands, and Marissa points to a woman in a brown jacket. "Nora, why don't you go first."

"Charlotte, did Alan Shaw ever let you out of the attic?" she asks.

I shake my head, and Marissa holds up her hand. "Please direct your questions to Cory, not Charlotte. And I'd like to remind you that we're not discussing her captivity. Are there any other questions?"

Most of the reporters put their hands down, but a bald man signals by waving his index finger. Marissa nods to him. "Go ahead, Paul."

"Mr. Weatherstone," he says, "it's been confirmed that Shaw molested his niece, but will you confirm they found evidence of another girl in the attic?"

I turn to stone as the room falls silent.

The One Before. They found The One Before.

The other reporters erupt in a wave of urgent chatter, raising their hands, shouting questions. "Another victim?" "Who is she?" "Where is she?"

Dad's face is white as he takes the microphone, his knuckles white too. "Last I heard, they couldn't find proof of another girl in the attic," he says, his voice controlled and steady, a direct contrast to the swirl and sway of emotions flooding my body.

"Dad, he said they have *evidence*," I say.

The reporters continue to bombard him with questions, but he shakes his head. "It's a police matter," he says. "I couldn't answer your questions even if I knew the answers."

The tenuous control I have crumbles, and I seek out the bald reporter, asking him the same questions everyone else is asking my dad. "Who was she? What was her name?" I ask him, plead with him. "What evidence did they find?" My inquiries only spur more questions from the other reporters, and soon my voice is lost among theirs, and I can't breathe. The One Before. They found The One Before.

Dad shouts something, and Alexa pulls me up and drags me from the office, Mom following close behind. Even in the kitchen with the door closed, I can still hear Dad and Marissa trying to subdue the roar from the reporters, and I still can't breathe.

An hour later, Dad's house is quiet. The demanding reporters are gone; Marissa is upstairs putting CiGi down for her nap; my family is in the family room, waiting for Agent Lindo.

The moment he walks in the door, I fly over to him. "You found her? Who is she? Where was she?"

"We didn't find her." He stomps the snow from his boots and sheds his gigantic, snow-frosted overcoat, and we settle around the coffee table before he tells us more. "But we found evidence of her."

"What kind of evidence?" Dad asks.

"We found a book in one of those blue storage bins he had in the attic. A library book from a middle school in central Illinois. Peoria. It took us a while to search their records, but earlier this week we learned the book was checked out seven years ago and never returned. The girl who borrowed it went missing a few days later. Thirteen years old, last seen walking home after a piano lesson. Never arrived."

The air is sucked from my lungs, the entire room, the entire world.

"Once we identified the girl as a potential victim," he continues, "we were able to compare her fingerprints from our records to the ones in the attic. And this morning, we found a match on a print that we got from one of those copper pipes in the back of the attic. It's only a partial, but it's enough to prove she was there. You were right, Charlotte. There was another victim. And she had long black hair."

As my family crumbles around me, I run emotions through my head, trying to decide how I feel:

Sorrow. As much as I was certain The One Before was real, it would've been better if she wasn't.

Relief. Relief that she's been identified, and now her family will no longer have to wonder what happened to her.

Grief. Grief that her family will know that what happened to her was horrible.

"How did he—" I struggle to push the words past the hands around my throat. "How did he get her all the way from Peoria up to his attic in Pleasantview?" What tricks did he pull? What lies did she believe?

"Unless he decides to cooperate and tell us," Lindo says, "we'll never know exactly how he did it. His business records show he was in Peoria the same weekend for a printing convention. Because he was there only that one weekend, we're assuming he didn't target her like he did you. He probably spotted her walking alone, saw an opportunity, and snatched her off the street."

I blink at him. "He targeted me?"

"You or your sister," he says. "We studied the videos of all the Dragon football games and practices that season," Lindo says. "He's in the crowd in a couple of them, wearing that Dragon hat. We also have a blurry security cam video of a man in a Dragon hat watching you and Lex at Iggy's Ice Cream Shop earlier that summer."

Iggy's Ice Cream: that was how he got me in his car after the football game. He asked me to help him get Glacier Bars from Iggy's for the team.

"He must have followed you two around for a few weeks until he was able to get one of you alone," Lindo continues.

I'm being crushed by a concrete slab of shock, but my parents don't look surprised at Lindo's news. He must have told them this before. Alexa, though, is frozen, rigid, white.

"Did you know that?" I ask her. "Do you remember seeing him?"

She shakes her head, and a strangled "No" escapes her throat. I know what she's thinking: if she'd been the one standing alone after the game, he would have just as eagerly taken her instead of me.

She's yanking her hair, and I can tell she's trying not to cry. I scooch closer to her.

"Agent Lindo?" I say. "The One Before—did she have a sister?"

He shakes his head. "Only child." He pulls a photo from his file and places it on the coffee table. "This is her."

She's in a park, sitting on the grass, arms wrapped loosely around her knees. Her long black hair is a little windblown, parted on the left, the right side held back in a clip. She's grinning, but when I look hard, I can see a hopelessness behind her eyes, as if somewhere deep inside her, she knows that she doesn't have much time left, that she'll never grow up, that what's left of her short life will be spent in pain, loneliness, and terror, locked in our Keeper's attic.

I blink and look again: the photo sharpens, and the hopelessness is gone from her eyes. It was just my own bad eye, playing tricks on me.

"What was her name?" I ask.

"Emily Alvarado."

The storm swirling in my mind quiets, and something unclenches inside me, loosens, lightens, opens up: a bird flying free from its cage. The One Before finally has a name: Emily. Emily Alvarado.

Oh, Emily. I'm so sorry you never made it home.

"Do her parents know?" Mom asks.

"I told them personally earlier today," Lindo says. His voice turns from just-the-facts to gruff and choked. "Drove through the snow. Just got back." Delivering that news wasn't easy for him. He clears his throat, and when he speaks again, he's back to his usual self. "They want Emily's remains so they can have a traditional funeral and bury her in the cemetery at their church. But we've already dug up his yard, tore apart his house and his copy shop. Came up empty."

"I take it he's still denying the whole thing?" Dad asks.

"He's clamped up even more than he was before," Lindo says. "His public defender is trying to make a deal for a lighter sentence if he talks, but he won't say a word. That son of a—" he cuts himself off. "Charlotte, are you *sure* he never told you anything?"

I take Emily's photo. Stare into her eyes. Reach deep, deep into my memory, force myself to remember things I never wanted to think about again.

I feel his hands close around my throat, but there's nothing in my memory of him telling me what he did with Emily Alvarado.

Defeated, I have to tell Agent Lindo no. "He never said anything."

He sighs heavily and pinches the bridge of his nose. "Then if he doesn't talk," he says, "we may never find her body."

No. I can't let that happen. He *has* to find her. We *have* to bring her home.

"Maybe you can make a different kind of deal with him." The idea comes unbidden, a venomous snake slithering from some dark and desperate place in my mind. "If he tells you what he did with her body . . ."

I try to stop it, but the snake strikes. ". . . I'll go visit him."

In the ensuing silence, I drag my gaze up to see their reactions, wanting them to agree, wanting them to refuse.

"Honey, no!" Mom cries. "Absolutely not," Dad says at the same time. Alexa's looking at me like I'm nuts, and Agent Lindo looks at me with pity, which is even worse.

"I told you, Charlotte," Dad says, "you will never have to see that man again."

I nod. I'll never see him again, not even in court, not even to make a deal to find The One Before.

But Emily Alvarado was more than The One Before. She was a real person, a real girl. She lived in Peoria, Illinois. She was an only child. She was thirteen years old. She went to middle school. She played piano. And unless Alan Shaw admits what he did with her body, all that's left of her will be a long-overdue library book and a partial fingerprint on a copper pipe.

chapter twenty-six

I sit in the center of an overstuffed couch in a pretty blue living room, trying to get air past the hands around my neck. People dressed in black crowd the house, speaking in low murmurs, occasionally glancing at me with a curious look in their eyes. When their curiosity turns to pity, I know they've figured out who I am.

My father is sitting next to me. He asked if I wanted to come with him today, and was incredibly pleased when I said yes.

Of course I'd said yes. I wouldn't miss Emily Alvarado's memorial service. I would have walked here, two hundred miles south, if I had to.

Now we're back at her house, sitting across from her mourning parents. Seven years of not knowing have etched deep lines of sorrow into their faces. And now that they do know, those lines are etched deeper still.

There are a million things I want to say to them:

I'm sorry Alan Shaw took your daughter too.

I'm sorry you had to live all these years—seven long years—not knowing if she was alive or dead.

I'm sorry she didn't survive.

I'm sorry the end of her life was filled with pain and terror.

I'm sorry I don't know where he hid her body.

I'm sorry you couldn't have a traditional funeral for her.

I'm sorry.

I'm sorry.

I'm sorry.

I want to say all those things, but I can't get them past my throat.

I look into Mrs. Alvarado's brown eyes, warm and wet with tears. Mr. Alvarado turns his head and clears his throat. They clutch each other's hands.

There's a piano against the wall. The fallboard is down, hiding the keys from sight. I wonder if anyone has played it since Emily disappeared.

On the wall over the piano are framed photos of Emily, at least two dozen of them, and she's smiling in all of them. Baby photos, soccer photos, school portraits starting at kindergarten. They stop after eighth grade. In one photo, she's in a red plaid dress, on stage next to a grand piano, curtsying. One picture shows her holding a stack of books so high she's resting her chin on it. Another photo is an action shot: she's running across a soccer field, throwing her arms up in victory.

Finally, there's something I can say to Mr. and Mrs. Alvarado without my throat closing up.

"I never met Emily," I tell them, "but I know she was brave. I know she was strong. I know she never stopped trying to escape. I know she fought. Hard."

Mr. Alvarado thrusts his chin out and nods. Mrs. Alvarado's chin trembles, and she presses her forehead into her husband's shoulder.

"I know she'd be relieved that you still love each other," I add, "and that her disappearance didn't drive a wedge between you."

Beside me, Dad clears his throat. "Charlotte."

But I'm not finished. If our fates were switched, and it was Emily talking to my parents instead of me talking to hers, she wouldn't be finished, either.

"And I know," I say, "that when you think of Emily, she wouldn't want you to think of how she died. She'd want you to think of her like she is in those pictures on the wall. Playing piano. Reading books. Playing soccer. Emily was amazing, and *that's* how she wants you to think of her."

Mrs. Alvarado crumples. She stumbles over to me, pulls me into her arms, and sobs.

chapter twenty-seven

Christmas Day is like Thanksgiving, custody-wise: Alexa and I spend half the day with Mom, and half the day with Dad. But both parents overload me with presents. Mom gives Alexa and me new matching comforters and blankets for our beds and things to decorate our room. Dad and Marissa give me all the gadgets I need to be a normal, regular, plugged-in teenager. I'm now the proud owner of a brand-new iPhone, a bunch of DVDs, an e-Reader loaded with so many books that I'll never have time to read them all, and my very own laptop. I spend all day programming my phone and setting up accounts on all the social media sites.

I wanted to give my family gifts too, but they all said my homecoming was the best gift I could ever give them. I did send cards to Agent Lindo, Dr. Goldbloom, my doctors, my physical therapist, and to Joel and Kev, the ambulance guys who found me. I sent a letter to Mr. and Mrs. Alvarado, telling them that as I celebrate Christmas, this year and every year, I'll be thinking of Emily.

I'm determined to celebrate Christmas, and celebrate it double, because Emily can't celebrate it at all.

Late that night, back at Mom's house, Alexa and I decide to have a movie marathon with our new DVDs. In the light of the Christmas tree, we lounge on the couch in our pajamas, eating sugar cookies shaped like reindeer and drinking hot chocolate garnished with mini candy canes, just like we used to do. The first movie we watch is a romance from three years ago. Alexa has seen it, but I haven't, of course. Two teenagers from the opposite sides of town meet, and they hate each other, and they bicker and argue, and then they realize they don't hate each other, not at all.

And then it happens.

They secretly meet on the beach one night. He sets out a blanket for her, keeps her warm under his arm. He kisses her neck, and she kisses him back. They touch each other, gently, slowly, falling onto the blanket, shedding their clothes, and he worships her with kisses.

There's no grabbing, no threats, no hands around her throat. No blood.

She doesn't cry while it's happening and she doesn't cry when it's over. Instead she lays her head on his shoulder and purrs, running her fingertips over his chest.

I take a pink teddy bear and pick-pull a seam in the leg. I knew what sex was before my Keeper took me. But until he took me, I never knew that sex *hurt*. I never knew that someone could hurt someone else with sex, that someone could force someone else to have sex with them. I never knew that an old man could have sex with a little girl. I never knew that sex and love could mean two different things.

My Keeper loves me. He told me that every day. He also did sex things with me every day. His sex was violent and wrong, and his love was violent and wrong.

I can feel Alexa watching me. "Sorry," she says. "I forgot about this part of the movie."

"It's fine," I say. I stare straight ahead at the screen, pretending this doesn't bother me, pretending that this beautiful, gentle love scene isn't detonating violent memories inside my mind, pretending his hands aren't around my throat, squeezing.

I pull a tiny bit of stuffing from the teddy bear and hide it between the couch cushions.

Who would ever want to have sex with me anyway, after everything he did to me? Who would even want to touch me?

"For what it's worth," Alexa says, "I've never had sex like the people in this movie. My first time was with some stoner guy in his basement one night after a party. It sucked."

"Why?"

She shrugs. "He was slobbery, he had beer breath, and his Xbox controller was jabbing into my back the whole time." She grimaces, angry at herself. "Shit. Sorry. That was nothing compared to what you went through."

"True, but what I meant was, why did you have sex with him?"

"I don't know." She shrugs again. "A million reasons. I was wasted. I didn't want to go home yet. Mostly I just wanted to see what it was like, I guess."

I keep my gaze on the TV; I keep my face expressionless. If Alexa sees how much this discussion disturbs me, she'll never confide in me again. "What about all those guys you go out with now?" I ask. "Do you have sex with any of them?"

"It usually ends up that way, yeah."

From the corner of my eye, I see her twist a lock of her white hair around her finger.

"It doesn't have to end up that way," I say.

But that's too much. I pushed it too far. Alexa yanks on her hair and shifts away from me. "This movie is stupid," she says. "Let's watch something else."

She puts in a different DVD, a comedy, but neither of us laugh. By the time it's over, I've pulled so much stuffing from the teddy bear that one of its legs is completely empty.

chapter twenty-eight

I'm still half-asleep the next morning when the doorbell rings. Dad's not scheduled to pick us up today, so it can't be him. Alexa's friends just honk from the driveway, and Mom's *No Trespassing* signs have ensured that no one comes to the door. Could Agent Lindo be here? Maybe he has news—maybe he finally got Alan Shaw to confess what he did with Emily Alvarado's body.

I jump out of bed and rush down the hall in my pajamas, just in time to see Mom opening the front door. A chipper voice says, "Mrs. Weatherstone, please don't send us away again. We just want to say hi to Charlotte. Please?"

It's Bailey Brandis! And Megan and Amber, too!

My mom shakes her head. "I'm sorry girls, she's still not ready for visitors. Maybe in a few weeks."

"Wait!" I cry. "Bailey! Don't leave!" I dash to the door, ignoring the pain in my knee.

Mom hesitates. "Charlotte, I don't know if this is . . ." She sighs, then turns to the girls. "Two minutes. And no questions about what happened."

Bailey nods solemnly, then bursts inside with a squeal. She squeezes me in a tight hug, and I hug her back even tighter. She still wears that vanilla perfume. She releases me, and I turn to hug Megan and Amber, who are standing stiffly in the doorway. Their hugs are stiff too, so I drop my arms and step back.

All three girls are wearing red and silver Sparklers jackets. They're taller now, of course, and wearing makeup. But their makeup is subtle; no heavy smears of black eyeliner like Alexa wears. Bailey has blond highlights in her brown hair.

Megan and Amber are looking at me the same way my cousins looked at me over Thanksgiving: they don't see *me*, only the things that happened to me. But not Bailey. She's looking at me with tears in her eyes and a smile that's filled with pure joy. She sees me, the real me. Not the broken little bird that my mother sees, or the Ambassador of Hope that my father sees, or the girl who was stupid enough to walk off with a stranger and ruin everyone's lives that my sister sees. Bailey sees me as I want to be: a normal, non-newsworthy, non-broken, non-disgusting sixteen-year-old girl.

Beautiful, beautiful Bailey. I squeal and hug her again.

"Oh my God, Charlotte, we missed you soooo much," she says. "Cheering hasn't been the same without you. When are you coming back to school?"

I glance at Mom, who looks horrified. "I don't know," I tell Bailey. "I'm being homeschooled for now."

Bailey pouts, her nose scrunching up. She still looks cute, even like that. Her gaze flickers to a spot behind me, and her spirit fizzles. "Hey, Lex," she says.

Alexa's leaning against the wall, arms folded across her chest. She gives a curt nod, her white spikes brushing up and down. "Hey."

"We came over to welcome your sister home."

"So I see."

Bailey bites her lip, clearly hurt. Intimidated, and maybe a little scared. She turns back to me and brightens, clapping her hands in quick little cheer claps. "You should totally come out with us tonight, Charlotte. Brandon Louis, remember him? It's his birthday, and we're all going to Stubby's, and you *have* to be there."

Stubby's: the pizza place from our Dream Book. Alexa won't go to Stubby's because all the Peps hang out there, and she's no longer friends with the Peps.

Bailey is more supportive of the Dream Book than Alexa is, and Bailey doesn't even know about it.

"Okay, yeah," I say. Excitement floods through me, and I clap my hands just like Bailey. Megan and Amber are uncomfortable around me, which means some of the others will be too. But if I stick with Bailey, things will be all right.

"You, um, you could come too, Lex," Bailey says. "You know. If you want."

"Can't," Alexa mutters, studying her fingernails. "I already have plans."

"Come on, Alexa—" I start, but Mom interrupts.

"I'm sorry, Bailey, but Charlotte can't go either," she says.

"Why not?" I ask.

"You've only been home for a few weeks," she says. "You're not ready to go out yet."

There's something pleading and desperate in her tone, in her eyes, and I can't bring myself to protest. Instead, I nod meekly. Bailey makes that cute pouty face again.

"Okay, girls, that's enough," Mom says. "Charlotte needs her rest. Thank you for stopping by." She practically pushes them out.

"Call me, Charlotte!" Bailey shouts, just as Mom shuts the door.

chapter twenty-nine

Mrs. Ridge takes her lesson plans out of her quilted bag, placing them in neat stacks on the dining room table. Today she has something in addition to her usual papers: an empty soda bottle, baking soda, and vinegar. "We're starting our chemistry unit today," she says. "We're making a volcano."

Making a volcano is a rite of passage for sixth-graders at Woodland Creek Elementary School. It was one of the things I was most excited about doing in sixth grade, but my Keeper took me just before the school year started.

"Oooo, a volcano!" Mom says from her desk across the room, where she's setting up her work. It's the middle of February, I've been home for four months now, and Mom still says I'm not ready to go to school or go out with friends.

Dad, on the other hand, is pressuring me to travel with him all over the country to comfort families in crisis as the Ambassador of Hope.

My Keeper is still not in jail. He's been transferred to a long-term care facility, where he remains under guard. But he's still refusing to confess what he did with Emily Alvarado's body.

A car honks in the driveway, and Alexa, dressed in her uniform of black-on-black-on-black, heavy black makeup, and spiked white hair, dashes to the door. "Jen's here," she says. "See ya later, sis."

The morning hours drag by as Mrs. Ridge goes through my lessons, one by one, in her prim and proper voice. Math. Social

Studies. English. And the volcano, which fails to live up to the expectations I had when I was eleven.

At precisely noon, I sit with Mom and Mrs. Ridge at the kitchen table and eat the lunch Mom made for me: vegetable soup, peanut butter and jelly on whole-grain bread, orange slices in the shape of a flower, and a protein shake.

Bailey calls me during her lunch period to say hi. She chatters on and on, but I can barely hear her over the laughter of the other students in the cafeteria.

I wait until Dad comes to pick us up on Wednesday night to make my announcement. He'll be thrilled with what I'm about to say, but I'll need his help convincing Mom. I'll need Alexa's help, too.

Dad arrives a few minutes early, as usual. I take my time in my room, pretending to get ready, until I'm sure Alexa, Mom, and Dad are all together in the foyer.

I tuck the Dream Book inside the pouch of my hoodie. Then I walk to the foyer, confidently, with pep and purpose, the way Bailey would, making sure I don't limp. I stand before my parents and take a deep breath. "I've been thinking about it," I say, "and I'm ready to go to school. Woodland Creek High."

As expected, Dad smiles so broadly that he lights up the whole house. "Excellent," he says. "Good for you, sweetheart."

Also as expected, Mom shakes her head. "You're too far behind."

"Mrs. Ridge says I'm ahead of schedule," I say. "I'll catch up the rest of the way at school. I can do it. I know I can."

"What do you say, Vickie?" Dad asks. "Charlotte's a bright kid. We'll start her off with some basic freshman-level courses, and she can get tutoring from Mrs. Ridge in the evenings."

Mom hasn't stopped shaking her head. "It's more than academics. She's not ready to go out in public."

"If you're worried about reporters," Alexa says, "they wouldn't be allowed on school grounds. But if they do try to bother her, I'll keep them away. You know I can do that."

Dad gives Alexa a slight frown, then says to Mom, "The socialization would be good for her."

Mom stops shaking her head as she considers it, but then shakes her head again, just once, with finality. "No. She's not ready. The answer is no. Absolutely not."

"You keep saying I'm not ready, Mom, but *you're* the one who's not ready," I say, and immediately regret it when a tremble starts in her chin and travels to her lip.

The same thing happened to her at the food court at the mall, when she told me that she blames herself for my disappearance because she was talking to the other moms instead of watching me.

Mom lost one daughter to abduction, her husband to divorce, and her other daughter to delinquency. Now she has one of us back, me, and I'm telling her that I want to leave her again. It's almost enough to make me back down, to stop pushing for school, to stay home with her forever.

But no. I reach in the pouch of my hoodie and touch the Dream Book to remind myself why I'm doing this. "I was locked away for over four years in that attic," I say, as gently as I can. "But now you're keeping me locked away too. I need to get my life back on track. Please, Mom. I want to go to school."

She does nothing for a long minute, just looks down at her feet and sniffles. Finally she says, "Maybe. I'll think about it."

I give a little squeal and jump, clapping my hands. *Maybe* is better than no, and *think about it* is one step closer to yes.

It takes a couple of weeks, but after getting a tentative thumbs-up from Dr. Goldbloom, and having several discussions with my doctors, meeting with the principal, guidance counselor, and social worker at Woodland Creek High, and promising to take an easy course load, to work with Mrs. Ridge three nights a week, to keep up with my physical therapy and my doctor appointments, and to tell my parents if I feel overwhelmed in any way, I finally get Mom's reluctant approval to go to school on a trial basis. I start next week.

This coming Monday, Alexa and I can finally start following the plans in our Dream Book. And I'm going to do it double, because Emily Alvarado can't do it at all.

chapter thirty

I have a closet full of clothes, and I don't know what to wear.

Definitely no skirts. Skirts are too open between my legs, and that will make everyone think about what happened to me.

I try on a yellow top. No, it's too tight and curves around my breasts. That'll make everyone think about what happened to me.

The blue hoodie? No, that's way too baggy. Everyone will realize I'm trying to hide what happened to me, which will make them think about what happened to me.

Finally I decide on a pair of jeans, a long ivory sweater with a chunky brown belt around the waist, and brown ankle boots. There. Sophisticated, yet bulky enough that everyone won't be reminded about what happened to me.

From my bed, Wiggles and the rest of the pink teddy bears are watching me. I resist the urge to take one and pluck out its stuffing. Instead, I take Emily Alvarado's photo from my bulletin board and tuck it between the pages of the Dream Book. I put them both in a pocket of my brand-new book bag.

Okay. I'm officially ready for my first day at Woodland Creek High.

Mom and Alexa are already in the kitchen. Alexa is eating Cheerios. Mom hands me a plate of scrambled egg whites, a banana, and a protein shake. I don't know if it's excitement about going to school, or nerves, or guilt about leaving my mom, or invisible hands around my throat, but I have to force the food down.

Mom isn't eating, and her chin is trembling again, but she's dressed in a gray skirt and black pumps. She's dressed for the office, her first time back since I've been home. She may not be ready for me to go to school, but at least she's trying. "You look nice, Mom."

"So do you." She smooths my hair and I try not to go stiff.

A car honks from the driveway. "That's Jen," Alexa says. She takes one more spoonful of her cereal. "Come on, Charlotte. Time to introduce you to the oh-so-wonderful world that is Woodland Creek High."

Mom rubs her hands up and down my arms. "You sure you want to do this?"

I don't want to spend one more day, not even one more second, sitting at the dining room table with Mrs. Ridge while Alexa and every other person my age is in school. "Yes, Mom. I'm sure."

"I wish you'd let me drive you."

"I want to go with Alexa." Mom would have too much time to change her mind if she drives me.

"Okay," she says, much too cheerfully, then gives me a tight-lipped kiss on my forehead. She turns away, but not before I see that she's trying to blink back tears.

"Do you want me to call you during lunch?" I ask. "I'll call you every hour, if you want."

She half-sniffles, half-laughs. "I'm being ridiculous, aren't I. Go to school, Charlotte. You're going to have a great day. You can tell me all about it when you get home." Then she adds under her breath, "This afternoon." As if she's convincing herself that I *will* come home this afternoon, and that I won't walk off with another pedophile and disappear again.

Alexa slides into the passenger side of her friend Jen's rumbling blue clunker, which means I get the back seat. It's littered with an empty pizza box, crumpled receipts, and a pair of dirty gloves.

"Charlotte, Jen. Jen, Charlotte," Alexa says with a wave of her hand. She gives Jen some kind of warning glance, then slumps in her seat and starts texting on her phone. I guess that's all we're going to get as an introduction.

Jen gives me a glance in the rearview mirror. "Hey."

"Thanks for the ride," I say back, playing it cool, not at all like I'm so excited-slash-nervous that my heart has turned into a jackhammer inside my rib cage.

I don't remember Jen from before, so she must have gone to one of the other elementary schools in our district. Her hair is the color of cinnamon, with bangs that are cut straight and short across her forehead. Her lipstick matches her hair color exactly. She's wearing black eyeliner that ends in a little swirl at the outer corners of her eyes.

She pulls out of the driveway and we head to Woodland Creek High. Every time I look up, she's looking back at me in the rearview mirror. I can't tell if her expression is curiosity or disgust or pity. Maybe it's a combination of all three.

Four blocks away, we pass a little boy standing at a corner, bundled up in an orange down coat and a Chicago Bears knit cap, with a backpack at his feet. "God *dammit*," Alexa shouts, and slaps the dashboard. "Stop the car."

Jen gives a long and heavy sigh, but she pulls over. "Here we go again," she mutters.

"Just watch him for me, okay?" Alexa snaps. "Charlotte, come with me."

"What's wrong?" I ask as we get out of the car.

"Just come on." She shouts to the little boy, "Hey, kid, where do you live?"

The boy points to a small brown-brick house two doors down, and Alexa takes me by the wrist and marches over there. She rings the bell and impatiently taps her foot. When no one answers within twenty seconds, she rings it again, then again.

Finally the door opens, revealing a tired-looking woman wearing a blue bathrobe and holding a coffee mug. "Can I help you?"

"Is that your kid?" Alexa demands, pointing to the boy on the corner.

The woman's eyes grow wide, all sleepiness gone in an instant. "Yes! Is something wrong?"

"Yes, something's wrong. He's standing out there all alone."

"He's waiting for the school bus," she says.

"*Alone*," Alexa says. "What if someone pulls up and tries to take him?"

The woman waves her off. "It's a safe neighborhood. And he's nine years old. He knows not to talk to strangers."

"Does he? Are you sure?" Alexa grabs my coat by the sleeve and gives it a little shake. "You see this girl? *She's* from this neighborhood, and *her* parents taught her not to talk to strangers too."

The woman pales, and I can feel the blood draining from my face, too. "Alexa, don't—"

"That's right," Alexa says to the woman. "You recognize her now, don't you. Charlotte Weatherstone. Alan Shaw took her in front of over a hundred people, and not a single one of us saw it. Your kid is standing out there all alone. *No one* is around. What do you think his chances are if someone tries to take him?"

The woman's face turns from pale to slightly gray.

Alexa moves from the doorway and gestures to the street. "Get out there and watch your kid," she says, and then her voice cracks. "Please."

The woman rushes from the house, dressed in only her bathrobe and slippers, and hustles to the corner. Alexa drags me back to Jen's car. "Alexa, you didn't have to do that," I say.

"Yes. I did."

Dad's using me as a message of hope. Alexa's using me as a message of fear.

I don't want to be used by anybody.

Jen is leaning back in her seat, smoking a cigarette, bored, as if Alexa has done this a thousand times before. Alexa watches the woman, making sure she stays with her son until the bus comes, even though she's shivering in the frigid air, gripping her coffee mug to warm her hands. Only once the boy is safely on the bus does Alexa nod at Jen, who then puts the car in gear and drives away.

⌒)

The second I walk into Woodland Creek High, I'm assaulted. With hugs.

I told Bailey about my return to school, and asked her to keep it quiet. But she must have told Amber and Megan and the cheerleading squad, because they're all waiting for me as I enter the building. The greetings tumble from their mouths, and I can barely make sense of them. I catch snippets: "Welcome back!" "We missed you so much!" "We're so happy you're back!" "I prayed for you every single day."

This is perfect. *Perfect.* My arms hurt from hugging everyone, my cheeks hurt from smiling so hard, and I'm so happy that I might explode into little bits of confetti.

I search for Alexa in the crowd and find her off to the side by a drinking fountain with Jen and a few others, all of them dressed in black. She's watching Bailey with narrowed eyes.

Bailey links elbows with me. "I'll show you where your locker is," she says. "There was an empty one four down from mine, and I asked them if you could have it, and they said yes."

I stop and look back for Alexa, but she's still standing by the drinking fountain, watching Bailey and me. Her chin is jutted out like she doesn't care.

"Alexa?" I say. "You coming?"

She looks at me and Bailey, then back at Jen and her friends, then back at me.

"Yeah, Lex, come with us," Bailey says.

Please, I beg her silently.

Alexa gives Jen an apologetic shrug, then shuffles over to Bailey and me. The three of us walk down the hall together.

Even though I'm sixteen years old and was ahead of schedule in my homeschool curriculum, at Woodland Creek High I'm only in remedial freshman-level classes. But I don't care, because the important thing is that I'm in school, which is exactly where I want to be. I'm officially a high school student. I have my own locker, #A329. I can go to pep rallies and basketball games and dances. I can complain about the gross food in the cafeteria. I can join clubs and activities, and say hi to my friends as we pass in the hall.

The only thing I don't love about Woodland Creek High is not having Alexa in my classes. When we were in elementary school, Mom and Dad always made arrangements for us to be in the same class. Alexa is far from the stellar student she used to be, but I still didn't test high enough to be with her.

She meets me after each class, though, to show me the way to my next one. Bailey does too. They stand together, jockeying for my attention, one dressed in pink with a perky ponytail, the other dressed in black with spiky white hair. As we navigate the halls, Bailey bounces, Alexa shuffles. Bailey gives everyone a cheery hello while Alexa stares everyone down.

I try to be more like Bailey, even though bouncing hurts my knee.

The hallways are crowded, and one time a bulky boy bumps into me, knocking me sideways. "Watch it, asshole!" Alexa shouts. The boy holds his palms up and rushes away.

I only recognize about a third of my classmates, but *everyone*— the students, teachers, admin, maintenance staff—knows who I am. Some of them treat me like I'm fragile and about to break, others are nervous, and others are overly casual, like it's no big deal that a famous kidnap victim is sitting in their classroom. I can see the questions behind their eyes, but no one asks about my ordeal. Maybe the principal warned them not to. Or maybe they're afraid of crossing Alexa.

By the end of last period, I'm exhausted, but I refuse to show it. Accompanied by Alexa and Bailey, I stop at my locker to get the textbooks I need to do my homework. Perky as ever, Bailey chirps, "Are you busy tomorrow after school? We have cheer practice, and Miss Klein, she's the cheerleading coach, she said if you want to come watch us, you can. I told her how good you were on the Dragonettes, how you were the first one of us to do a backflip and all that."

"Really?" I have physical therapy tomorrow, but not until six. I can definitely go to cheer practice.

"Yeah," Bailey says. "I mean, we have a full squad already, but you could learn the routines. And then in May, when we have tryouts for next year, you'll be ahead of the game."

"Okay, thanks!" I'm bursting. *Bursting*. I beam at Alexa, but she's pretending to study her chipped black fingernails.

"You too, Lex," Bailey says. "You should come too. Really. I mean it. I want you both on the squad next year."

Alexa glances up, and for just an instant, the defiance in her eyes is replaced by excitement, and she looks like the Alexa I remember, the Alexa from my attic daydreams, the Alexa I know she truly is. "I don't know," she says. "Maybe."

When we get home, there are two cars in the driveway: Dad's white car, and a brown one I don't recognize.

"That's Lindo's car," Alexa says as we trudge past it.

It's not our night to go to Dad's house, but he may have stopped by to ask about my first day of school. But there's no reason, no reason at all, why Agent Lindo would be here, unless something is horribly, horribly wrong.

chapter thirty-one

Mom, Dad, and Agent Lindo are sitting in the family room when Alexa and I enter the house. Agent Lindo is his usual massive, serious self. Dad looks slightly stunned, and I think Mom might be crying.

"What's wrong?" I ask. "What happened?" So many horrors flood my mind: he escaped, and he's kidnapped another girl. He escaped, and he's headed here. He escaped, and he wants Alexa.

Mom sniffles and wipes her eyes. "Oh, Charlotte, nothing's wrong. We have *good* news."

Good news? I don't even have to ask what it is. There's only one piece of good news Agent Lindo could possibly deliver: they found her. They found Emily Alvarado.

Mom gives a weird, choked little laugh. "Charlotte, he's dead."

The realization of what's happening grips my heart with icy claws. I know what she's going to say, there's only one answer she could give, but I have to ask. "Who's dead?"

"Alan Shaw. This afternoon," she exclaims. "He's *dead*, Charlotte!"

I'm frozen. I can't move. I can barely speak. The room tilts, narrows. "But he was getting better. Stronger."

"He was getting stronger," Agent Lindo says. Anger roils just under the surface. "So much stronger, in fact, that he was able to kill himself."

Agent Lindo's words are scrambled. They make no sense. I couldn't have heard him correctly, because I'm slipping, I'm plummeting, I'm drowning. "He—he *killed* himself? You said he was under guard."

"The guard was stationed outside the room," Lindo says. "He used his IV cord as a garrote. He ratcheted it around his neck and knotted it, closing off his jugular. Resulted in ligature strangulation."

"But there's supposed to be a trial," I say. "I'm supposed to testify."

"And now we don't have to worry about that, Charlotte." Dad gives Lindo a congratulatory pat on the back. "It's over."

It's over. He's dead. I never have to see him again. Alan Shaw is dead.

Then why are his hands creeping up around my throat and squeezing, squeezing, squeezing? My Keeper is dead, but he still won't let me go.

Eventually, Agent Lindo leaves, and then my dad. Alexa and I do some homework. We eat dinner. Then more homework. Mom watches the news, and Alan Shaw's suicide is the first thing they report. It's on every station. It's all over the Internet. Bailey texts me, then calls. I don't answer. I change into my pajamas. I brush my teeth in the dark. I go to bed. The storm swirls, churns, rumbles in my mind.

That night, long after Mom and Alexa have fallen asleep and the house is silent, I lay in my bed and pick-pull the stitching on another pink teddy bear.

I pluck out a bit of stuffing. "He's dead," I tell Emily.

But I can't tell her that she's free.

There is an awful keening noise coming from somewhere. It doesn't stop, it doesn't stop, it doesn't stop, this horrible, haunting, howling cry.

It's only after Alexa calls out and Mom comes running and they shake me that I realize the noise is coming from me.

But still, the cries don't stop.

chapter thirty-two

I don't stop crying all night long, so Mom won't let me go to school the next day. She and Dad take me to Dr. Goldbloom instead. She rearranges her appointments to fit me in.

My eyes are puffy and I'm exhausted. My throat is raw, and I have a headache from all the crying. I don't want to talk to Dr. Goldbloom. I don't want to sit on her soft lavender couch in her sunny white barn. I don't want her to gaze at me with her warm, kind eyes, or smile at me with her gentle, patient, nonjudging smile. But that's exactly what she's doing.

I don't say anything. I look at my hands so I don't have to look at her. I wish there was a pink teddy bear in here, but there's not. I take a lavender throw pillow and pick-pull at a seam.

I feel a tear slip down my cheek, and I swipe it away before she can see it.

Too late.

"So," she says in her soft accent. "Alan Shaw is dead."

"Yep." I swipe away another tear.

"How do you feel about that?"

I shrug. "I'm happy."

"According to your mother, you were extremely upset about it last night."

I shrug again. "I don't know what that was all about. I should be happy that he's dead."

"Why do you think you *should* be happy about that?"

"Because he's gone," I say. "Forever. There won't be a trial. I won't have to testify. I won't have to see him, ever again. He can't hurt me anymore, or anyone else."

"But he's still hurting you," Dr. Goldbloom says.

"No he's not. He killed himself, and I'm glad. I'm glad he strangled himself. I'm glad he died like that." His hands creep up around my neck. "That was the perfect way for him to die."

"Then why are you crying?"

I swipe more tears from my cheek. "I don't know."

Dr. Goldbloom gazes at me. I look away for as long as I can. When I look back, she's still looking at me. "I think you do," she says.

I squeeze my fingers into the throw pillow. "No I don't. You're just like Agent Lindo, asking me things I don't know." I shove the pillow from my lap, and it falls to the floor soundlessly. "If you think you know so much, then you tell me why I can't stop crying."

"Okay," she says. "You're crying because he died before you could say goodbye."

"Goodbye?" I cry. "I hate him. Why would I want to say goodbye to him?"

"Not to him. To the fear."

I sniffle. "Yes. But he's dead now, so there's no more fear."

"But . . ." she says, and waits.

"But I wanted him to *pay* for what he did to me." I pick up the pillow from the floor, stand, and this time I throw it. Hard. "To me, to Emily Alvarado, to Julia Hogan." With each name, I throw another pillow. "I wanted him to go to trial, and be convicted, and spend the rest of his life locked up in a tiny little prison cell. And now he won't!"

Dr. Goldbloom doesn't react to my tantrum. She nods slowly. She smiles gently. She waits patiently.

"I'm pissed that I went to school for just one day and it went really well and then he had to go kill himself and now I had to miss school to come here," I say. "It's like he picked yesterday on purpose. Like he *knew* just the right day to kill himself."

I want to punch things. I want to throw things. I punch another pillow, then throw it.

"I wanted to see him again," I say through clenched teeth. "I wanted to see him. I wanted to—" I slam another pillow to the floor. "I wanted him to see how much he hurt me. How much he hurt my mom, and my dad, and my sister, how he destroyed my family . . . I wanted to tell him that he can't just take a little girl away from her family, that she's a *person*, and he has no *right* to use her and hurt her just because he's sick and twisted and bigger and stronger and she can't fight back. I wanted to see him again, there was supposed to be a trial, and I was going to testify, and he was going to spend the rest of his life in prison, but he died, he *killed himself*, before any of that could happen."

I take another pillow, slam it to the floor, and stomp on it. I howl when it hurts my knee. "Now I can never show him how much he hurt me. He'll never understand. He'll never pay. And he did it to himself! It's like he did it on purpose, just to hurt me one last time. He took everything from me, everything! My freedom. My body. My family. And now he took away the last chance I had to see him again. He took it all!"

There are no more pillows left to throw, but they are too soft, too silent, anyway. I grab a heavy ceramic vase from the coffee table, glance at Dr. Goldbloom, and when she nods, I erupt in a scream and hurl it across the barn as hard as I can. It shatters against the wall with a loud, satisfying crash.

Fists clenched, heaving air in and out in high squeaky gasps, I turn and face Dr. Goldbloom.

"What else," she says.

"He wouldn't tell anyone what he did with Emily's body, and now he never will," I say. "Agent Lindo keeps asking me if he ever told me anything, and I think and think and think, but there's nothing. All he ever said was that she's dead because she didn't behave, and if I don't behave, he'll do to me what he did to her and then replace me with my sister. He never told me what he did with her body, and now he's dead, and now we'll never find her."

My breath is coming in short little gasps. I swipe at my throat. "And he keeps strangling me! He's dead, but he still won't let me go!"

Dr. Goldbloom nods again, slowly. Then she unfolds herself from the sofa, and her anklet jingles as she glides across the barn to a closet. She takes out a broom and a dustpan, then glides back to me, where I'm standing among the pieces of the shattered vase. "What he did was a cowardly thing," she says. "His life was cowardly. His death was cowardly. But he is dead. Gone forever. And you, Charlotte, you are still here. You are alive."

She hands me the broom, and together we sweep up the broken vase. By the time we finish, I've stopped crying, and I can breathe again.

chapter thirty-three

Algebra. Biology. English. Language Arts. Social Studies.

I don't know how I thought I could miss four and a half years of school and then jump right back in. I missed all of sixth, seventh, eighth, and ninth, and half of tenth grade. I'm taking the easiest, most basic classes that Woodland Creek High offers, but my textbooks may as well be written in another language. I downloaded a dictionary app to my cell phone, and I spend more time looking up vocabulary words than I do reading the text.

Only one fact sinks in through the clutter, in History, where we're learning about World War II. After class, I show Alexa a black and white photo in my textbook. She recognizes it instantly.

"This is the same plane you drew on your laptop," I say, pointing to the circled R on the tail. "The *Enola Gay.*"

"Yeah, so?"

"So you named yourself after the plane that dropped the first atomic bomb? Why would you do that?"

She shrugs, moving her chewing gum from one side of her mouth to the other. "I just liked it. Thought it fit. Enola is also *alone* spelled backwards."

"You're not alone anymore, Alexa."

"It's Lex," she hisses, and shoves past without another word.

Knowing what *Enola* means somehow makes it even harder to concentrate. But when the school's social worker calls me to her office to ask how I'm doing, I tell her I'm doing great. It was hard enough to convince Mom to let me come back to school after my meltdown the other day. If she even suspects that I'm struggling, she'll make me go back to homeschooling with Mrs. Ridge. And then I'll never be a Sparkler. And neither will my sister. She'd never join the squad without me. Not as Alexa, and definitely not as Lex Enola.

I'll just have to work harder. I keep the Dream Book tucked in my book bag. Every time I see a long paragraph of confusing words, or a math problem with weird, indecipherable symbols, I reach into my bag and find the Dream Book. I will not quit. I can't quit. I have to keep going, for myself, for Alexa, and for Emily Alvarado, who will never be found.

After school a couple weeks later, Bailey meets me at my locker to take me to cheer practice. She's all smiles in her red and silver practice uniform, and her hair is pulled up in a high ponytail. Ooo—why didn't I think of that? I have practice clothes on—a sweatshirt and loose yoga pants—but I don't have anything to pull my hair back with.

"Hey, Bailey, do you have an extra hair tie I can borrow?" I ask.

She hands me one from her bag, an elastic band threaded with red and silver ribbons. I use my fingers to comb my hair in a high ponytail.

He would hate this. He likes my hair down.

He touches my hair, brushes it, smooths it. *There, all done. Now come to bed—*

"Perfect!" Bailey's squeal jars me, brings me out of the attic and back to the school.

He's not touching my hair. He's dead. He is *dead*.

"You look soooo cute like that," Bailey continues, all sparkle and shimmer and sunshine.

Since I won't look in a mirror, I have to trust her. I smile, soaking in some of that sunshine.

We wait for Alexa, and when she doesn't come, we go looking for her. We find her at her locker with a huge, hulking boy who's jamming his tongue down her throat. He's holding an unlit cigarette in one hand, and his other hand is on her breast. She's not in the throes of passion or anything, in fact she seems kind of bored, but she's kissing him back.

"Alexa," I say.

She pulls away and wipes her mouth with the back of her hand. "Gotta go, Danny," she tells the boy. "I'll meet up with you later." He pulls her back and shoves his tongue in her mouth again until I step in and yank her away.

"We have cheerleading practice," I hiss, sharply, as much to him as to her.

The boy sneers. He has long brown hair that curls around his ears and impossibly long eyelashes, and I suppose I would consider him good-looking if he wasn't such a scumbag. He slides the cigarette behind his ear and slinks off.

"Well, should we go?" Bailey asks, overly perky, with just a trace of apprehension. "We don't want to be late!"

Alexa shuffles along as we go with Bailey, and I can't tell if she feels guilty for kissing that awful boy or resentful that I pulled her away from him. I want to say something, to scold her, but I hold it back. It would only make her defensive, and I don't want her to quit cheerleading before she's even started.

In the field house, Bailey introduces me to Miss Klein, the cheer coach. She looks a lot like Bailey: young and pretty, and her long blond hair is in a high ponytail. I'm extra glad that I put my hair up. I give her my cheeriest, peppiest smile, which she returns. She glances at Alexa like she's afraid of her.

"Why don't you two join us for the warm-up?" she says. "But, um, Lex, you'll need to take out your piercings."

When Alexa hesitates, I give her a pleading look until she reluctantly pulls out her multiple studs and rings. I nudge her a thank you, then put a bounce in my step to join the squad. Alexa drags behind, but she comes.

I don't recognize half of the cheerleaders. Only Bailey, Megan, Amber, and a couple others were on the Dragonettes. There are boys on this squad.

Miss Klein starts the music and leads the warm-up routine. My physical therapy sessions have increased my stamina and improved my muscle tone, but I'm sweaty and huffing and puffing before the end of the first song. I try to follow the moves, but by the time I figure out one eight-count, they've already moved on to the next one. My knee is killing me, enough to bring tears to my eyes, but I pretend I'm wiping sweat from my forehead and wipe my eyes with my sleeve.

But Alexa is loving this. I can tell. She's pretending not to, but she can't hide the sparkle in her eyes. And she's *good*. Not as good as the rest of the squad, but she picks up the moves after only one or two tries.

Miss Klein comes over to us, her ponytail bouncing behind her. "Lex, that was fantastic," she says. Alexa is trying so hard not to smile she has to bite her lips shut.

When Miss Klein turns to me, though, I know she's going to tell me to forget it. "You did well too, Charlotte," she says. "I know you've been . . . out of commission for a few years. But with a little practice, you should be up to speed soon enough."

I think I love Miss Klein.

She tells Alexa and me to sit on the bleachers to watch the squad do their competition routine. My physical therapist signed off on cheerleading only because I promised not to do anything too demanding, to limit myself to standing cheers and arm movements, so I try not to limp as we cross the field house.

The squad gets in formation, the music starts pumping, and they break out into a fast-paced choreographed routine of flip flops, twists, V-jumps, leaps, lifts, tosses, and dozens of stunts.

In my peripheral vision, I can see Alexa watching me, not the squad. "You okay?" she asks.

"I'm great."

"You were limping pretty bad."

"No, I wasn't."

On the mats, the boys lift the girls up over their heads. They touch them all over. Their waists. Their hips. Their legs. Their hands slide up and down the girls' bodies.

I forgot how much touching there is in cheerleading.

Alexa's still watching me. "You don't have to do this, you know. They're only letting us come to their practices because of who you are. If your knee hurts too much, or if the boys—"

I shake my head. "I want this." Being a Sparkler is in the Dream Book. It's one of the few things left in the Dream Book that I can do. This was the first time I've seen Alexa happy, even if it was only for a millisecond.

chapter thirty-four

Marissa and the replacement baby are in the car Friday night when Dad picks Alexa and me up for our weekend visit. CiGi's car seat is in the middle of the back seat, so Alexa and I have to sit on either side of her. She immediately tries to grab my hair.

Dad has a foundation board meeting later this evening, and Marissa doesn't feel like cooking, so we swing into the Woodland Creek Plaza, a strip mall with a bunch of stores: a dry cleaner, a dog groomer, a 7-Eleven, carryout restaurants. Behind the stores are the woods and the creek that gave our town its name.

"What'll it be, girls?" Dad asks. "Taco Grande, Blue Sea Sushi, Schneider's Red Hotz?"

"How about Schneider's?" Marissa says.

"Tacos," Alexa says flatly, immediately after.

I can't speak. My stomach is seizing at the sight of Schneider's Red Hotz. *He* went there once, one night after a bad beating. He brought the food back to the attic in a white paper bag printed with *Schneider's Red Hotz* in cheery red ink, then sat on the bed and ate his cheeseburger and fries while I scrubbed my blood from the floor with bleach. He didn't share his food with me that night, but I was in too much pain to eat anyway. I remember thinking the words on the paper bag were so much redder than blood.

"Charlotte," Dad says, "you're the tie-breaker. Schneider's or tacos?"

I squeeze my hands into fists to keep them from trembling, take a deep breath to clear my nostrils of the bleach smell. My stomach is spasming and I'm not hungry at all anymore, but I say, "Tacos." It's on the opposite side of the shopping center from Schneider's.

Dad pulls into a parking spot in front of Taco Grande. It's drizzling a little, and chilly. Marissa hooks CiGi's carrier over her elbow and rushes inside, her blond corkscrews bobbing up and down. Alexa follows a few steps behind. I don't mind the rain; it cools my skin and eases my nausea. Dad strolls next to me, pushing his hands deep in his pockets.

"How ya doing, sweetheart?" he asks.

"Fine. I'm really happy to be back at school."

"Any more meltdowns since the other night?"

"No." Suddenly I feel guilty. He thinks I'm strong and brave, and my meltdown has proven otherwise. "I'm sorry."

"For what?"

"I disappointed you."

"You went through a huge ordeal, Charlotte," he says. "A meltdown was to be expected. It's healthy to release your emotions rather than keep them inside. If you weren't as strong as you are, you wouldn't have bounced back from it so quickly. And now you're even stronger."

Even a meltdown makes Dad think I'm strong.

"How's your mom?" he asks as we step around a puddle.

"She's great," I say, pleased that he's asking about her. "I was worried she'd start drinking again when I started school, but she hasn't."

"That's a relief. And Lex? How's she doing?"

I shrug. "I don't know. She hates everybody. She acts like she's my bodyguard. But she went with me to cheerleading practice. She pretended that she didn't like it, but I know she did."

"That's a step in the right direction," Dad says. "I tried for four years to get through to her, taking her to Dr. Goldbloom, sending her to Bright Futures. But you're the one who's getting through to her. To your mom, too."

He's smiling, so proud of me. And for the first time, I don't mind.

He pulls one hand from his pocket to open the door to Taco Grande, and I hear a gasp. A woman clutching a carryout bag and wearing a dirty orange coat is staring at me. Skin gray, lips pale, eyes sunk deep in their sockets, cheekbones casting sickly shadows down her face.

Under her knit cap, her shoulder-length hair is stringy . . . and black.

And that's how I know who this woman is.

We stare at each other. Breathless. Frozen.

Alexa steps in front of me. "Leave her alone, lady," she growls.

But this pale, horrified woman isn't about to attack me or question me. She's not a curious bystander or an eager reporter.

She's Julia Hogan. Alan Shaw's niece. His first victim.

I step around Alexa. I want to talk to Julia. I *need* to talk to her.

But before I can say anything, she blurts, "I—I'm sorry. I'm so sorry," and flees from the restaurant.

"Wait!" I cry. "Come back!" I chase her into the fading sunlight and drizzling rain. She slips into a rusty green sedan, starts the engine, and rumbles away.

Dad, Alexa, and Marissa come up behind me in the parking lot. CiGi whines, and Marissa tucks her blanket around her. "Do you know that woman, Charlotte?" she asks.

"I think that was Julia Hogan," Dad says, watching her car turn onto the street.

I nod. "It was. Maybe now that her uncle's dead, she felt safe enough to come home."

"Why did she say she was sorry?" Marissa asks. "What is she sorry for?"

The silver stud in Alexa's eyebrow shines in the light of the overhead street lamp. "She never told anyone what Alan Shaw did to her," she says. "She blames herself for what happened to Charlotte. That's why she's sorry." She swings her booted foot at a loose piece of asphalt, and it goes flying. "And she should be."

"It's not her fault," I rush to say, because I suddenly feel very protective of Julia. "You don't know what it was like for her, Alexa. How much power he had over her. Maybe she was too scared. Maybe she was too ashamed."

But Alan Shaw is dead now. He can't hurt her, or me, ever again. And now that Julia is home, she can recover, just like me.

chapter thirty-five

A boy wearing a backward White Sox cap holds something out to me, pinched between his fingers. Alexa slaps his hand away. "What the fuck, Jonah? Charlotte doesn't do pot. Get that away from her."

"Just trying to be friendly." The boy takes a drag and slumps away. "Bitch."

Alexa calls after him, "Asshole."

I'm not surprised there's pot at this party, but I'm astounded that Alexa actually considers these people her friends.

Dad had to leave for the foundation board meeting after dinner, and when Alexa asked Marissa if she could meet up with her classmates to work on a research paper, Marissa was pleased to say yes. Not wanting to be alone with Marissa and CiGi, I asked Alexa if I could go with her. Now I know why she had been so reluctant to agree: there was no study group, no research paper. Alexa was sneaking out to a party.

I'm not even sure whose house this is. People are crawling all over the place, and Alexa and I are on a musty couch in the basement, which is unfinished with old cast-off furniture and stained area rugs. Music is pumping loudly, everyone's drinking beer and all sorts of other stuff, and the air is pungent from all the pot. In the corner, a guy's snorting a line of coke with a rolled-up dollar bill.

"I thought you were done with all this," I say to Alexa.

She takes a swallow of her beer. "With what?"

I gesture to the beer in her hands, to the party around us. "With all of this. What about rehab?"

"I haven't hung out with my friends since you got back, okay?" she says. "They started giving me shit for hanging out with the Peps and going to cheer practice. I just need to—" She stops, and her gaze fixates on the stairwell. "Oh, fuck."

A boy in a black trench coat lumbers into the basement. His eyes search the smoky room, then land on Alexa. She swigs the rest of her beer and lifts her hand in a casual wave.

"Who's that?" I ask as he weaves his way over.

"No one. Just some guy."

The boy slides down next to Alexa, slinks one arm behind her, and crosses his booted ankle over his knee. His eyes are sharp and predatory, his dark hair is long and unruly, and he's got the beginnings of a soul patch under his lip. He caresses Alexa's shoulder with his thumb while he studies me, up and down. "Who's this?" he asks her.

"My sister," she says.

"The chick who was—"

"Yeah."

"Huh," is all he says in response. I hate him so, so much.

He slides a glance at Alexa. "You two have the same face."

"That's because we're twins, Einstein," she says.

"Her hair is prettier than yours, though," he slurs, and slides his hand into her white spikes and pulls them. "You should grow yours out and dye it back to black."

"Go to hell, Cam." But she doesn't stop him when he kisses her neck.

Ugh. "Let's go, Alexa," I say.

She closes her eyes, letting him slurp on her like he's sucking venom from a snake bite.

"Alexa. Let's go." I grab her arm, but she shakes me off.

So. I guess that's how it's going to be. I slip away and push my way upstairs.

The air is clearer and fresher in the kitchen, where a boy in a green Pleasantview High School football jersey hands me a cup of beer. "Thanks," I say. What the hell, if Alexa can drink, so can I. I take a big gulp.

Gross. It's warm and bitter and disgusting. But I can make myself do lots of disgusting things, so I take another gulp.

The boy smiles at me. His lips look soft. His eyes are soft, too, and they match his jersey exactly. "You new here?" he asks.

This boy doesn't know who I am.

He doesn't know who I am.

"Yeah," I say, in all of my coolness.

We sip our beer, and he makes small talk, and I reply with my own. Maybe. I can't concentrate. I don't know what I'm saying, but it must be funny, because he chuckles, and then his gaze lingers on mine.

I swallow hard. He's looking at me like he *likes* me.

So I stay.

Because a normal girl, a girl who wasn't held captive by a pedophile for four years, would stay.

A normal girl would not have invisible hands constantly squeezing her neck.

A normal girl would not want to puke at the thought of someone touching her.

A normal girl would *want* to kiss a cute boy who smiles at her.

A normal girl would step forward, reach out, and touch him.

A normal girl would go with him upstairs, without being afraid that he's leading her to a secret room at the top of the house.

A normal girl would close the door to the bedroom. A normal girl would sit on the bed next to him, and put her hand on his leg.

A normal girl would like the feeling of his lips on hers.

A normal girl wouldn't freeze when he puts his hand under her shirt. A normal girl wouldn't quietly start crying when he kisses her.

A normal girl would not have to separate her mind from her body and take herself far away as she goes through the motions.

A normal girl doesn't have a twin sister who flies into the room and tears her away from the boy as she's kneeling between his legs.

"What the fuck are you doing?" Alexa roars.

I flinch instinctively, but she's yelling at the boy, not me.

"What—Hey!" he yells. He jumps up, and I realize my top is off and his pants are down around his ankles.

"You think just because she's Charlotte Weatherstone that she'll have sex with you?" she snarls as I scramble to put my sweater back on.

The boy sputters. "That's—Charlotte Weatherstone? You're Charlotte Weatherstone?" He wipes his mouth. "Oh, God. I wasn't . . . *You* came on to *me*. I didn't . . ."

Alexa shoves him with both hands. "Get out of here, you *ass*hole."

The boy rushes away, tripping as he pulls up his jeans over his briefs, giving me one last horrified glance.

Alexa kicks the door shut behind her and stands over me, fuming. "*You* came on to *him*?"

"So what?" I shout back. How dare *she* be angry with *me*? "You have sex all the time, with any guy who wants it. You probably just had sex with that guy in the basement!"

"No, because I had to stop and go find *you*. What the fuck, Charlotte?"

"It's my body," I say. "I own it. I can do what I want with it." I press the heels of my hands into my eyes before any tears can form, but it's too late. The tears extinguish my anger, leaving me feeling hopeless and ashamed.

"I just wanted to have sex on *my* terms for once, you know?" I say.

"Yeah." She says it as a long, slow sigh as she sinks next to me on the floor. Together, we lean against the bed. She rests her head on my shoulder. The party pulsates below us, but we sit in the dark. Quiet, still, and together.

"Alexa?"

"Yeah?"

"That boy? He wiped his mouth. When he realized who I was, he wiped his mouth."

She nods, then says nothing for a long time. Then: "The people here suck. Let's go home."

chapter thirty-six

When my homework goes hazy, I blink my eyes to clear the blur. I notice the time, then pick up my phone and hit #2 on speed dial.

He answers on the first ring. "Hello?"

"Hi, Agent Lindo. It's Charlotte."

"I know, honey. It's eight o'clock. Time for your nightly call."

"Any updates on Emily?"

"Not today. Sorry."

"Julia Hogan's in town."

"Yes, your dad told me you saw her. She's staying with her mother in Pleasantview."

"Maybe she knows what happened to Emily."

"I questioned her, but he took Emily after Julia left and before he took you. Julia has no idea what he could have done with her remains."

"You're still looking for her, though, right?"

"Of course."

"You won't quit?"

"Never."

"I'll call you tomorrow night, then."

"I know you will. Good night, Charlotte."

"'Night."

chapter thirty-seven

"Make a left on the next street," I instruct Bailey from the front seat of her little red Volkswagen Beetle.

"I still think this is a bad idea," grumbles Alexa from the back. Bailey turns left anyway.

Maybe it *is* a bad idea to go see Julia Hogan, but I don't care. I'm doing it anyway. She's back in town, living with her mother. It had been easy enough to find their address online, and even easier to punch that address into the map app on my phone. The hard part was convincing Bailey to take me there after cheerleading practice. "Why?" she'd asked.

I couldn't answer her, because I don't know why I want to see Julia. All I know is that I must.

Bailey, being a good supportive friend, agreed to take me. Alexa, being an angry protective sister, insisted on coming too.

On the next road, a green metallic sign on a metal post sticks out of the ground. In white block letters it says simply, *Entering Pleasantview: Population 8163.*

My heart vacillates between beating much too fast and not at all. I don't let myself think about how close we're getting to Alan Shaw's house, and instead I look at the architecture that Pleasantview is known for. The houses in this town are just as old as they are in Woodland Creek, but here they're bigger and fancier, with brick exteriors instead of aluminum siding. The trees are taller and more majestic. The stores are more exclusive. Even the McDonald's has a unique, elegant design—no golden arches here. I wonder if this was the McDonald's he went to all the time.

I need to stop thinking about him. I sip in air, forcing it past the hands around my throat.

The map on my phone says to turn left. On the right side of the street is a large park with a playground. Two children, a boy and a girl, are swinging on the swings.

"Stop!" Alexa shouts, and Bailey slams on the brakes.

"What's wrong?" I ask.

". . . Nothing," Alexa says eventually. "Just making sure those kids aren't alone. But I see their parents, over there at the picnic table. They're watching them."

Bailey pulls ahead, and a few blocks later, it's my turn to panic. My heart stops, then starts again, so fast that I start shaking. His house. Right there. Brown shingles, dark red shutters, yellow-and-black police tape wrapped around the massive tree trunks. The attic window looks out over the yard and the world narrows until that attic window is the only thing I can see.

Time slows, then stops, or maybe it's just Bailey. Because as soon as Alexa snaps, "Bailey, what the hell? Get Charlotte away from here," Bailey speeds down the street. Time goes back to normal, and his hands release my throat.

Donna Hogan's house is a few blocks away from her brother's. It's smaller, with black shingles instead of brown, and white shutters instead of dark red. The sun is setting, and the trees cast long shadows over the yard.

Alexa and Bailey open their car doors, but I tell them to stay put. "You sure?" Bailey asks.

"Yeah. I'm sure. Stay here." Alexa is so resentful of Julia, and I can't let her blow up at her. And I need Bailey to keep Alexa in the car.

I shrug against the April wind—I swear it wasn't this cold in Woodland Creek—and climb the two steps up to the front porch. It's swept clean of dirt, and a pair of wooden rocking chairs sit in front of a lace-curtained picture window. Except for the *No Trespassing: Violators Will Be Prosecuted* sign on the door, exactly like the one my mom has, there's no indication that the woman who lives here is the sister of Pleasantview's most infamous citizen. I wonder how many reporters have knocked on her door.

I take a breath for courage and reach past the No Trespassing sign to ring the doorbell.

When no one answers, I ring it again.

And again.

Finally, the lace curtain moves, just an inch. A few seconds later, the front door drags open.

Mrs. Hogan stands in the doorway, wringing her hands. Her floral dress falls limply over her hips. She seems smaller now than she had when she came to my dad's house, a few days after my rescue. Sadder. Grayer. I can picture my mother in about fifteen years, if I'd never returned home.

"Charlotte, hello," Mrs. Hogan says with a question in her voice.

Breathe, I remind myself, breathe. "Hi." Then I'm silent. I don't know what to say or why I'm here.

"Would, um, would you like to come in?" she asks.

I glance back at Bailey's car. Bailey is watching with wide eyes. Alexa is watching with narrowed eyes. "I'd better stay out here."

Mrs. Hogan nods. "You look . . . good. You have color in your cheeks now."

"Thank you," I say. My cheeks have color because my heart is beating too fast.

Her gaze flicks up from my face and locks on my hair. It must be messy from cheer practice because I wouldn't look in a mirror to fix it. Either that, or Agent Lindo told her that her brother liked girls with long black hair.

I push my hair behind my shoulders.

"I came to talk to Julia," I say. And with those words, I realize I do know why I'm here. I still don't know exactly what I'll say to Julia; I just want to connect with her. We can help each other. We can give each other strength. I want to know if she can still feel her uncle's roaming, clawing, squeezing hands; hear his rough, gravelly, sinister voice; smell his heavy coffee-smoky breath. I want to know if she still feels dirty, and contaminated, and used. I want to know if she changes her clothes in the dark, if she can't look at herself in a mirror.

Mrs. Hogan twists her lips. "I don't know if that's a good idea. It was hard enough to get her to come home. She's very . . . fragile. Talking with you would be too much for her right now."

"But talking with me may help her," I say. "It'll help both of us."

"Maybe in a few months." She says it with firmness and finality.

I nod, but my disappointment must be evident, because she adds, "For what it's worth, I didn't have a funeral for him. I didn't even claim his body. He's somewhere in the county graveyard with a cement paver instead of a headstone. I haven't been to visit. I never will."

Something twists inside my gut. That is unfair. That is *so* unfair. His body is unclaimed, buried somewhere in the county graveyard with a cement paver instead of a headstone, but Emily Alvarado doesn't even have that.

"Mrs. Hogan, do you have any idea what he did with Emily's body?" I ask. "Where he hid it? Could he have buried it somewhere?

Or left it somewhere? Or—" My mind draws a blank about what
else he could have done with her. I can't think about it without his
hands creeping up around my neck.

"I don't know," Mrs. Hogan says. "I'm sorry."

"He must have said something to you one day, or gone
somewhere different, or acted strangely . . ."

"The police have already asked me the same questions," she
says, shaking her head. "I can't think of anything. Have *you* been
able to think of anything?"

"No. But he killed her before he took me," I say, and Mrs.
Hogan flinches at the word *killed*, and again at the word *took*.
"He never told me what he did with her body," I continue. "So
you need to think harder, Mrs. Hogan. Please. You knew him his
whole life. You're the person who knew him best."

"Everything I thought I knew about my brother was wrong,"
she says. She hesitates, then adds, "*You're* the person who knew
him best, Charlotte. Maybe *you* need to think harder."

The wind goes still, and she shuts the door.

Alexa is twisting her white hair around her finger as I climb back
into Bailey's car. Bailey is chewing her lip. "How'd it go?" she asks.

"Alexa was right," I say, sliding down in my seat. "It was a bad
idea to come here." I got nothing accomplished. I can't talk to
Julia, and Mrs. Hogan was no help in my search for Emily's body.

Alexa says nothing, just yanks on the hair twisted around her
finger as Bailey drives away. She takes a different route out of
Pleasantview. It takes a few minutes longer, but we avoid driving
past my Keeper's house.

It's almost full dark now. Bailey's phone is connected to her car
stereo, and her music app is playing a pop playlist. I turn up the

volume and try to absorb the cheeriness. All three of us are silent until we reach my mom's house. Bailey pulls into the driveway and turns off her headlights, but doesn't stop the engine. "Charlotte?"

"Yeah?"

She whispers, "What was it like?"

She doesn't elaborate, but I don't need her to. I know what she's asking.

Alexa does too. She kicks the seat. "Damn it, Bailey," she mutters. "Charlotte doesn't want to talk about it."

"Yes," I say. "I do." And it's true. Bailey's looking at me, not with anger and reluctance like Alexa does, or with hunger like the reporters do, or with that strange mixture of repulsion and pity like everyone else does. Bailey's looking at me with eyes wide with fear and concern. Like she doesn't want to know, but she needs to know, because I am her friend.

And I'm going to tell her, because she is mine.

I turn down the music and stare out the window, no longer seeing the dark sky, or Bailey's car, or my yard, or my house. Instead I see him standing over me in the attic, smell his coffee-smoky breath, hear the lock of the door, the snap of his belt, the creak of the bed.

"He says he loves you," I say. "Every day he tells you he loves you, that you belong to him, and he will never share you with anybody. But to him, you're not a person with thoughts and feelings and a name. You're a thing. A pretty little thing that he owns."

"Charlotte, stop," Alexa whispers from far away.

But I don't stop. I can't. "At first you think he'll let you go, or the police will find you, or your parents will find you. But day after day after day passes, night after night after night, and eventually you realize that he'll never let you go, the police will never come. No release, no rescue, no escape. No more Mom, no more Dad, no more sister. Only him, and the attic, and the locked door with claw marks on it from The One Before, and the wire crate, and the tub with lion paws, and the creaky bed."

Bailey is staring, eyes swimming, hand over her mouth.

"Charlotte, please. No more," Alexa whispers. She opens her door a little, like she's going to leave. Icy wind howls and rushes in, but she stays.

"Even if you could escape, you wouldn't," I say. "You don't even let yourself think about leaving him. If you do, he'll replace you with someone else: your sister. And you would never let that happen to her. So you stay. You stop hoping. You stop wishing. You stop praying. The only thing you do, is endure."

A sob shatters the quiet. From Bailey? From Alexa? My cheeks feel cool, my eyes hot. Maybe the sob was from me.

"You never know what's going to make him angry," I continue. "He tests you, he tricks you. He hurts you. But he's everything to you. He's the only person you ever see. The only voice you ever hear. He's your only source of food, of water. Of air. You need him so you can stay alive. And even though you're miserable and lonely and hurting, and you know that all there will ever be for you is more misery and more loneliness and more pain, you want to stay alive. Because if you die, he'll replace you with your sister. So you try to be a good girl for him. You stay quiet because he doesn't like noise. You scrub your blood from the floor because he doesn't like messes. You fight through the pain, but you don't fight him. When he touches you, you separate your mind from your body and take yourself far away. And you endure."

I have to pause to suck in a breath past my Keeper's hands. Bailey is staring, frozen, not even blinking. Alexa is no longer begging me to stop. She's a shadow in the back seat, breathing in ragged bursts.

"The only thing that keeps you . . . *you*," I say, "is thinking about your family. Your mom and dad and sister. But it hurts to think about them, sometimes it hurts even more than the beatings, because you know you'll never see them again. More than anything you want to go home, but you know you'll never go home. So the only other thing you want is for your family to find some kind of peace and happiness. You wish so, so hard for them to be happy that you begin to believe it. And when he's on top of you, or he's beating you, or when he locks you up and leaves you all alone, you think about your family. You know your mom and dad are still madly in love. You know your sister is following the plans you made in your Dream Book, and she's doing it double, because you can't do it at all. Knowing your family is happy is the only peace you have. But it's enough, because it has to be."

Now, I'm done.

The hands release my throat.

Bailey pulls me in for a hug that's much too tight.

Alexa pushes the car door all the way open, and goes inside the house without a word.

chapter thirty-eight

Whether I sleep at Mom's house or Dad's, first thing every morning before Alexa wakes up, I take the pink teddy bear that I pick-pulled at the night before and hide the stuffing in the bag in the back of my closet. Then, in the bathroom, I shower and brush my teeth and hair in the dark, and then I go back to the bedroom to wake up Alexa and get dressed.

But this morning when I wake up, Alexa isn't in her bed. Her bed is unmade, which isn't weird, because she never makes it. But I didn't hear her get up, or even taking a shower or drying her hair. Which *is* weird, because Alexa is anything but quiet.

She was so upset last night after I told Bailey about my time in the attic. She was irritated and snappy all evening long. Maybe she's sleeping in the other bedroom, Dad's old office, where she slept while I was missing.

I get out of bed and look, but she's not there. Her sex offender map is still on the wall, and some of her clothes are sticking out of the drawers, but the bed is made up and hasn't been touched in months.

I pad past Mom's closed bedroom door, down the hall to the kitchen. Empty. She's not in the family room or dining room, either. I even look in the garage. Alexa is nowhere in this house.

Ice shoots through my veins. He took her. I *know* it.

No. He's dead. He strangled himself. He's been dead for two months. Now he's in a coffin, buried under six feet of dirt in the county graveyard with a cement paver as a headstone.

But what if it's a trick? What if he faked his suicide? What if he faked his death and escaped from the hospital, and came here and took Alexa?

"Mom!" I choke. "Mom!"

Mom comes running in her nightgown, hair disheveled. "What is it? What's wrong?"

"Alexa! She's not here!"

Her panic dissipates, turns to anger. "She probably snuck out to be with one of those boys again."

"Mom, we have to call the police! Call Agent Lindo!" We have to tell him Alan Shaw has her. He took her. I know it. I *know* it. He locked her up, he's beating her, he's raping her. His hands are around her neck, and he's squeezing . . .

"Charlotte, honey, relax. I'm sure she's fine," Mom sighs. "Let's call her cell phone first. If she doesn't answer, we'll call Agent Lindo, okay? But we won't need to. She's fine. She'll be grounded, but she's fine."

But I can't move. A high, strangled noise comes from my throat.

Then, from the other side of the house, the front door creaks open. I go running. "Alexa?" *Oh please, oh please, oh please . . .*

It's her. Tight black clothes, spiky white hair. Her black eyeliner is smudged and tear-tracked.

My muscles turn to jelly and I collapse into her. She's alive, my sister's alive, he is dead, and she's alive. "Are you okay? Where were you? What happened?"

But Alexa says nothing, just looks behind me.

Mom is standing there, shaking her head. She starts to say something, but then she sighs and walks away. "You'd better hurry if you want to get to school on time."

"That's all I get?" Alexa says.

Mom turns and blinks at her.

Alexa glares back. "Charlotte was missing for two seconds and you called the cops, the FBI, and every single TV station in America, and I'm gone for seven hours and all I get is *you'd better hurry?* You come in our room and stare at Charlotte every night. Did you even look on my side? Did you even notice I was gone?"

Mom sighs again. "I don't know what else to do, Lex." She heads down the hall, and mutters over her shoulder, "You're grounded for a month."

Alexa storms after her. "You don't care about me at all, do you?" she yells. "Charlotte was gone, but you still had me, and you didn't even care! You were so wrapped up in her disappearance that I barely existed for you. At least Dad cared enough to send me to rehab. All you did was drink. And now Charlotte's back, but all you still care about is *her!*" Alexa roars, then stomps to our room and slams the door so hard the entire house rattles.

Mom and I stare at each other in the screaming silence. She's frozen, hand covering her open mouth. She takes a robotic step toward the bedroom, but I stop her. "I'll talk to her."

My sister is right. Our mother never gave up on me, but she gave up on Alexa long ago.

"Alexa?" I call through our locked bedroom door. "Can I come in?"

For a minute there's no reply, no sound, then the knob turns and the door swings open. Alexa stomps past me, her face skewed into a scowl. "I'd better hurry if I want to get to school on time," she mimics, and marches to the bathroom.

I shuffle behind. She stands at the mirror, squeezing a tube of gel into her palm, then scrapes it into her hair so it spikes. I stay just far enough in the hallway that I can see Alexa but not the mirror.

"Where were you?" I ask her.

"Why do you even care."

I want to say: *Because for one horrifying minute I was sure my Keeper wasn't dead and he took you, that's why.* But instead I say: "Because I do."

She smears black eyeliner around her eyes. "If you must know, Cam texted me to meet him last night so I snuck out." A clear trail appears in the black rings around her eyes as a tear slips down her cheek. She fills in the trail with more eyeliner, but the trail appears again. "Fuck."

"What happened?"

"He wanted to . . . you know. In the back of his truck. And I realized that I don't want to be used like that anymore. That I don't want to sleep around anymore. So I told him no."

"Good. Alexa, that's good." I'm so proud of her.

"Yeah, but I've never said no to anyone before. So he said," she makes her voice go low in an imitation of Cam, "When did a slut like you turn into such a frigid bitch?"

I sip in air. "You can't let him talk to you like that."

"I know. So I broke up with him."

"Really? Good!"

"Yeah." She sniffles and tries to apply her eyeliner again. "He got *super* pissed. Like, scary pissed."

I imagine Cam swinging his belt, or squeezing his hands around Alexa's neck. "Did he hit you?" I check her arms and neck for bruises.

"He was about to. He got all red and his hands were in fists, and so I reminded him that my dad is friends with the FBI and that he's eighteen so he'd go to real jail, not just juvie. But I made the stupid mistake of breaking up with him while we were in Brunsville instead of waiting until we got back to Woodland Creek."

Brunsville is a farming town, almost an hour away. "Why were you in Brunsville?"

"That's where Cam gets his coke. He said to get in the truck and he'd take me home. But he was driving really fast, blowing through stop signs, and I told him to slow down. So he pulled over and kicked me out. Like, he opened my door and literally kicked me out. He left me on the road by some corn field and drove off."

"In the middle of nowhere?"

She nods. "I called Jen to come pick me up. I had to use the GPS on my phone to tell her where I was." Her lip trembles.

"You stood out there in the dark for an hour until Jen came? Why didn't you call *me*?"

"Because how could that have helped? You don't have a car. You can't even drive." She clutches her eyeliner and fills in the tear-tracks. "You would've told Mom, and Mom wouldn't care. So then you would call Dad, and Dad would pick me up and drive me straight to rehab. Even though I was trying to do the right thing for once."

"Lex?" Mom's quivery voice calls from down the hall, and Alexa goes stiff. When Mom approaches, timid and unsure, Alexa sets her jaw and circles black liner around her eyes again.

"Lex, I need to talk to you," Mom stammers. "I'm so sorry. You're right . . . I neglected you . . . I've been neglecting you this whole time." She steps into the bathroom, and I step out. "I was so wrapped up in Charlotte's disappearance that I couldn't see beyond it," she says. "But you needed me too, and I . . . I failed you." She releases one raw, aching sob as she realizes the weight of her mistake.

I slip away to get dressed, leaving Mom and Alexa alone to talk. That day, I go to school, and they go to see Dr. Goldbloom. When I get back, they're on the couch, and Alexa is sleeping with her head on Mom's lap.

chapter thirty-nine

This is it. Cheerleading tryouts for next year's squad.

I have my hair up in a high ponytail and tied with red and silver ribbons to show my school spirit. Alexa's hair is still too short to put in a ponytail, but she's dyed it back to black, and she has a sequined red and silver bow in it that pins her bangs back. Without that heavy black eye makeup, her blue irises shine and sparkle. In fact, she's sparkling all over, glowing from the inside out. She's as excited as I am.

I went to all the cheer clinics, I know the group routine, Bailey helped me choreograph an amazing individual cheer, and last night I finally did a backflip. I'm going to make the squad—I *have* to make the squad—so I don't know why I'm so nervous. My palms are even a little sweaty. I wipe them on my Woodland Creek T-shirt and sink to the floor to stretch some more. My knee is sore from all the practice lately, but it's not too bad. The physical therapy has really helped me. I'm super flexible, and there's no limit to my stamina.

The air is electric in the field house. There are forty of us trying out for the twenty spots on the varsity squad. The members of the current squad almost always make it again, so really, the only open spots are the ones left by the graduating seniors. That leaves nine. Three of those spots will go to boys, so that means six will go to girls. And two of those girls will be Alexa and me.

Miss Klein claps her hands and tells us to line up according to the number pinned to our chests. Alexa and I grin at each other. Numbers were assigned alphabetically by last name, so that means we're going at the end, which is bad for my nerves, but good because we'll be in the same group for the dance routine.

We settle on the bleachers to watch the first groups try out. Bailey is flawless, of course, and easily the best of the bunch. She flies through the routines. Her voice is loudest too. I make a mental note to amp up my volume during my turn. When Bailey does her individual cheer, she may as well have a spotlight on her, because she lights up the entire field house. She gets the most enthusiastic applause of anyone.

After waiting for what seems like hours, it's finally time for Alexa and me to do our group routine with four other girls and two boys. I put an extra bounce in my step and an extra lift to my chin as we line up in formation in front of the judges. Alexa and I are in the middle. From her seat in the bleachers, Bailey holds a glittery sign over her head: GO CHARLOTTE! GO ALEXA!

The music starts pumping, and carries me away.

It's simple. It's easy. It's *fun*. My moves are sharp, my kicks are high, my smile is bright, and I'm so filled with joy I could soar into the sky.

I'm doing it. I'm no longer the girl in the wire crate, no longer the girl in the attic, no longer the girl everyone feels sorry for. I am Charlotte Weatherstone, Woodland Creek Sparkler.

I've earned it.

I make sure to make direct eye contact with the judges, and Miss Klein is beaming at me.

The music stops and we all hoot and holler and kick our legs up and wave our arms, then it's time for our individual routines. Within our group of eight, Alexa is sixth, and I'm seventh. I'm glad I have a chance to rest while numbers one through five go, because my knee is starting to throb.

No. No, it's *not*. My knee is fine.

Miss Klein calls Alexa's number, and she squeezes my hand and hops up, then runs to the mat. Individual cheers are the most nerve-wracking part of tryouts, because you're all alone on the mat. There's no music or dancing; this part is pure cheer.

But Alexa doesn't look nervous at all. I've never seen her so happy and confident. She starts off on one knee, her chin down. Then she jumps up into an X, pops her head up, and in a clear voice that sails around the room, she cheers, "It's time . . . To let your spirit shine!" Each move is exactly as she practiced, original and sharp and clever. I can already see her in the Sparkler uniform, cheering at football and basketball games and performing at competitions. She finishes with something she didn't rehearse: a series of flip-flops all the way down the mat, ending with her hands up in a high V.

The crowd on the bleachers goes crazy. The applause for Alexa is just as loud as it was for Bailey, and Bailey is cheering the loudest of all.

Alexa skips back to the bleachers next to me, giving me a big hug.

This is the Alexa I remember. Happy, energetic, excited. No more angry, defensive, trouble-making Lex Enola. I *knew* bringing her back to cheerleading would bring her back to me.

"Number thirty-nine," Miss Klein announces.

That's me. I squeeze Alexa's hand the way she squeezed mine, then skip to the mat. Bailey hoots for me and I get some applause from the other girls, and I haven't even started yet.

My knee doesn't hurt.

It does *not*.

I smile, stand straight, chin up. I put my hands on my hips, and begin.

"Silver and red . . ."

My moves are sharp, but I'm not loud enough. I say the next part louder.

"We're always ahead . . ."

Shhh, girl. No noise. Good girls don't make noise.

His voice is in my ear, much louder than my own, louder than Alexa's, louder than the people shouting for me in the stands. My knee wobbles during my lunge but I force it back into place.

"Woodland Creek Sparklers . . ."

Louder. I have to be louder.

"We're always ready . . ."

When I land after my half-split, I have to put most of my weight on my left leg to get up.

"Woodland Creek Sparklers, we're solid steady!"

I said no noise!

The hands around my throat are NOT really there. I run a few steps, swing my arms back to wind up, then fly into a round-off, twist into a perfect backflip—

There's a great snapping sound like the world is breaking in two, and pain explodes in my knee and shoots into every limb, every cell.

I land flat on the mat. The crowd gasps; Alexa screams. Everyone is running to me, crowding around me, and I can't move, and why are they all looking at my knee when my Keeper is squeezing my throat and I can't breathe, I can't breathe, I can't breathe.

I didn't make the squad. I'm not a Woodland Creek Sparkler.

I busted my knee so badly that I'll need surgery to fix it. There will be no cheerleading for me. Not next year. Not ever.

Miss Klein comes over to tell me in person, while I lay on my mom's couch in a big, bulky stupid leg brace and surreptitiously pick-pull at the seams of another pink teddy bear. "I'm so sorry, Charlotte," Miss Klein says. Her hair is up in a ponytail, but it's limp. She looks as devastated as I feel, and her voice isn't nearly as squeaky as usual. "I was really rooting for you."

I don't ask for my final score. I don't know what would be worse: not making the squad because my score was too low, or getting a high score but failing to make the squad anyway.

"If I'd known that your knee was still bothering you that much," Mom said, and Dad said, and Miss Klein said, "I would never have let you try out."

"It didn't bother me until tryouts," I mumble, but that's a lie, and by their sighs, I know that they know it's a lie too.

"What about Alexa?" I ask Miss Klein.

She swallows and turns to Alexa. "You made it," she says, weakly, as if she's apologizing for telling her in front of me.

Under her short black hair, Alexa's eyes go a little wide. Her skin goes a little pale. Her head gives a little shake. But before she can say anything, I catch her eye. A thousand silent words pass between us in one moment.

Then, keeping her eyes on mine, she thrusts out her chin and says aloud, "Okay. I'll do it double."

Thank you, Alexa. That's exactly what I want her to do. She's going to do it double, because I can't do it at all.

chapter forty

Alexa is keeping her promise to do it double. For the past two weeks she's embraced the Woodland Creek Sparklers with the same devotion she once had for the Dragonettes. She's embracing everything now, even school, with the same enthusiasm she had before I disappeared. At this moment, Thursday night at seven o'clock, she's out with a group of classmates, preparing for their history presentation tomorrow.

Mom is in the family room, filling out an online form to get her fitness certification reissued so she can teach again. She has the local Top 40 station playing on the radio, and she's singing along.

I'm on my bed in my room, my bad leg propped up on pillows, doing my math homework.

That last part is a lie. I'm on my bed in my room, and my bad leg is propped up on pillows, but I'm not doing homework. I'm plucking the stuffing from a pink teddy bear and paging through the Dream Book. There isn't much stuffing left in the bear, and now that cheerleading is gone, there aren't many dreams left in the Dream Book that I can do.

I stop plucking long enough to flip over the "Make the Woodland Creek Sparklers Squad" page, and Emily Alvarado's photo slides out and lands on my leg brace. She smiles up at me, young and innocent, her black hair spilling over her shoulders.

She wants to be found. I can *feel* how much she wants to be found. Her final days were spent in terror and pain, and she never had a chance to follow any of her dreams. Now she wants to be laid to rest in the cemetery at her parents' church. A place that's peaceful, a place with sunshine and trees and flowers, a place where her mom and dad can visit her.

"I'm trying," I assure her silently. "I call Agent Lindo every night. I even asked Donna Hogan if she has any idea what he did with your body."

She keeps staring at me.

When he was in the hospital, he refused to say what he did with her, or even admit that he'd taken her. Agent Lindo has looked everywhere for her remains, and he still can't find her. Donna Hogan knows nothing.

I'm the one who knew Alan Shaw the best. *I* need to think harder.

Think, I command myself. Think *harder.*

I pluck more stuffing from the teddy bear and think. I squeeze my eyes shut and think. I separate my mind from my body, take myself back to the attic, and think.

But as always, the only thing that comes to mind is our Keeper's hands squeezing my throat, his muddy eyes flashing, his rumbled threats hissed in a fit of fury: *Don't make me do to you what The One Before made me do to her.*

I force my eyes open, force his voice from my head, force a breath past his hands.

From her photograph, Emily is still staring at me.

He told me he killed her, but he never told me what he did with her body. Of that, I am absolutely positive. But still, I'm Emily's last hope. I'm her only hope.

"I don't know where you are," I tell her aloud. "But I know where I can go to figure it out."

Alexa's busy with her study group. Mom's busy with her application. Dad's busy with Marissa and the baby. But none of them would take me where I need to go anyway.

I pick up my phone and dial. "Bailey?" I say when she answers. "Can you come get me? I need to go somewhere . . . Yes, right now . . . Because I've already put it off for too long."

Fifteen minutes later, Bailey pulls her little red Beetle into the driveway. I tell Mom I'm going out with Bailey to work on a project—not a lie—and I'll be back in a couple hours. I don't give her a chance to protest before I hobble out on my crutches. The sky is deep indigo, almost black, and the air smells like longing and desperation.

Bailey helps me into her car. My leg in its brace juts out straight in front of me, and I slide my crutches in the little area between our seats.

"Where to?" she asks as she backs out of the driveway.

I'm scared she won't take me if I tell her where I want to go, so I say, "Head to Chapman Street first."

Bailey follows my directions out of the neighborhood. "That sucks about cheerleading," she tells me for the millionth time. "I really wish you would have made it."

"I'm just happy Alexa did."

"I'm happy she made it too. I missed her. After you disappeared, she kind of did too, you know? She became this whole different person, and I tried to keep being her friend, but she wouldn't let me, no matter what I did. But now you're both back."

I can't reply, because the further we get from Woodland Creek, the harder it becomes to breathe. I tell Bailey to turn left at the next light, then right at the stop sign, and soon we're driving past the green metal sign that says *Entering Pleasantview: Population 8163*.

Bailey throws a suspicious glance at me. "Am I taking you to that woman's house again?"

I shake my head.

She slows the car and murmurs, "Am I taking you to *his* house?"

I nod.

"Why?"

"He never told me what he did with Emily's body," I say, "but if I go to his house, maybe I'll make a connection and figure it out."

She rolls past a streetlight, and her face is white. "I don't know, Charlotte."

"Please, Bailey. I have to do this," I say. "I'm her last hope. I'm her only hope."

Bailey's hands tighten on the steering wheel, and her lips tighten into a straight line. But she nods, a curt, one-time nod, then turns onto Mill Road, Alan Shaw's street.

Red and blue lights flash rhythmically in the black sky.

"What's going on?" Bailey asks. "A car accident?"

No. There's no car accident. Along with the red and blue lights, there's also a flickering yellow. The scent of charred wood. The air is smoky.

No, no, no. Please no.

A house is on fire, and I know—I *know*—whose house it is.

A police officer is in the intersection, directing traffic. He motions for Bailey to turn around.

"We can't get through," she says, relieved. "Why don't we go to Stubby's? We can split the chili cheese fries."

"Pull over." I have the door open before I finish the sentence.

Bailey screeches to a halt and I jump out, pulling my crutches with me. "Wait!" she cries. "What are you doing?"

I hobble down the street, swinging on my crutches, past the brick houses, past the towering trees, past the curious neighbors gathered on the sidewalk.

Two fire engines are parked in front of my Keeper's house, spraying it with water. Flames shoot out the windows. I inhale ash.

Shoving through the crowd, I get as close as I can until a police officer holds out his arm and stops me.

I back away, weave my way through the crowd. Someone's put up a barrier of plastic sawhorses to keep the spectators away. I slide under them, dragging my crutches and my bad leg behind me. Duck behind one of the fire trucks. Limp through the flickering darkness along the fence to a big tree in the front yard, and hide behind it. The tree still has yellow-and-black police tape wrapped around it, and the loose end flaps furiously in the wind.

His house is on fire. I was too late. Emily needs me, but I was too late.

My fingers curl around the handles on my crutches. I was too late.

I plant my crutches in the grass and swing, propelling myself closer to the house, behind another tree.

Emily needs me, she needs me to go to the attic, she needs me to *think harder.*

But I was too late.

My breath comes in deep smoky rasps, and I swing on my crutches again, close enough now that my eyes and cheeks burn from the heat. My ears pop from the pressure.

Emily needs me to go to the attic. She needs me to *think.* She needs me to find her.

I plant my crutches in the grass and—

Someone grabs me from behind.

"What the hell, kid? Are you nuts? Get out of here!" A firefighter hoists me under one arm, and my crutches drop to the ground as he whisks me away.

"No! Wait!" I claw at him, but my fingers don't make a dent in his thick canvas clothes. "I need to *think*! Please!"

He carries me to a police officer and hands me over. "Found this kid in the yard. I think she was trying to get inside," he says before rushing back to the flames.

I implore the officer to let me go, but he hauls me out to the street, past the fire engines, and deposits me in the back of a squad car. I push against him, but I have no strength left. Only now do I feel the pain in my knee, throbbing, radiating, making me dizzy, making everything red.

I was too late. A day too late, an hour too late. I could have triggered a memory, made a connection. I could have found Emily. But I was too late.

The officer kneels, and I must look completely pathetic, because his expression is sharp but not unkind. "That house is empty, so I know you don't live there. Why would you—" he stops, peering at my face. "Charlotte Weatherstone? What are you doing here?"

He looks back at the burning house, then at me again. "Did you set this fire?"

chapter forty-one

At the Pleasantview police station, Bailey confirms she picked me up from my house, so there was no way I could have set Alan Shaw's house on fire. She's pale and crying, and doesn't stop even after her mom comes to pick her up. When she leaves, she looks back at me, and for the first time, there's pity in her eyes.

Dad arrives first. Mom rushes in a few minutes later. Agent Lindo comes a few minutes after that, and tells the cops to release me.

At home, I sit on the couch, wrapped in a blanket and sipping a cup of flavorless tea. I smell like smoke and ash and defeat. Mom gives me a pain pill for my knee.

Mom, Dad, Agent Lindo: all three of them stare at me.

"I didn't do it," I mumble into the teacup. "I didn't set that fire."

"We know," Lindo says. "But why would you go back to that place?"

"I went there to look for clues for Emily," I confess. "When I saw it was on fire, I just . . ." I can only shrug.

"Were you really trying to get inside?" Dad asks.

"No." Maybe. I don't know.

"Agent Lindo is looking for Emily," Mom says. "That's his job. Not yours. I know how desperate you are to find her, but honey, you could have been killed."

"But Agent Lindo can't find her!" How can they not care about finding Emily as much as I do? "Mrs. Hogan can't think of anything. Which means it's up to *me* to find Emily. *Me.* I thought going to the attic would trigger a new memory, or help me make a connection. I was her last hope, and now there's no hope left."

The silence that follows lasts an eternity, until Lindo deflates with a sigh onto the armchair. He scrubs his big palm over his face. "You may be right, Charlotte. If there was any evidence left in that house, it's gone now. Even the yard was contaminated by the firefighters. And now there's another crime to solve," he adds. "The fire marshal suspects arson. Whoever set that fire destroyed an active crime scene. That's a federal offense."

"But who would do such a thing?" Mom asks.

The front door opens, and Alexa walks in.

I see it happening in slow motion: Mom and Dad see Alexa. Mom's face goes white. Dad's face goes red. Agent Lindo frowns and looks Alexa up and down.

They think Alexa did it. They think Alexa burned down Alan Shaw's house.

"No," I say. "She didn't do it. There's no way."

"Do what?" Alexa asks. "Charlotte, are you okay? What's going on?"

Agent Lindo stands and hoists his pants higher on his belly. Takes a step toward Alexa. "Where were you this evening, Lex?"

Alexa steps back, eyes wide, a mouse caught in a trap. "At a study group."

One of Lindo's eyebrows hooks. Mom and Dad say nothing. They aren't accusing her, but they don't necessarily believe her, either.

"What?" Alexa says, infuriated. "I wasn't doing anything wrong. I wasn't doing drugs. I wasn't drinking. I was at a study group. They drove me home and they weren't drinking either."

More silent glances. More dubious looks.

"She didn't do it," I say. "I know it. I know she didn't."

"How do you know that, Charlotte?" Agent Lindo asks. "Were you with her this evening?"

"No, but she would never do it. Alexa, tell them you didn't do it!"

"Didn't do what?" She stomps her foot. "Will someone please tell me what's going on?"

Wringing her hands, Mom quivers. "Someone burned down Alan Shaw's house tonight."

Alexa stumbles back. "You think it was me?"

"You have the motive," Lindo says. "And you've been arrested before, for harassing sex offenders. Twice."

"Yeah, but egging a house is a lot different from burning it down," she cries. "I was at Tyler Hanson's house with Janice Kim and Josh Swanko and we worked on our European History presentation. You can ask them."

"I will," Lindo says. "But your friends aren't the most trustworthy of witnesses."

"She has new friends now," I say. "Dad, do something! Mom!"

But they're staring at Alexa, confused, doubtful, disappointed.

I grab my crutches and struggle to my feet. "She didn't do it." I move to stand in front of her, guarding her like she's guarded me so many times before.

Lindo sighs and looks at my dad. "Cory, I hate to do it, but I wouldn't be doing my job if I didn't follow up on this. There've been too many incidents involving Lex. I have to question her further."

Behind me, Alexa gasps. "But I swear I—"

"Lex, don't say another word," Dad says. "I'm calling my lawyer."

I stand in front of Alexa, keeping her safe behind me. No one is taking her away from me. If Lindo arrests her, he'll have to arrest me too. I'll hit him with my crutches if I have to.

Dad punches numbers into his phone, calling his lawyer, then holds it to his ear. At the same time, Lindo's phone rings.

The two of them mumble into their phones. Mom cries. Alexa cries. I stand guard, every muscle tense, ready to strike.

"Don't worry," I promise Alexa. "I won't let anything happen to you."

Lindo hangs up and slides his phone back into his jacket. "Well, Lex didn't do it." He sounds stunned. "They found the person who did."

My body sags with relief, and I half-lean on my crutches and half-lean on Alexa. She wipes angry tears from her eyes. "I told you it wasn't me." She glares at everyone—Lindo, Mom, Dad—for not believing her.

Dad clicks his phone off. Shame-faced, he says, "Alexa, I'm sorry." He hugs her. She goes stiff, but then she hugs him back.

Mom joins in the apologies and hugs too. Alexa draws me in, and for one brilliant, shining moment, we're one family again. Until Dad pulls away.

"Who was it?" he asks Lindo. "Who set the fire?"

Lindo gives us a grim look. "Julia Hogan."

Julia Hogan. My Keeper's niece. His first victim.

"Her mother found a note," Lindo says. "She said she wanted that house gone."

"Did they arrest her?" Alexa asks.

"There will not be an arrest." For the first time, the giant man looks small and vulnerable. "They found her body. It was in the attic."

Those icy claws grip my heart again. "She's dead?" I say aloud, because I have to hear myself say it to believe it.

"Oh, her poor mother," Mom whispers.

"She set the fire and couldn't get out in time, right?" I ask. "It was an accident, right?"

Please say yes. Please say that's what happened.

But I know he's not going to say that.

"She said in her note that she couldn't stand the guilt," Lindo says. "She blamed herself for what her uncle did to you and Emily. She wanted to get rid of everything that had to do with him. Even herself."

chapter forty-two

I can feel the meltdown coming; it builds up inside me, rumbling and churning. The storm is about to break. A tornado, a hurricane, a tsunami.

Mom sits up with me all night. Alexa keeps her arm around me. Even Dad stays. When the sun rises in the morning, they take me to see Dr. Goldbloom.

When I enter her barn-shaped office, she's waiting for me, holding a large cardboard box filled with old coffee mugs, ceramic plates, and soup bowls. Heavy, chipped, mismatched: breakable.

She hands them to me one by one, and I hurl them against the far back wall. And I scream.

Julia Hogan, the attic, my hopes of finding Emily. All three burned up in the fire, reduced to ashes and smoke, and are now gone forever.

When I'm done throwing, done breaking, done screaming, Dr. Goldbloom hands me a broom. Together, we sweep up the mess on the floor.

Then we settle on her lavender couch to sweep up the mess in my head.

chapter forty-three

Even though I won't look in a mirror, I can see in my peripheral vision that my hair is wild and frizzy. The hot, humid Florida air settles heavily in my lungs. My knee is sweaty inside my new brace, but at least I'm done with crutches.

I'm not in Florida to go to Disney World, although that's a page in the Dream Book. That dream will have to wait. I wouldn't want to go to Disney World without Alexa, and she's at a Sparklers retreat this weekend. I'm in Florida because I've finally agreed to go with Dad on one of his foundation trips. He came to help organize the search for a little boy who never made it home from school four days ago. I came to comfort the little boy's family.

Zachary is his name. Zachary Russo. Seven years old, red hair, brown eyes, freckles, forty-eight inches tall, fifty-one pounds. Last seen getting off the school bus, wearing blue shorts, a Miami Dolphins T-shirt, and a Superman backpack.

A black cloud of activity and panic surrounds the Russo house. Police rush around, their walkie-talkies emitting static and muffled speech. In the living room, Dad gives directions to a group of volunteers. Mr. Russo is talking to a detective. I'm sitting on the couch, holding Mrs. Russo's hand.

In Mrs. Russo's other hand is the pink teddy bear I gave her earlier. A reporter made sure to capture that gesture on camera.

Mrs. Russo hasn't showered in days. Or slept. Her auburn hair is greasy, her eyes are sunken and red. She hasn't cried, at least not since I've been here, but she keeps staring off into space. Maybe she's all cried out.

Was this what my mom was like, the entire time I was missing? Is this what Donna Hogan is like, now that her daughter is dead?

I wanted to go to Julia's funeral. Surprisingly, so had Alexa. She was more torn up about Julia's death than even I was. But Mom said no, our presence would complicate things too much for the Hogans. And the reporters, Mom added with a shudder: just as things were calming down, Julia burned down Alan Shaw's house, killing herself in the process, and the reporters returned. Going to the funeral would only feed the media frenzy.

So Alexa and I stayed away from the funeral, and I felt utterly and completely useless.

Now, on this foundation trip to Florida, maybe I won't be so useless.

I pat Mrs. Russo's hand. "I'm going to get you something to eat," I tell her. "And then you should take a nap. If there's any news, I'll come get you."

She looks at me with wide eyes, desperate eyes, as if she believes that because I came home after being kidnapped, I must have some magical power that will make her son come home too. She nods at my suggestion of food and sleep.

I hobble to the kitchen to make a plate for her. Neighbors and volunteers have been dropping off platters of cold cuts, julienned veggies, and brownies all day long.

Dad comes in as I'm spreading mustard on a roll. His golden-brown hair is tousled, his pink tie loose. He's clearly tired, but he gives a volunteer, an old lady with white hair, a gentle pat on her shoulder as a thank you. He's busy but calm, purposeful but passionate.

When he sees me, he says, "You're doing a great job, sweetheart."

"I'm not doing anything," I reply. "I don't know what to say to anyone."

"You don't have to say anything. Just being here is enough."

His cell phone rings, and as he answers it, I look around the Russo's kitchen. It's decorated in peach and mint. Soft, happy colors.

Dad hangs up the phone. "That was Marissa," he says. "The *Shannon Symond Show* called again. She wants to interview you. It would be broadcast as a primetime special."

The most popular and respected TV journalist in the country wants to interview me. She wants to broadcast it in prime time. Millions of people would watch it. Millions of people would see me.

I look up at my dad. "You want me to do it, don't you?"

"People care about you and want to see how well you're doing. The interview would lead to more donations, and we could help more missing children and their families," he says. "I want you to do it, but only if *you* want to do it. It's your decision."

On the Russos' refrigerator door, attached by a palm tree magnet, is a watercolor painting of a house under a rainbow. Three stick figures stand outside the house in a row, one small between two big, holding hands. Zachary's name is printed on the bottom in large wobbly letters. The drawing flutters as a bearded police officer rushes by it.

"It's never going to end, is it?" I say to Dad.

"What?"

"Missing kids. Even if we find Zachary today, another kid will go missing tomorrow. Another search party to organize, another family to comfort. It'll never end."

"No," he says. "It won't."

"What if he's . . ." I lower my voice to a whisper. ". . . never found? Or found dead? How can I give people hope when there's nothing left to hope for?"

"Some stories won't have a happy ending," he says. "But there's always hope that the next one will. Hope is everything, Charlotte.

Even when there's nothing else. Especially when there's nothing else."

The bearded police officer returns, zipping past the refrigerator on his way through the kitchen, and Zachary's watercolor painting swoops to the floor. I pick it up and return it to its place on the fridge, securing it with the palm tree magnet, and then an additional magnet of a silver star.

"Dad?" I say. "Tell Shannon Symond I'll do the interview."

I return to the living room with food for Mrs. Russo and make sure she eats half of it. Then I lead her to her bedroom and put her to bed. I prop the pink teddy bear onto the pillow next to her, and stay with her until she falls asleep. "He'll come home," I whisper to her. I don't know if that's true, but for right now, for this moment, hope is everything.

chapter forty-four

"How do you feel about doing the Shannon Symond interview?" Dr. Goldbloom asks me in her clipped accent. The sun streams through the tall windows, which are open, and the sheer lavender curtains sway gently in the breeze. The air smells like grass and springtime.

"I feel good about it," I say. "It'll raise awareness for the foundation, and we'll get more donations. We can help more people."

"That's true," she says, and waits.

"I'm just . . ."

She waits.

"I'm just scared she'll ask me questions I don't want to answer," I admit.

"Such as?"

"Questions about the attic," I say, then change direction. "And millions of people will see me."

"Ah." She folds her hands in her lap. "You know, Marissa called me the other day to tell me something about you. Something that's been concerning her."

I slide a throw pillow onto my lap, holding it against my stomach like a shield. "What?"

Dr. Goldbloom's anklet jingles as she tucks her legs under her. "She told me that when you're in the bathroom, you never turn on the light. She noticed it the first time a few months ago, and it's still happening."

Stupid, snooping Marissa. Just because she's married to my dad does not mean she has the right to spy on me, and she certainly doesn't have the right to call my therapist and talk about me. I tighten my hold on the pillow. "Why would she tell you about that?"

"Why do *you* think she would tell me about that?"

I shrug. "Because it's weird?"

"Do you think it's weird?"

I shrug again. "Maybe. Yeah."

"So why do you do it?"

"I don't know."

"Does the light hurt your eyes?"

"No."

"Do you turn on the lights in other rooms?"

"Yes."

She blinks, waiting again, for me to speak.

"I—I don't like not having clothes on," I tell her. "Having the lights on when I'm taking a shower makes me feel . . . exposed."

"That's understandable," she says. "But Marissa says you also brush your teeth in the dark. You even brush your hair in the dark. Why is that?"

I dig my fingers into the pillow. "I don't know."

She waits.

I say nothing. Dr. Goldbloom's job is to make me feel better, but she's making me feel worse. She's still looking at me, her locks of silver hair sparkling in the sun, waiting patiently for me to tell her why I keep the lights off in the bathroom.

"I don't know," I insist. I change the subject before invisible hands can creep up around my neck. "My mom's doing really well," I offer. "So's Alexa."

"Good," Dr. Goldbloom says. "I'm glad."

We talk about Mom and Alexa for a while, and how happy I am that they're happy. We talk about my physical therapy. We talk about how sad I am that Zachary Russo, the little boy from Florida, hasn't been found yet. We talk about how I had to miss CiGi's first birthday party because I was sick. We talk about how school is ending in a week and I'm still way behind, but I'm going to take summer classes.

At the end of my session, I hop up and head for the door. I'm about to leave when Dr. Goldbloom puts a hand on my shoulder.

"I have an assignment for you, Charlotte," she says. "Something I want you to do before you come back next week."

She's never given me an assignment before. "What is it?"

"I want you to turn on the light when you're in the bathroom."

"Okay. See you next week." I open the door to go.

"Not so fast," she says. "And then, I want you to look at yourself in the mirror."

"But—but I already know what I look like," I stammer, lamely.

"Do you?"

I take a breath to respond, but the words evaporate before I can say them. I shake my head instead.

"When was the last time you looked at yourself in the mirror?" she asks.

"Not since . . . before."

"That's a long time. Almost five years," she says. "Why haven't you looked at yourself, Charlotte?"

I swallow the lump in my throat. "I don't want to see . . . what everyone else sees when they look at me."

"And what do you think they see?"

The lump returns with a vengeance, and I cannot swallow it. "They see the girl who was kidnapped. They see the girl in the attic. They see the girl who was raped every day for four years."

"Would you like to know what I see when I look at you?"

"No."

She tells me anyway. "I see the girl who was strong enough to survive."

The bathroom is dark, almost pitch black. In one hand I hold the Dream Book. My other hand rests on the light switch. Both hands are trembling.

Through the wall, I can hear the music Alexa is playing in our bedroom. I can hear the vacuum my mom is running in the family room.

I can do this. I survived being kidnapped. I survived four years of captivity in a dim attic. I survived four years of loneliness, terror, and pain. I can survive flipping this tiny little switch in my own bathroom in my own house. I am the girl who was strong enough to survive.

I can *do* this.

I close my eyes. Take a breath.

All it takes is a flick of my index finger—*flip*—and the light turns on.

I force myself to open my eyes.

My eyes are staring at my hands, which are now gripping the sink. Now my eyes are staring at the fake marble countertop. Now they're staring at the chrome faucet. Now they're staring at the drain.

My eyes may as well be anchored with lead, they feel that heavy. But I force them to raise, to pull away from my white-knuckled grip on the sink, and to look in the mirror. To really look.

Look.

I see a girl. No. A young woman. She's thin, but not too thin. Her cheeks are flushed. Her lips are full and pink. Her eyes are big and blue. Haunted. But behind that: strong and determined. Her hair . . .

Her hair is black. Thick. Messy. Long. It tumbles halfway down her back. When she was eleven, she had thick bangs, but she hasn't had a haircut in almost five years, and now her bangs have grown out.

Her Keeper loved this hair. *My* hair. He loved to wash it, to brush it.

I can still feel his hands in it, combing it with his fingers, then suddenly wrapping it around his fist and tugging, snapping my neck back.

I hate my hair. I *hate* it. That's what drew him to me: my long, black hair.

I should cut it.

I want to cut it. I need to cut it.

I yank one of the drawers open, digging through the clutter. Scissors. Where are the scissors? Only Alexa's makeup is in this drawer. I slam it shut and open the next. A straightening iron, a bottle of hair gel, an unopened kit of white hair bleach. With a sob, I slam that drawer shut too.

My hair is burning my scalp now. I have to take it off. I have to get rid of it. I want it off I need it off I have to cut it off *cut it all off*.

I open each drawer again, then the medicine cabinet, then the cabinet under the sink. I pull everything out. Cosmetics, toothpaste, deodorant, lotion. But there's no scissors. I can't find the scissors. Don't we have any scissors in this house?

"What are you doing?"

It's Alexa.

"I need scissors," I say. "Where are the scissors? I need scissors!"

She dashes off, then returns with a pair of scissors with a red handle. "You want me to cut off a tag or something?"

Next to the Dream Book, the kit of hair bleach lies on the pile of junk on the counter. *Yes.* I need to do what Alexa did after I disappeared: cut my hair short, bleach it white. The exact opposite of long and black. The exact opposite of what my Keeper would like.

I grab the scissors with one hand and grab a handful of my hair with the other. I open the scissors and—

—wait.

I drop the scissors. Stare at my sister. My twin sister.

"That's why you changed your hair," I say. "Because you knew he wouldn't like it."

Her face becomes as white as her hair used to be.

"You knew who he was," I say.

She steps back, shakes her head.

I take a step toward her. "You knew who he was, didn't you? Admit it."

"I—I didn't know *who* he was. I noticed him following us around, at Iggy's Ice Cream and places like that. Coming to our practices and games."

"You told me, and Agent Lindo, that you never saw him before. Why did you lie?"

She opens her mouth but only a squeak comes out.

"Why did you lie, Alexa?"

I remember now: eleven-year-old Alexa, all playfulness and joy, walking around town with a wiggle and a skip, tossing her long black hair. "You knew he liked your hair."

She's folding up into herself, breath hitching with each inhale. "He touched it, once, at the park. He said it was pretty. So after that, whenever I saw him, I . . ."

"You tossed your hair. Oh my God, Alexa, you *flirted* with him."

"But I didn't think . . . I didn't know he would . . ."

A ball of fire ignites in my chest. "He wanted *you*, Alexa! He wanted you, but he took me by mistake. I stayed with him and did what he wanted to protect *you*. But you knew he took the wrong one, didn't you?"

Mom is here now, standing in the hallway, her mouth hanging open. "Alexa? Is this true?"

With a whimper, Alexa backs away. "You disappeared, but we didn't know someone took you until they found that video footage a couple weeks later." Her words pour out of her mouth. "I was too scared to say something then because I thought I would get in trouble, because it was my fault, I knew it was my fault . . . And the longer I didn't say anything, the more trouble I knew I would be in."

Her cheeks are colorless. Her blue eyes dart side to side, trapped rodents seeking escape. "And then I thought you had to be dead, it was too late . . ."

A sheet of red descends over my vision. "You blamed me for destroying our family," I hiss. "You destroyed my half of our bedroom. You threw the Dream Book at me and said I ruined everything because I walked off with him! But all along, it was *your* fault. And you *knew* it!"

Alexa takes another step back. "But there was nothing I could do! I didn't know his name!"

"You could have described him to the police! You saw him following us around town. You knew he lived nearby!"

"Charlotte, please! I'm sorry! I was only eleven years old. I know it was wrong and stupid not to tell anyone, and I've never stopped hating myself for it. I *hate* myself! I'm sorry. I'm so, so sorry."

"Sorry isn't going to give me my four years back. You ruined my life! You ruined all of our lives!" I swipe the Dream Book from the counter and hurl it at her. It hits her square on the chest, but she doesn't flinch.

All energy drains from me. My heart is heavy, like a rock thrown in a creek, falling deeper and deeper until it hits bottom. I sink to the floor. I can't even cry.

My twin sister crouches next to me, reaches for me. "Char—"

"Get away from me, Lex Enola."

That makes her flinch. She emits a helpless, violent whimper, then bolts down the hall. A few seconds later, the front door slams.

Mom is still standing there, frozen, hands over her mouth.

The pages of the Dream Book are scattered on the floor. On my hands and knees, I pick up each sheet, crumple them up, and throw them all in the trash.

I hate my sister. I hate her. I hate her. I hate her.

chapter forty-five

There is no meltdown. There is no storm. I can't. I'm too empty.

The rest of the day drags in hollow, heavy silence. Or maybe it speeds by. I don't know. I don't remember any of it. Suddenly it's nighttime, and I'm in the kitchen, pushing my dinner around with a fork instead of eating it.

Mom hangs up the phone. "I just talked to your sister," she says wearily, her shoulders slumped, her face sagging. "She's at your dad's house."

"Hm." Why is she telling me this? I don't care where Lex is.

"She asked me if she should live with him from now on."

"What did you say?"

"I told her it's up to you."

I push my food around some more. "I say she should live with Dad."

Mom breathes once, twice, three times before she replies. "That's . . . probably for the best."

I go to my room. It's *my* room now, not mine and Lex's. She'd better come pack up her stuff when I'm not here. We'll have to change the custody arrangements so on the days I go to Dad's house, she goes to Mom's.

I wonder how she'd react if I trashed her side of the room and ruined all of her stuff, the way she destroyed mine?

I think about how Lex used to skip and toss her hair, full of youth and innocence and playfulness and joy. I think about my

Keeper following us around town, to our practices and games, to Iggy's Ice Cream Shop, and how she *knew* he was doing it. She knew he liked her hair. She tossed her hair for *him*.

And she never said anything when I disappeared, because she was afraid of getting in trouble? When she knew the trouble I was in was much, much worse?

Fuck her.

She blamed me for our family falling apart, when all along it was her fault. She really is the *Enola Gay*. She carried a weapon inside herself, an atomic bomb of lies, and she dropped it on our family.

I wish my Keeper *had* taken her instead of me.

Early, early the next day, while darkness is still clinging to the sky, I go into Mom's room. I'd spent the night pick-pulling the seams of a pink teddy bear and plucking out the stuffing. I've made a big decision, and I want to tell Mom so we can get started today, this morning, this minute. But Mom, surprisingly, is deep asleep.

I sit on the edge of her bed. "Mom?" I whisper. "I want to take Uncle Tim up on his offer. I want to move to Georgia."

She doesn't respond.

"Mom, did you hear me?" I say. "Let's move to Georgia. Things aren't working out here. I just want to forget everything and start over. You and me. I have it all figured out. Lex can stay here with Dad, and you and I can go to Georgia. A fresh start. That's what you want, right? I don't want to live in Woodland Creek anymore either. Too many bad memories."

Still no response. I reach to shake her awake, and touch something hard and smooth. It moves and hits something else, making a tinkling sound.

I snap on the light. An empty tumbler and a glass bottle lie on the bed next to my mother. The bottle is a quarter-full with clear liquid. Vodka.

"Mom?"

Her skin is cold, tinged with blue. She takes a stuttery breath and lets it out.

She does not breathe again.

chapter forty-six

The ambulance arrives just in time. They pump Mom's stomach and take her away. At the hospital, she's diagnosed with alcohol poisoning.

I stay with her in the hospital all day. She's going to be all right, eventually, but she has to stay at their inpatient alcohol rehabilitation program for a few days. They won't let me stay with her, which means I have to go to Dad's.

Lex is staying at Dad's. There's *no way* I can be in the same house as her.

Dad understands. As soon as he brings me back to his house, he tells Alexa to pack up. He's made arrangements for her to stay with a friend of Marissa's.

I stay in the kitchen while Lex packs. She stops in, dressed all in black, more black clothes dangling from an overnight bag. "Charlotte?" she squeaks. "Can we please talk?"

I turn my back. I can't look at her. My throat is closing up, but now it feels like Lex's hands around it, not my Keeper's.

"Lex, not now," Dad says. Only after he takes her away do I drag myself upstairs to get ready for bed. I keep the light off in the bathroom.

In the bedroom, I go through the dwindling pile of pink teddy bears and choose an extra furry one to pluck the stuffing from tonight. I'm just about to crawl into bed with it when Marissa comes in, and my stomach seizes when I see CiGi on her hip.

"Please don't," I tell Marissa, before she can say anything.

"Don't what?"

"Please don't ask if I'm okay."

"All right," she says.

"Thank you."

She remains in the room, and when I say nothing else, she says, "I talked with Lex while you were at the hospital with your mom. We talked for a long time."

When I still say nothing, she continues. "She told me she's been punishing herself for the past four years. Quitting cheerleading, the crowd she hung out with, the drugs. She slept around with all those boys because she didn't feel she deserved anything better."

"She doesn't deserve anything better," I say. "She'll never deserve anything better."

"I'm not trying to defend her, but you should know that Lex is more upset with herself than any of us are."

"Good. She should feel bad," I say. "But it's impossible for Lex to hate herself more than I hate her."

Marissa comes further into the room. She hesitates, then says, "Charlotte, she told me that a couple years ago she was planning to kill herself. She was going to purposely overdose on heroin. But then she changed her mind. She said that she didn't even deserve to die. She needed to live so she could continue punishing herself."

That shocks me, and I almost—*almost*—feel sorry for her. "Do you think she's upset enough to try to kill herself now?"

"I was worried about that too," Marissa says. "The friend of mine who your dad is taking her to stay with is a suicide prevention counselor. She'll keep her safe."

My mom is staying at an alcohol detox center, and my sister is staying with a suicide prevention counselor. What a mess.

I'm holding the fluffy pink teddy bear on my lap, and I realize that I've already started pick-pulling at a seam. I don't stop myself. "Marissa, can I ask you a question?" Pick-pull.

"Anything."

Pick-pull. "Why did you marry my dad?"

"Because I love him."

"No, I mean, why would you *want* to marry my dad, when our family is so screwed up?"

Marissa puts CiGi down and comes to sit next to me on the bed. The baby toddles over to the pile of pink teddy bears in the corner. I have to hold myself back from dragging her away from them.

"It wasn't an easy decision, marrying your father," Marissa says. "My friends, my family, they all tried to talk me out of it." She gives a sarcastic chuckle. "I get it. There's a big age difference between us, but that's minor compared to everything else. His ex-wife had a drinking problem. One daughter was an uncontrollable delinquent who hated everyone and everything, including me, and his other daughter was missing and probably dead. Every hour he spent outside of work was spent on the foundation. Every dollar he made went to the foundation."

"Then why did you marry him?"

"Because every time I look in his eyes, I can see how much love he has to give. He had all this love, and no one to give it to. Your mother kicked him out; Lex wanted nothing to do with him. You were gone."

I bite my lip to keep it from trembling. Pick-pull.

"Your father's a good man," Marissa says. "A loyal man. He's devoted to you, Charlotte. To you *and* Lex, even though she's made it difficult for him. Even when he thought you were dead, he was devoted to keeping your memory alive. That's why I love him. He was so broken, and I was so honored to be the one who could take the pain out of his eyes and give him the tiniest bit of happiness."

CiGi toddles to the bed, holding one of the teddy bears. "Bear!" she declares, and offers it to me. I scooch away from her, my stomach churning.

Marissa scoops CiGi up and nuzzles her nose with her own, making CiGi giggle. She glances at me. "Okay. Now it's my turn to ask you a question."

I steel myself. "What is it?"

"Why do you hate CiGi?"

"I don't hate CiGi." I pick at a seam, pull at a stitch.

"I know it was a shock to find out your dad has a new wife and a new baby," Marissa says. "I didn't expect you to accept us at first sight. But you've been home for eight months, and you've never played with her. You've never touched her. Your dad thinks you're jealous of her, like she took your place. But you're too old for that."

"I'm not jealous of her." Pick-pull. "But she did take my place. She replaced me."

"You think your dad and I had a baby to replace you?"

"You gave her my name."

"We named her in honor of you, Charlotte Grace. In memory of you. So every time we said her name, we would also think of you."

"Oh. That's pretty nice, actually."

She studies me from behind her blond corkscrews. "But I think it goes deeper than that. It's not just the replacement thing."

Pick-pull. "What do you mean?"

"You can't even look at CiGi without dry heaving. Something like that is instinctual. Psychological. I wonder . . ." She tilts her head. "After your rescue, when the doctor examined you, she said you didn't have a baby. But . . ."

"No." Pick-pull-pick-pull-pick-pull. "Whatever you're thinking, you're wrong. So stop thinking it. Please."

She starts to speak, then clamps her lips shut.

But then she says it anyway: "Charlotte, was the doctor mistaken? Did you have a baby?"

My stomach seizes, my throat closes. "No. There was no baby." I clutch the teddy bear and stumble from the bed. "There was never a baby."

I back away and trip over something, another stupid teddy bear, and land hard on the floor. Hands . . . neck . . . can't breathe . . . Oh God, can't breathe . . .

"Charlotte," Marissa cries. "I didn't mean to make you feel threatened—I'm calling your dad—maybe I should call Dr. Goldbloom . . ."

She fumbles for her cell phone as I struggle to breathe. My stomach clenches, my vision narrows. The room swirls around me.

And then it stops.

I have to say it. Out loud. I have to say, out loud, the one thing I haven't ever let myself think about. It's the only way I'll be able to get his hands off my neck. The only way I can breathe again.

"There was no baby," I whisper. "But I did get pregnant."

Marissa freezes, and his hands disappear. I inhale a full, deep, shuddering breath.

"I didn't know it at first," I say. "I was nauseated all the time. Constantly throwing up. I thought I was sick. But then I figured it out, and . . ."

I breathe again, and again, and admit the next horrible truth.

"And I was *happy*. For the first time in the attic, I was happy. I wanted that baby," I choke. "She was a girl, I have no proof of that, but she was a girl, I could feel it. I knew it was wrong to want her, but I did. I *wanted* her. I wanted someone to love, someone who loved me back—the real kind of love. The right kind of love. I wanted someone who would stay with me so I wouldn't be so alone."

"Oh, Charlotte. Oh, sweetie."

"But he figured it out a couple weeks later," I say. "And he got so mad, madder than he'd ever been, before or after. He was furious.

He—he—" I take another deep, jerky breath. "He punched my stomach, kicked it, and he wouldn't stop, not until I was bleeding. Not until . . ."

"Not until you lost the baby," Marissa whispers.

"And he still kept hitting me, punishing me for trying to bring someone between us. Because I belong to him, and only to him, and he's never going to share me with anyone. Not even a baby."

I'm rocking back and forth now, barely getting the words out. Marissa is on her knees next to me, her arms wrapped around me, rocking with me. From the corner of my eye, I see my dad in the doorway, frozen.

"When he stopped, he picked up the—mess. The *baby*," I say. "It was just blood, pulpy, lumpy blood, but I know she was in there somewhere, just a teeny tiny thing . . . He yelled, *Look at this! Look what you made me do!* and then he dumped her in one of those blue storage bins. A little one, like a shoebox. He said he needed to go take care of it. He needed to hide it. And then he left. He locked me up and he took the baby away."

I inhale another ragged, jagged breath. Breathe . . . Breathe . . . Breathe . . .

"When he came back, he had a bag of food with him, but he didn't give me any. He gave me a bottle of bleach and a scrub brush and told me to clean the blood from the floor. I was scrubbing, still cramping, still bleeding, and he sat on the bed, eating a cheeseburger and fries from Schneider's Red Hotz. He told me to stop crying, that everything was okay now. He said he hid the little blue bin somewhere safe, someplace where no one would ever find it, and now it's just him and me again. A few days after that, he started making me take a birth control pill every morning."

Marissa's fully weeping now. CiGi's starting to cry too. Even Dad has tears in his eyes. He's clutching the doorframe with white knuckles.

I am breathing.

"When did this happen, Charlotte?" Dad asks, swallowing hard. "How long ago?"

"I'm not sure, but . . ." I point to CiGi.

"Oh, God. Oh, no," Marissa moans.

My baby, if she had survived, would have been the same age as CiGi.

chapter forty-seven

That night, I don't sleep. I don't pick-pull at the seams of a pink teddy bear.

Instead, I breathe.

In the middle of the night, CiGi cries, a quiet little whimper. I get up and go to her nursery.

Her night-light emits a soft glow. She's standing in her crib in little pink footie pajamas. Little rosy cheeks, little blond curls. When she sees me, she points to the floor with her little chubby hand. "Bear," she says.

There's a teddy bear on the floor, with light pink fur and a big pink nose.

I give the bear to her, and she gives a big smile to me.

"CiGi," I say. "CiGi Hope." I run my finger down her cheek. It's so soft. Like silk.

She holds out her arms, and I pick her up. I take her to the rocking chair and put her in my lap, then tuck a blanket around us. She smells like fresh powder.

"CiGi, CiGi, CiGi, I'm your big sister," I whisper-sing. With a contented sigh, she nestles her head in the crook of my arm, plops her thumb in her mouth, and closes her eyes.

This is the way it should be. This is how a baby should live: with loving parents and a loving sister, with food and clothes and toys. A warm, soft, safe place to sleep. Sunshine and grass and sky.

If my baby had survived, she would have had to live in the attic with me. Our Keeper would have locked her up every time he left. No food, no toys. No school, no friends. No sunshine, no grass, no sky.

Just me and our Keeper. One loving parent, and one monster parent who had all the power. When the baby cried, he wouldn't hold her. When she had a cold, he wouldn't tenderly wipe her nose. When she was teething, he wouldn't give her a chamomile-soaked washcloth to chew on. He would only punish her for making too much noise. He would eventually replace me with her, and I would no longer be around to protect her. He would do the same horrible, painful, disgusting things to her that he had done to me.

CiGi coos in my arms. She is safe, and she is loved.

I close my eyes, and I breathe, and I fall asleep.

When I wake up, I'm still in the nursery, still in the rocking chair, still holding CiGi. Cloudy sunlight filters through her curtains, rain patters rhythmically on the roof. I brush my lips over CiGi's warm cheek, place her in her crib, and tiptoe back to my room.

Something's bothering me, itching at me, pestering me. It's not CiGi. It's not my father and his foundation. It's not my mother and her drinking. It's not my sister and her betrayal.

It's Emily. The One Before.

I can feel her. She's close.

I close my eyes and breathe . . . breathe . . . breathe.

And then I know.

I open my eyes, pick up my cell phone, and dial. "Agent Lindo?"

"Charlotte? It's six in the morning. Is everything all right?"

"It will be. Can you come pick me up?"

"Now? Why?"

"Because I know where Emily's body is."

chapter forty-eight

An hour later, Agent Lindo, Dad, and I arrive at Woodland Creek Plaza. Schneider's Red Hotz is closed this early in the morning, but we didn't come here for breakfast. I instruct Lindo to drive behind the building, and we get out of the car.

We zip up our jackets and put up our hoods to shield ourselves from the cold drizzle. A dirty delivery truck rumbles away. Old dry, dead leaves rustle in the wind. A pair of squirrels forage for discarded food around the dumpster.

"She's here," I say.

"If he threw her body in the dumpster," Lindo says, "she's long gone."

"Not there," I say. "He loved her, in his own twisted way. He wouldn't have just tossed her in the garbage."

I turn my back to the building and face the woods that surround the plaza. The trees stand tall before us, their leaves fully green. A flock of blackbirds squawk; the creek babbles in the distance.

"He buried her somewhere in these woods," I say. "She's in a blue storage bin."

"You're sure?" Dad says.

"I'm sure."

"You said he never told you what he did with her body."

"He didn't. But she's here."

"How do you know?"

"Because my baby is somewhere in these woods too."

Within an hour, Agent Lindo has cordoned off the area, and his team is searching the woods, dredging the creek. As the hours wear on, he tells me I should go home. Dad insists on taking me home.

I refuse. I will not leave Emily. I won't abandon her. I'll stay until the end.

The gray clouds continue to drizzle as Dad and I stand behind Schneider's Red Hotz, staying dry but not warm under a blue tent-like tarp, passing out coffee and food donated by Schneider's to the search team. There are no reporters; Dad has promised not to alert the media about the search. Not until they find Emily.

Just before noon, my cell phone rings: Lex. Instead of answering, I hit Ignore and shove the phone in my pocket.

Midafternoon, I take my phone back out and dial.

"Calling Lex?" Dad asks hopefully.

I shake my head. "Hospital."

I ask to be transferred to the alcohol detoxification unit, and when a nurse answers, I identify myself and ask how my mother is doing.

"She's resting," the nurse tells me. "Would you like to talk to her? I'll transfer you."

"No, let her rest," I say. "But please let her know that I called, and that I'm okay, and that I love her." Mom doesn't know I've figured out where Emily is. She doesn't know about the baby. I want her to know; I'm aching to crawl into her arms and tell her everything. But I need her to get better first. She needs to take care of herself right now.

"Dad?" I say after I hang up.

"Yes, sweetheart?"

"Why did you leave Mom?" The question is as unexpected to me as it is to him.

"Your mother left *me*, Charlotte. She asked me to leave. She demanded that I leave."

"You could have said no. You should have said no."

"I did say no. At first. But it got worse. Living with a wife and daughter who want nothing to do with you isn't the easiest thing in the world."

"But they did want you. They needed you. They just couldn't show it."

He sighs. "I know that now. But at the time, I couldn't see past my own pain. Being at home brought more pain. The more I tried to help them, the more they pushed me away. I had to do *something*, so I started the foundation and had a memorial for you as a way to get closure and move forward. That was the breaking point for your mother. When she told me to leave, I did. I was certain it was temporary. At least, that's what I'd hoped."

"If you still had hope that you and Mom would get back together," I ask, "why did you start a new family?"

"My God, Charlotte." The fine lines on his face tighten into a road map of loss and devastation. "You were gone. Lex was out of control. Your mom wanted nothing to do with me. I'd lost *everyone*. Then Marissa came along, and for the first time in a long, long time, I was happy."

I study my father: shoulders broad, hair gold, eyes blue and aching and pleading. "You really love her," I say.

"I do, Charlotte. I do."

When I was in the attic, all I'd wanted was for my family to be happy. And my dad was the only one who found a way.

But I'm still not done. He's standing a couple feet from me, and I take a step closer. He stuffs his hands in his jacket pockets.

"Dad?"

"Yes?"

"Do you think I'm disgusting?"

"What? No, of course not. Why would you think that?"

"All those things he did to me. All those things he made me do. You don't think I'm disgusting? Ruined?"

"Sweetheart, no. He's the one who's disgusting. What he did to you was disgusting. But *you* aren't disgusting. *You* are perfect."

I nod, but I'm still not satisfied. I take a step closer. He doesn't step back, doesn't move, except for pushing his hands deeper in his pockets.

"You never touch me," I say. "Since I've been home, you haven't hugged me, haven't touched me. Not even once."

He looks stricken, guilty. He draws his hands from his pockets, but keeps them at his sides. He taps his fingers on his legs, hesitant, unsure.

"I'm a man," he says, with a tinge of repulsion. "And it was a man who hurt you. I haven't touched you, Charlotte, not because I think you're disgusting, but because I don't want you to feel threatened by me. It would kill me if you were scared of me, if you thought I would, or could, hurt you."

I take another step toward him, closing the distance between us even more. "I could never be scared of you, Dad. I know you'd never hurt me." I take another step. We're inches away now.

He opens his arms a little, then hesitates. "You sure?"

I step into his arms and wrap my own around him. "I'm sure."

Finally, he hugs me. Tight. And I am warm, and safe, and loved.

All day long, Dad and I huddle against the wind and drizzle in the back lot of Schneider's Red Hotz. He keeps me warm under his arm. I let him take me home only after the search team has quit for the night, and I make him take me back when the sun rises the next day.

Yesterday's rain has moved on, leaving today's sky blue and sunny, making things easier for Agent Lindo and his search team. Occasionally, Lindo comes tromping out of the woods to give us updates, but I can always tell by his slumped shoulders and heavy sighs that the search team hasn't found anything. "Keep looking," I tell him. "She's in there somewhere."

Marissa stops by late that morning to visit. CiGi grips her hand, her blond curls bouncing as she wobble-runs over to Dad and me on her plump toddler legs. She squeals with delight as a bushy-tailed squirrel dashes across the back lot. Sweet, innocent baby; she's clueless about the true, dark purpose of our vigil here at the edge of the woods. I dread the day my little sister learns that there are bad people in this world, and I vow to do everything I can to protect her from them.

Later that afternoon, I distribute more hot dogs and fries to the search team. When I turn around, I see my mother, talking with Dad and Marissa. "Mom!" I rush over, hug her tight. "What are you doing here?"

"The hospital released me this morning." She draws back, her lips trembling. "Your father called and told me where you were. He told me everything. Oh, honey. I should've been there for you. You needed me, and I—"

I stop her before she starts crying. "You're here now. You came at the perfect time. We're finding Emily today."

She inhales a shaky breath, lets it out. Pulls a pamphlet from her back pocket and shows it to me.

"Alcoholics Anonymous?" I say.

"There's a meeting tonight at the church on Chapman Street. I think I'll go."

"Good, Mom. I'm proud of you."

My phone dings—it's Lex again, texting this time. *I don't blame you if you never talk to me again, but please know that I am so, so sorry.*

Mom looks over my shoulder as I delete the text. "You and your sister, when you were little, I sometimes forgot you were two individual people."

"Me too," I say, and I have to chuckle. "We were Charlottealexa. And you and Dad were Mommydaddy."

"I never expected our family would end up like this."

"Me neither."

"When your father had that memorial for you," she says, "I thought he was going through some kind of mental breakdown. I didn't realize the person having the breakdown was me."

In the distance, twigs snap as the search team walks through the woods.

"But I couldn't give up hope that you would be found one day," Mom continues. "I thought I'd be able to forgive him once you got home, and he'd come back and we'd be a family again. But then he got married and had a baby, and I realized he was never coming back. And I hated him even more."

"Do you still hate him?"

"No. I'm disappointed. In myself. I wasn't strong enough for him. Or for you, or for Alexa. Even after you came home, I wasn't strong enough. I dumped all the liquor down the sink except for one bottle that I kept hidden in my closet. I avoided it for months, even when you went back to school, even when you had that meltdown after Alan Shaw died. I truly thought I would never need it. But when Lex told us what she did, it was too much. I went straight for the bottle. I wasn't strong enough to stay away."

"You're getting strong now, Mom. That's what's important."

"You're the strongest of all of us."

Together, we look out into the woods, and we wait. Our shadows stretch long before us.

Just before the sun slips behind the horizon, Agent Lindo comes out of the trees. His shoulders are slumped, his face is drawn.

He stops in front of me and says three words: "We found her."

chapter forty-nine

Agent Lindo tells us they found Emily's remains inside a big blue storage bin that was wrapped in duct tape, embedded in mud at the bottom of the creek.

Ten minutes later, they find a little blue bin, the size of a shoebox, a few feet away.

Emily Alvarado and my baby are finally going home.

And I can finally breathe.

chapter fifty

Dr. Goldbloom is curled up on her velvet couch next to me, legs tucked under her, waiting patiently for me to speak. I know she wants to discuss everything that happened since we last met: looking at myself in the mirror, my sister's betrayal, my mother's alcohol relapse, accepting CiGi, finding Emily's body, my pregnancy.

But I don't want to discuss any of that.

I have a pink teddy bear in my lap. Wiggles, my original pink teddy bear. I brought it from home. It's still whole, the seams still intact.

I say, "Before my first session with you, my sister said you'd give me a doll and tell me to show you where the bad man touched me."

Dr. Goldbloom chuckles. "I've never done that, but is it something you'd like to do? I have some dolls over there." She gestures to the wooden toy chest at the front of the barn.

"Not with a doll." Instead I take Wiggles, and pick-pull at the seam on its leg. I pick-pull until a stitch breaks. I dig my nails into the seam and pull. Pull again. Pull some more, until the silence is broken by a ripping sound as more stitches break.

With my finger and thumb, I pluck out some stuffing. Then more. And more. I keep pulling and tearing, pulling and tearing, until I can pull out handfuls of stuffing at a time. Soon piles of stuffing lay scattered around me, and the bear is flat and deflated. Empty. A carcass.

"That's where he touched me," I say. "Everywhere. Inside and out. He gutted me."

Then I pick up all the stuffing and push it back inside the bear. As soon as I get home, I'll sew the seams back up and make Wiggles whole again.

chapter fifty-one

"You sure you want to go in there alone?" Bailey asks me.

"I'm sure. Thanks." I climb out of her car, and alone, I enter the county graveyard.

I search the gravesites, row by row, one by one. My knee is sore, but I keep going. I finally find the one I'm looking for, in the very back, separated from the others. A simple cement paver is all that marks it. No pithy expressions of love, no wishes for a peaceful rest are engraved on the marker. No *Beloved Son* or *Beloved Brother*, and certainly not *Beloved Uncle*. Only his name, and the dates he poisoned humanity with his life.

Alan Shaw's grave is isolated, quarantined, in the very back of the graveyard, where it won't contaminate anyone else's peaceful deathly slumber.

"You don't deserve this." I kick at the cement paver with my toe. "Your name is on your grave marker, and you never called me by my name. I'm sure you never called Emily by her name, either. And I didn't even get to give my baby a name before you beat her out of me."

I kick the paver again, and again, until I swing too hard. My knee gives out and I fall to the ground. With my bare fingers, I start pulling out the grass. I claw at it, pulling up huge chunks of it, digging up dirt. My fingernails break, my skin is cut. I punch the ground, then pound on the paver with my fists, ignoring the pain that shoots up my arm.

A fist holding a large rock appears in front of me. "Here. Use this."

I sniffle and sit up. My sister stands above me, dressed in black. Her hair is black, too.

"What are you doing here, Lex?" I wipe my face with my arm and it comes back dirty.

"Mom told me you went to Stubby's with Bailey so I went there to talk to you. But when you weren't there, I figured you made her take you on a detour. I knew this is where I'd find you."

She sinks to her knees, raises the rock above her head, and smashes it into the cement paver. It echoes with a dull thud.

"That's illegal, you know, desecrating a grave," I say.

"It's not his grave. It's just his headstone. And so what if we desecrate his grave? He desecrated our lives."

She hands the rock to me. It's solid and heavy and fits perfectly in my hand. I take a deep breath, raise the rock over my head, and with a war cry, I *slam* the rock on the paver.

That felt good. Great. Powerful. I finally have the power over him. I can scream at him, I can beat him, I can hurt him, and he can't punish me. *I'm* the stronger one now.

Again, I raise the rock over my head, and slam it on the marker. Soon Lex joins me with a rock of her own, and we take turns screaming and pounding. First we make some dents in the concrete, then the letters of his name get nicked. Pieces of cement chip off. Some fly away. I don't stop until my throat is raw and my voice is hoarse and the paver looks old and broken.

Finally I collapse to the ground, exhausted, panting, crying, but feeling so fierce and victorious that I end up laughing.

But Lex is still going at it. She's smashing her rock into the paver, screaming, tears are flying along with the little chips of concrete.

"Lex," I say.

She doesn't stop. Again and again, she smashes her rock into the paver. She howls when she catches her pinky between them, and I spring over. "Alexa! Stop!" I tug at her arm and pull the rock from her hands.

She looks at me with wild eyes, sobbing. "I hate him. I *hate* him!"

"Me too," I say. "Me too."

"I *liked* the way he looked at me," she says. "Before. When he followed us around town and came to our games. I tossed my hair, wiggled my hips the way the older girls did. It never occurred to me—" Her breath catches. "I never thought he would—" She howls, doubling over, wraps her hands in her hair. Tears streak through the dirt on her face. "I wanted to die. I wanted to kill myself."

"I know." I lift her up, ignoring the pain in my knee, and we limp over to sit against a tree. "I'm so, so glad you didn't."

Her sobs slow to hitching breaths. I take her hand, and she puts her head on my shoulder. "I'm sorry, Charlotte."

I squeeze her dirty hand with my own. "It's not your fault."

"Yes it is."

"It's *not* your fault," I say. "It's not Julia's fault for not telling anyone. It's not Donna Hogan's fault for not knowing. It's not Mom's fault for not watching me more closely that day after the game. And it's not my fault for walking off with him. The only person to blame for anything, is *him*."

chapter fifty-two

There's a corner of the backyard at my mom's house that's always in the sun. It's in that corner I dig a small hole in the ground, just big enough for a little wooden box. I place a small blanket in the box and lay a tiny pink teddy bear on it. Then I close the lid and put the box in the ground. My baby doesn't really have a body I can bury, so the teddy bear will have to do. And now I have a place to come visit her.

I cover the box with dirt and sprinkle wildflower seeds on top. Then I sit back on my heels and look up into the blue sky.

I canceled that interview with Shannon Symond. I also told my dad I'm not going to be the Ambassador of Hope. And, I asked him to change the name of the Charlotte Weatherstone Foundation to the Never Lose Hope Foundation.

I'm not trying to deny what happened in the attic. I'll never forget it; I'll never be able to forget it. I'll never forget Emily or Julia, either. They'll always be my sisters, as much as Alexa and CiGi are my sisters. But Emily and Julia wouldn't want their short lives to be defined by one horrible man, and I refuse to let that man define who *I* am, or who I'll become.

Maybe I'll change my mind one day and do the interview, and work for the foundation. I don't know what my future will bring. But for now, I'm going to go to school. Hang out with my friends. Audition for plays. Get my driver's license. Eat chili cheese fries at Stubby's. Be normal. I deserve that much.

I stand slowly, accepting the pain in my knee, and, no longer trying to hide my limp, I head toward the house. Alexa's on the patio, waiting for me. Our hair is almost identical now, in both color and length. She's letting hers grow, and I've cut mine to just past my shoulders.

We don't have a Dream Book anymore. But we don't need one.

resources

If you need help, or know someone who needs help:

RAINN (Rape, Abuse & Incest National Network)
www.rainn.org
800-656-HOPE (800-656-4673)

> Call RAINN to be routed to a crisis center near you. Confidential, 24 hours a day, 7 days a week.

National Center for Missing & Exploited Children
www.missingkids.org
800-THE-LOST (800-843-5678)

> Contact this organization if you think you have seen a missing child.

CyberTipline
www.missingkids.org/cybertipline

> This congressionally authorized site is a means for reporting crimes against children.